# THE WILDERNESS MINE

"'TRY THE KNOB TO THE LEFT,' HE SAID. 'THEN IF YOU CAN REACH THE CRACK—'"

—*Page 255*

# THE
# WILDERNESS MINE

BY
HAROLD BINDLOSS

AUTHOR OF
PARTNERS OF THE OUT-TRAIL,
THE LURE OF THE NORTH,
PRESCOTT OF SASKATCHEWAN, Etc.

NEW YORK
GROSSET & DUNLAP
PUBLISHERS

Made in the United States of America

COPYRIGHT, 1920, BY FREDERICK A. STOKES COMPANY
PUBLISHED IN ENGLAND UNDER THE TITLE "STAYWARD'S VINDICATION"

ALL RIGHTS RESERVED

# CONTENTS

## PART I — CREIGHTON'S PATENT

| CHAPTER | | PAGE |
|---|---|---|
| I | MRS. CREIGHTON'S EXTRAVAGANCE | 1 |
| II | THE RECKONING | 11 |
| III | THE SPIRIT TANK | 21 |
| IV | STAYWARD FINDS OUT | 32 |
| V | MRS. CREIGHTON REFUSES | 41 |
| VI | RUTH IS MOVED TO ANGER | 49 |
| VII | RUTH'S ADVENTURE | 58 |
| VIII | MRS. CREIGHTON'S JEALOUSY | 70 |
| IX | RUTH GETS TO WORK | 81 |
| X | GEOFFREY'S NEW POST | 92 |

## PART II — THE RIDEAU MINE

| I | THE BUSH | 103 |
|---|---|---|
| II | GEOFFREY ENGAGES A COOK | 112 |
| III | SNOW | 122 |
| IV | THE MINE | 131 |
| V | GEOFFREY TRESPASSES | 140 |
| VI | CARSON EXPERIMENTS | 151 |
| VII | THE DAM | 161 |
| VIII | CARSON RESUMES HIS OCCUPATION | 172 |
| IX | GEOFFREY'S HOLIDAY | 181 |
| X | CARSON'S ADVICE | 191 |
| XI | GEOFFREY'S TRIUMPH | 200 |
| XII | CARSON'S LAST JOURNEY | 211 |

# CONTENTS

## PART III — THE STRUGGLE

| CHAPTER | | PAGE |
|---|---|---|
| I | GEOFFREY'S RETURN | 221 |
| II | GEOFFREY MEETS MISS CREIGHTON | 229 |
| III | THE SHIELING | 238 |
| IV | THE STACK | 249 |
| V | RUTH'S PERSUASION | 259 |
| VI | THE BROWN CAR | 270 |
| VII | MRS. CREIGHTON'S WEAK MOMENT | 281 |
| VIII | THE BROWN CAR STOPS | 289 |
| IX | RUTH GOES TO NETHERCLEUGH | 298 |
| X | THE PORTRAIT | 308 |
| XI | RUTH REBELS | 318 |
| XII | MRS. CREIGHTON RETRACTS | 328 |

# PART I
## CREIGHTON'S PATENT

# THE WILDERNESS MINE

## CHAPTER I

### MRS. CREIGHTON'S EXTRAVAGANCE

THE drawing-room window at Iveghyll was open, and Creighton, lounging on the seat in the thick wall, listened while Mrs. Creighton talked. This was his habit, for Mrs. Creighton talked much, and as a rule expected him to agree. She was resolute and, by concentrating on her object and disregarding consequences, had so far been able to satisfy her rather mean ambitions. Now Creighton saw the consequences must be faced. In fact, it was getting obvious that Janet must pull up, but he doubted if he could persuade her.

Although Iveghyll was not a large country house, Creighton knew it was too large for him. It occupied a green hollow at the bottom of a dark fir-wood that rolled down the hill, and a beck brawled among gray bowlders across the lawn. The lawn was wide and a rhythmic hum mingled with the drowsy splash of water as the gardener's boy drove a pony mower across the smooth grass. Behind the belt of red and white rhododendrons, a greenhouse glittered in the last beam of sunshine that slanted down the fell. A sweet resinous smell from the fir-wood drifted into the room.

Creighton was fond of Iveghyll. After the smoke and ugliness of the mining village where he spent his days, its quiet beauty was soothing. Moreover, the old house gave its occupants some standing in the rather lonely neighborhood, and Mrs. Creighton valued this. She was the daughter of a small landlord, who had died in debt but had been unable to borrow money on the property her mother had left her. Only her lawyers knew how small the income she derived from her tied-up inheritance really was.

For all that, Creighton might have lived at Iveghyll without much strain, had his wife been content to study economy and had he been firm. The trouble was, Mrs. Creighton was firm and he was weak. In a short-sighted way, she was clever, and her main object was to keep up the traditions of the landowning stock from which she sprang. In order to do so, she had urged on her slack and careless husband, and by and by meant to marry her daughter well. In the meantime, there was no reason why Ruth should not develop her musical talent. The girl had no social ambition and not much beauty, but now-a-days talent brought one recognition.

"You must get me the money," she declared. "Although I cut short my stay in town, I was forced to borrow from Christine. Then there are many bills, and Ruth's going to Munich is an expensive business. She must have a proper outfit and allowance. One cannot tell whom she may meet, and my daughter must not be shabby."

"One understands students are generally poor," Creighton remarked.

# MRS. CREIGHTON'S EXTRAVAGANCE 3

"Ruth must be able to meet the other kind," Mrs. Creighton rejoined. "She is, of course, a little unconventional, but this is, perhaps, because she is young, and when one has talent, a touch of originality is not a drawback. Ruth will not forget she springs from the Hassals."

Creighton yawned. He was tired of hearing about the vanished glories of his wife's family, and after all they had not been people of much importance. Their fame had not gone beyond the secluded North of England dale. The last Hassal's death was, however, regretted by numerous disappointed creditors.

"Oh, well," said Creighton. "How much do you want?"

When Mrs. Creighton told him he moved abruptly and tried to brace himself.

"I can't get you this sum," he replied. "When I wrote the last check, before you went to town, you declared you wouldn't bother me again for long. For that matter, I thought you ought not to go at all."

Mrs. Creighton gave him a cold glance. "Before I married, I spent every season in town, and now you grudge me two or three weeks! I gave up much for your sake, but one cannot be altogether a recluse. Do you expect me to be satisfied with three or four dull neighbors and such amusements as one can get at this bleak, lonely spot?"

Creighton hardly thought she expected an answer and for a few moments he mused and looked about. The drawing-room was expensively furnished, but without much hint of taste; the lawn and garden his view commanded were good. This was his province, although Janet had urged him to build the new greenhouse and get help for the gardener, and he would have been happy at Iveghyll, pottering about his grass and flowers, had she left him alone. Still, keeping things in shape was rather a strain; he ought not to employ a gardener, but Janet encouraged his spending money on the grounds. She liked Iveghyll to grow the finest flowers and earliest fruit in the dale.

He studied her rather critically. She had kept something of her beauty, although her face and hair were getting thin. Her mouth and eyes were good but hard, and on the whole she looked querulous and dissatisfied. Janet was not robust and sometimes used her weak health as a means for extorting concessions Creighton knew he ought not to make. He had a touch of cynical philosophy and admitted his feebleness. Now, however, he must try to be firm.

"We have been spending too much and must stop," he said. "I can't give you the money you want. Our account at the bank is very low and it's lucky Stayward is too occupied to look at the books. I'm rather afraid there'll be trouble when he finds out how much I've drawn."

"You are Stayward's partner."

"That is so. As the law stands, I'm justified in using the house's money; ethically, I'm not. I invested nothing when Stayward built the coke ovens, and he has spent remarkably little on himself. In fact, John uses Spartan self-denial; I don't know how the fellow lives."

"You did invest something. Stayward could not have started the coke ovens but for your invention."

Creighton agreed. He was slack and careless, but he had a talent for chemistry and had some time since

# MRS. CREIGHTON'S EXTRAVAGANCE 5

patented an apparatus for refining tar. It was typical that after a few disappointments he had given up his efforts to get the invention used and had done nothing with it until Stayward built the coke ovens. Indeed, it was then owing to Mrs. Creighton's urging that he talked about his retorts and condensers to Stayward, who saw the invention might be profitable and gave him a share in the business.

"To some extent, I suppose your argument is good," he said. "The coal in our neighborhood is not adapted for coking; the stuff's too soft to stand a heavy load and blast-furnace owners pay us some shillings a ton less than they give the Durham makers. If it was not for the by-products we distill, I doubt if we could carry on. But you know something about this——"

"It's important that Stayward knew."

"Oh, well," said Creighton. "Stayward is shrewd and obstinate. If he had not been obstinate, we should have been forced to stop some time since. Our experiments were expensive; we had no money behind us, and couldn't borrow, because Stayward had mortgaged the ovens. He has worked early and late, and spent nothing except on the new plant. You see, the interest on the mortgage was a steady drain. Now our stuff is getting known, and although money is very short, it begins to look as if we would soon turn the corner. All the same we have got to use stern economy. There's the trouble, because if we could spend a sum on better retorts, it would help our progress."

'In the meantime, I must pay our debts and Ruth

must go to Munich. Christine needs the money she lent me and our creditors cannot be put off."

Creighton's smile was ironically resigned. "I have preached retrenchment, but I suppose there is no use in talking about this. We have got the things you wanted and must try to meet the bill, although whether they were worth the price or not is another matter. We have outshone our neighbors when we gave a dinner; you and Ruth have gone to London when Harrogate satisfied your friends, and our name has been pretty near the top of local subscription lists. I don't know if it was charity, but we gave more than we ought. Now Ruth is to go to Munich with an allowance that will no doubt excite the other students' envy. Well, I grudge this least, but all the same I'm bankrupt and the bill has come in."

There was a new note in Creighton's voice and Mrs. Creighton looked at him rather hard. He was a handsome man, but one remarked a hint of indulgence that had not been there when he married. Then Tom had begun to look old; there were lines on his forehead and wrinkles about his eyes. For all that, Mrs. Creighton did not mean to be disturbed. Tom had long talked economy, but he had left her to pinch.

"I don't think I have been extravagant," she replied. "It has been a struggle to keep up our position with insufficient means. But I must have the money——"

She stopped, for a small car rolled up the drive and vanished behind the shrubs. A few moments afterwards a girl carrying a violin case opened the glass door on to the terrace and came into the room. Ruth Creighton was tall, with a slim, well-balanced figure and graceful pose. Her look was frank and her gray eyes were steady; her mouth was rather large and her skin was colorless. As a rule, strangers did not think her attractive, but her friends declared Ruth had a charm that gradually got stronger for people who knew her well. Perhaps the characteristics one noted first were her frankness and honesty.

"Had you a pleasant afternoon at Carrock?" Mrs. Creighton asked.

Ruth sat down and smiled. "Yes; at least, I know the performers had, although it's possible our friends were bored. We took ourselves rather seriously and gave them the best music we could play. Jack Fawcett's friend from town is, of course, one of our famous amateurs."

"He is well known," Mrs. Creighton agreed. "What did he think about your playing?"

Ruth hesitated for a moment, as if half disturbed, and then looked up frankly.

"He talked about it—I expect he knew why I was asked to play. Perhaps I imagined something, but while he encouraged me I don't think he was enthusiastic."

"You can play," Creighton declared. "Some of these fellows feel they ought to be critical."

Ruth smiled. "I imagine he felt he ought to be kind, and this was perhaps the worst. An artist's admiration is, so to speak, spontaneous when he meets real talent. Of course, serious music demands all one can give and I haven't studied hard very long. He talked most about my technique and I liked that. One can get the mechanical training at a good school and I ought to make rapid progress with the Munich masters." She paused and resumed, rather anxiously: "You do mean to let me go?"

"I understand your mother promised," Creighton replied. "The fellow hinted you needed training in technique?"

"Yes," said Ruth, thoughtfully. "At least, I imagine so, and in a way, it was encouraging. One can get control of wrist and fingers and develop the proper muscles. If this is all I need, I oughtn't to be afraid; but it means close study and proper teaching."

Creighton nodded. "You won't shirk the study. I suppose it wouldn't carry you very far by itself?"

"Not without clever teaching," said Ruth. "One needs good masters, and I want so much to go." She stopped for a moment and resumed in an apologetic voice: "If I have any talent, it's for music, and since I was a very little girl I've meant to be a player. Sometimes I think it's possible and sometimes I doubt, but I feel if I want to make my mark it's the best chance I've got. I'm not very pretty, I'm not a clever talker, and I know no useful work. But this is not important; I love music and think I could play."

Creighton was moved. He knew Ruth felt keenly. Moreover, she was tenacious; it was not a romantic ambition she had indulged. The girl was very dear to him and he could not refuse her.

"You must get your chance," he said. "Besides, your mother promised. We will let you go."

Ruth gave him a grateful glance, and he went out on the terrace and lighted his pipe. The sun had left the hillside, the woods down the dale were getting dim, and the dew had begun to fall. A thin streak of mist touched the highest trees, which rose from the vapor in blurred, dark spires, and the crying of lambs came down from the moor. Except for the splash of the beck, all was very calm, but Creighton felt moody.

He was glad he had agreed to let Ruth go; hers was a clean ambition and she must follow her bent. For all that, the extra expense would be an awkward strain just now; Janet had been horribly extravagant, and since he had no money, he had used his partner's. To some extent, perhaps, he was justified; the invention that enabled them to start the business was his, but the works had hardly begun to pay and their capital was nearly exhausted. In fact, he sometimes doubted if they could hold out until the tar-refining plant worked properly. The alterations they were forced to make cost much.

Creighton, however, banished his disturbing thoughts. His habit was to put things off and he began to muse about his life since he married. He did not think the Hassal family approved him, but Janet was not often baffled, even when she was young. Creighton remembered with ironical amusement that he was then rather a handsome, romantic fellow, and believed in his ability to make a career. He had taken a degree in science and occupied a post in the laboratory of a famous works. Moreover, he had some money; not as much as the Hassals thought needful, but enough to relieve him from the necessity to work.

He saw the money had been a drawback, although his carelessness and lazy good-humor to some extent accounted for his not making progress. Janet had persuaded him to give up his post, and he had rather amused himself by than labored at private chemical research, until he realized with a shock that his fortune was nearly gone. After this he abandoned his experiments, and left things to Janet, who took firm control. Janet was clever; Creighton did not know how she had satisfied their creditors and kept the foremost place she loved, but for a time she had done so without much help from him. Creighton owned that he had loafed and got the habit of indulging while his talent rusted.

Then Stayward built the coke ovens and when he was offered a partnership Creighton pulled himself together. At the beginning, he was happy, but Janet soon gave up the economy she had been forced to use and their debts got burdensome. Creighton, in a sense, had staked all upon the success of Stayward's venture, enjoying his share of the profit they hoped for, before it was earned, and now he wondered whether his rashness had not made success impossible. Stayward had been absorbed by the struggle with mechanical difficulties, and although he was sternly parsimonious, had not studied their accounts. Yet Creighton knew he must do so soon. It was, however, not his habit to meet trouble until he was forced, and getting up, he went back to the house.

## CHAPTER II

### THE RECKONING

A WEEK or two after his talk with his wife, Creighton and Ruth one morning left Iveghyll in the small car. A quantity of heavy luggage was strapped on the back, and when Mrs. Creighton kissed her daughter at the steps, she felt she had in an important sense done her duty to the girl. Smart clothes meant much to Mrs. Creighton; they were a sign of the rank that she rightfully enjoyed. Yet she would not go with her husband to put Ruth in the train. Excitement and emotion were not good for her, since her heart was weak, and Creighton smiled with bitter humor when she stated why she could not come. Janet's weak heart was a convenience now and then.

His feelings were rather mixed as he drove down the dale. He noted that Ruth's hands trembled as she pulled up the rug, although she had some color and her eyes sparkled. She was young and had never gone away alone; after all, to leave her quiet home for a foreign city was something of an adventure for a girl. Yet Ruth had pluck, and he knew that in spite of some natural shrinking she meant to seize the chance he had given her.

Creighton was glad he had done so, although he would miss Ruth much. She was kind and staunch, and he turned to her for comfort when his wife jarred on him. Ruth was not a fool; he saw she knew his slackness but hid her disapproval. Well, he had arranged that she should study at Munich for a year, and now, while he sympathized with her high hopes, he wondered rather gloomily whether he had been rash. In a sense, it had not cost him much, but he was embarrassed by Janet's extravagance and the expense might, so to speak, be enough to turn the scale. So far, he had somehow kept the balance even; now the beam was obviously tilting.

By and by the car ran out of the dale and in front brown moorland and thin pasture rolled down to the sea. The landscape was stern and bleak. Ragged stone walls marked off the gray squares of fields, since the starved grass was never really green. The small farmsteads were, for the most part, tarred to keep out the rain, and bitter winds had bent the ash-trees that grew about the walls. In the distance were villages, surrounded by chimney stacks and colliery winding-towers, and long trails of smoke from the furnaces blew along the shore.

"The low country's charm is not very obvious, and I doubt if its look is deceptive," Creighton remarked. "One wonders why men were allowed to build villages like these. Ugliness is not needful, as some people think; I don't know if it's always cheap. If I were a free-agent, I think I'd stay in the dale, where all's green and quiet and one is out of the wind."

Ruth smiled. She knew her father, but she loved, and made allowances for him.

"You don't like ugliness," she said. "Yet men do useful work, and money's earned, at the furnaces and in the coal pits."

# THE RECKONING

"Sometimes money's lost," Creighton rejoined. "Anyhow, it's horribly hard to earn and one gets tired."

Ruth gave him a sympathetic nod. She had seen the lines on his forehead get deeper recently.

"I know! It is not the work, but the wondering. Things would be easier if one knew one would make good. But you and Stayward are near success."

"Stayward believes this. John is never despondent and tired. He's indomitable—I think it's the proper word—like your mother. I don't know if it's unlucky we're not all like that."

"Pluck is a great thing," Ruth said thoughtfully. "One can remove many obstacles when one is not afraid."

"But not all, I think," Creighton remarked.

Ruth knitted her straight brows. "You mustn't daunt me, father. I need encouraging. You have been very generous, and, for your sake and mine, I feel the venture I'm making must be justified. The trouble is, I really have not much pluck, and now when I try to be confident, I doubt. One can get mechanical skill, if one works hard enough; but suppose I haven't the vital spark of genius? If there is a spark, one can help it to burn by study, but one cannot light it. Unless it springs up spontaneously, your art is dead and cold."

"You have the spark," Creighton declared. "I knew long since, when we heard the boys sing in the cathedral. You were very young, but I do not think you moved and I saw your eyes shine, as if the treble voices called and you meant to follow. I wondered where."

"Oh!" said Ruth, "they carried me to a world where nobody ever fails and there is nothing ugly and mean. I often think about that evensong—the light fading behind the pillars, the glimmer of the big red and green window, and the voices echoing along the high roof. You taught me the beauty of music then, and now you have given me another gift; the chance I'll always remember, if I succeed or not——"

She paused and resumed with some emotion: "I'm frank because you always understand. I mean to be a musician, if it's possible, and you have helped me to find out if it is. That is very much. You see, dear, it would be dreadful to look back afterwards and feel one might have been a great player and was not because one had never been allowed to try one's powers. Now, if I do fail, I'll know I could not have gone far along the path I love, and I hope I'll have the pluck to take another."

"You have pluck," said Creighton quietly. "It's your mother's gift. Mine was less desirable; I taught you to feel——"

He broke off, for they ran through a mining village, where children whose clogs rattled on the stones were going to school, and soon afterwards he stopped the car at a bleak, smoke-stained station by the sea. They had not long to wait and when the train rolled in Ruth put her arms round Creighton's neck and kissed him.

"I shall miss you and perhaps you will miss me. I'd rather like you to, but you mustn't bother at all; I'm going to be absorbed in work," she said. "When you write, tell me about the invention and the retorts.

I expect they will make you and Stayward famous before I come back."

The whistle blew and Creighton jumped down from the step. Ruth waved her hand, he saw her face at the window for a moment or two, and then the train rolled through an arch and she was gone. Creighton walked back to his car, feeling strangely flat. He had sent her off, found her the longed-for opportunity to try her powers, and now, when he was lonely, he must meet the bill. The bill was not large. Indeed, it was strange he could help Ruth at so small a cost, but as he drove to the bank he thought bitterly about his wife's shabby ambitions and extravagance.

The bank was small and dingy. Soot grimed the windows that shook with the measured throb of a big mining pump. While Creighton waited at the counter there was a harsh rattle as a loaded cage came up a neighboring coal pit. Putting down the check he had given his wife, he said to the clerk:

"Enter this sum to Mrs. Creighton's account, and then she can draw the money when she likes."

"Certainly," said the clerk, who took the check and went behind a partition, where Creighton heard him put a heavy book on a desk. Then a door opened quietly and Creighton frowned, because he thought he knew what this meant.

"Mr. Evans would like to see you," the clerk stated when he came back.

Creighton followed him to an adjoining room, and did not feel much comforted when the bank manager, sitting in front of his big desk, looked up with a friendly smile. He knew Evans, who was urbane but firm.

"A fine morning, Mr. Creighton, although the wind is cold," he remarked. "Well, about this little check; we will, of course, meet Mrs. Creighton's demands to the full amount; but I expect you'll need the usual sum for wages and the payment you generally make the builders at the end of the month?"

"That is so," Creighton replied. "In fact, since we have been forced to use an extra lot of fire-bricks, we'll need a larger sum."

"Oh, well," said the manager, smiling, "I expect you will soon get your money back. To keep one's plant up to date is an excellent plan. Still, you see, in the meantime——"

His pause was significant and Creighton tried to brace himself. Stayward left him to look after their accounts and he had known money was very short, but he had for some time neglected to find out exactly where they stood. This was not altogether carelessness; he had been half afraid to study the books. Now, however, it looked as if the reckoning he had weakly put off had come.

"I suppose you mean we will be in the bank's debt when the wages and the builders are paid?" he suggested.

"A little on the wrong side," the manager agreed urbanely. "The improvements you are making are, no doubt, a sound investment. All the same, you will need a good sum at the end of the month and the balance is against you."

"How much?" Creighton asked anxiously.

When Evans told him he made an abrupt movement. From the beginning Stayward and he had not had enough capital and his invention had not worked well at first. They had been forced to alter the ovens and distilling plant as they went on; spending on improvements money they got for their coke. Although it had been a struggle, they had kept going, and but for Mrs. Creighton's demands Creighton imagined they might have continued to do so. Things, however, were worse than he had thought, and the last check, so to speak, had tipped the beam.

"Well," he said as coolly as possible, "we are pretty good customers and expect to get two or three large sums before very long. Our accounts with the blast-furnace owners are sent in quarterly."

"This leaves you on the wrong side for some time. Besides, I expect you find one's debtors don't always pay when they ought."

"That is so," Creighton agreed. "However, the people who use our stuff are honest and generally punctual. The time is not long, and as soon as we get paid I'll send the checks across."

Evans shook his head, regretfully. "The trouble is our directors don't allow a manager much discretion; head-office rules are strict, you know. Then one can't tell when a traveling auditor may arrive."

"You mean, if you are to cash our checks, you must have a guarantee for the over-draft?"

"Something like that," said Evans, in an apologetic voice. "A matter of form! We won't be very particular about the security; anything we can show an auditor will meet the bill."

Creighton's forehead got wet. He had no security to offer and doubted if Stayward had. Yet it was obvious they must find something to pledge, or the works must stop. One could not put off the payment of wages, and he could not give the bank a bond on the buildings and ovens, because they were already mortgaged. But this was not all. Stayward, concentrating on another side of the business, had left the books to him, and he had let things go until the house was threatened by bankruptcy. Stayward had staked his all on the venture and was very hard. Creighton shrank when he thought about his anger. Yet, if they could hold out for a few weeks, things might improve and Stayward need not know.

"Then, I suppose you really cannot wait until we get some money from our customers?" he said with a carelessness that cost him an effort.

"I'm sorry," the manager replied. "I'd have liked to help, but rules are rules, you know. Bring me something we can use to satisfy the auditor and we'll meet your demands."

Creighton nodded, although he was not deceived. He knew the security he brought Evans must be sound.

"Very well! I must talk to Stayward and see what we can do."

He thought Evans looked rather hard at him, but he remarked that this was the best plan and Creighton went out. When he reached the works he found some spirit they distilled from the tar would not stand the proper tests and for two or three hours he was occupied in his laboratory. Then Stayward joined him at the plain lunch that was brought to the office, and went off a few minutes afterwards. Stayward was not given to talk. When he had gone, Creighton returned to the laboratory and puzzled about the impurities in the spirit. To account for them was an awkward problem, but Creighton knew something about chemistry. The trouble was, he had forgotten much in the years when he loafed, and indulgence had blunted his skill. It was sometimes obvious he had once been a better man.

All the same, his work engrossed him and concentration was something of a relief. When evening came he had solved the problem and began to grapple with another that was worse. Stayward had gone off with a colliery manager. They did not keep a clerk, and Creighton was alone in the small office when he opened the safe.

For a time he studied books and documents, made calculations, and tore up the papers; and then pushed back his chair and wiped his face. His skin was wet with sweat and his brows were knit, but for some minutes he sat still, absorbed by gloomy thought. The day laborers had gone and the works were nearly quiet. A plume of steam went up outside the window and big drops fell on the iron roof. Now and then a shovel clinked and he heard the rattle of a truck.

Creighton pulled himself together. Although there was nothing he could lawfully pledge, he must not be fastidious. Money must be got, and he thought he saw a plan. He had long been rash and now must run another risk. It was the worst he had run, but if things went well, he would be on safe ground again when payment for the coke arrived.

They had stock on hand, coking coal that Evans would, no doubt, take as guarantee for a loan. Since the coal was not paid for, Creighton admitted that it did not really belong to them, but Evans did not know this and before long he would be able to redeem the stock. He would have to give Evans some kind of a formal transfer and must see him about this in the morning. In the meantime, he was tired after a disturbing day, and locking the office, he went for his car.

## CHAPTER III

### THE SPIRIT TANK

BRIGHT sunshine and speeding shadow touched the bleak moorland. A boisterous wind blew in from sea, but the morning was warm and Creighton's mood was tranquil while his car ran down hill. For one thing, Ruth was happy at Munich and declared she made good progress. The letter Creighton had got before he started related some compliments her masters had made her. Then Janet had not bothered him about bills, and the coke ovens were going well. In a few weeks, he could pay off the banker's loan and Stayward would know nothing about the transaction.

Creighton was careless; things did not bother him long, and when he had put off a trouble he forgot about it. Moreover, he had put a generous dose of brandy in the coffee he had drunk while he smoked a cigarette after breakfast. He did not know if Janet knew about this or not, but he had got the habit when he drove to the works on bitter winter mornings. When the condensers were not turning out good stuff and he expected a hard day at the laboratory, he took a larger dose.

As the car ran down hill the stone walks along the road gave place to ragged thorns. Rusty pit-rope spanned the gaps the wind had made, and the bent trees about the farmsteads were blackened by smoke. Clouds of dingy fumes from the blast-furnaces trailed across the sky, and clusters of chimney stacks dotted the green sweep of corn by the coast. The bleak landscape was stained by the grime of industry, but the sun shone and the wind was bracing. Creighton felt cheerful as he smoked his cigar.

When the car rolled into a mean, black village he slowed the engine. Children played about the street, lean whippet dogs ran across, and here and there a broken bottle threatened his tires. Some of the strongly-built men lounging about the doorsteps gave him a nod and some a dull glance. All knew Creighton of the coke ovens, where a number worked, but the North-countryman is not, as a rule, remarkably gracious to his employer, and Stayward was hard. Yet the strange thing was, although the hands disputed with Stayward and his partner was indulgent, they did better work for the man who generally beat them than for Creighton. After all, Stayward sprang from their stock; he was blunt and forceful, and they understood his philosophy. He swore, in their own dialect, when Creighton smiled.

The car turned a corner and Creighton threw away his cigar. A high wall ran along the road, and in one place, a streak of flame leaped up through the smoke from the ovens. The flame ought not to be there; it was near the tank into which spirit was pumped, and a row of small houses fronted the wall. Creighton remembered that they had been puzzled to find a place for the tank, and the spot on which they had fixed did not altogether comply with the rules. He had left the thing to Stayward and did not know how

# THE SPIRIT TANK

he had satisfied the local council. Stayward's habit was to carry out his plans.

Creighton drove through a gate and stopped. Not far off, a group of men stood about a jet of fire that shot up and broke into a shower of blazing drops. It burned furiously, without slanting from the wind, as if forced up by strong pressure, and smoke that had a strangely pungent smell eddied about the neighboring tank and blew across the wall. Some of the men had shovels and were throwing sand into the flame, which sprang from a hollow like a crater at the top of the pile. Creighton imagined the stop-valve that controlled the supply of spirit to the tank was beneath the sand. The spirit was obviously burning at the valve and he did not see how they could put it out. To begin with, however, the blaze must not be allowed to excite alarm in the village.

"Shut the gate," he said, and turned to a man who had wrapped a greasy red handkerchief round his hand and wrist. "Have you stopped the pump? How did the fire start?"

"Pump's stopped. I reckon spirit's running back from tank; she's mair nor half full. When I com't in, fire was weel alight. Carruthers found valve leaking in t' dark and when he was looking what was wrang she fired from his lamp."

Creighton nodded. The vapor the spirit gave off was strongly inflammable, but there was no use in talking about the carelessness of the man who had used an open engineer's lamp to examine the leaky joint.

"Have you tried to screw down the valve?" he asked.

The other held up his bandaged hand and Creighton saw his skin was blistered above the greasy handkerchief. Moreover, he noted raw red spots on the man's face.

"Yes; I tried 't, but couldn't get hold with spanner because of flame. Neabody else wad gan near and I'll no' try again."

It looked as if his resolve was justified. The jet of fire broke at its top into a shower of burning liquid; the men had buried the valve, and in order to reach the hole from which the blaze sprang one must stand amidst the shower. Nothing could be done to stop the leak, but while Creighton knitted his brows Stayward and a young man ran across the yard. Creighton imagined the young man was his partner's nephew and they had just arrived by the office entrance. Stayward did not ask questions; his plan was to deal with essentials first.

"We must empty tank," he said and pushed one of the men. "Gan to station for benzol car and see you bring her; shunting engine's in the yard." Then he turned to the others. "Tak' your shovels. We're gan t' dig."

They followed him to the tank, and seizing a spade, he marked out a trench. Creighton got a pick, for although he was not given to physical effort the need was urgent and he saw Stayward's plan. The tank was not large, but it held a quantity of explosive spirit, and Stayward meant to run off some of the liquid. This would lessen the risk, but it was not enough. The tank was thin and sparks rained about its top; the spirit was volatile and the vapor it gave off could hardly be kept in by the caulking at the joints. If the tank bursts, the burning liquid must be turned into the trench before it could flow about the yard and into the street.

They got to work and Creighton noted that Stayward's nephew, who had thrown off his vest and jacket, used the shovel well. He was an athletic young fellow and looked good-humored and frank. Fresh men came to help, the trench got deeper, and presently a small locomotive snorted up the line that ran into the yard, and pushed a big steel cylinder up to the tank. Black smoke and sparks blew round the engine, and the driver looked out.

"It's nea a varra safe job you're giving us," he said. "Hooiver, we'll try 't if you'll fix your pipe quick."

"Two's enough to help him," Stayward remarked. "The rest of you will dig."

Creighton, digging and watching the men at the pipe, was conscious of keen suspense. It looked as if the steel cylinder filled very slowly, the blaze had leaped up higher, and one could not tell when a spark might start an explosion. There was some leakage round the joint where the pipe was screwed to the tank. The thing was horribly risky, but the men went on digging and nobody looked disturbed. They were slow North-country folk and hard to move.

At length the engine whistled and rolled away with its load. Some of the dangerous stuff was gone, the pressure was eased, and the flame sank a little. Creighton, with a feeling of keen satisfaction, stopped to get his breath and straighten his aching back. Next moment, however, he dropped his spade, for there was a sharp crack, and he saw the tank split along a joint of the plates. It opened, as if torn apart, a heavy report shook the ovens, and a column of fire leaped up. Then thick smoke rolled about the yard, and Creighton saw a burning flood run across the ground. His face and hands smarted, and he thought he noted dark spots with smoldering edges on his clothes.

The men went back for a few yards, and then stopped when Stayward shouted. Creighton saw him run forward, into the smoke, with his nephew close by; but for the next few minutes he was desperately occupied. Waves of fire overflowed the trench and broke against the bank behind, bent figures loomed in the smoke, and one heard the furious clink of shovels. The men's job was plain; they must hold back and, if possible, smother the fire. They needed no orders and Stayward gave none. He worked where the fire was hottest and when he ran to meet a fresh wave of burning spirit his nephew followed.

In the meantime, the roar of the explosion had alarmed the village. Clogs rattled on the stones outside and shouts came from behind the gate.

"Keep it shut," Stayward ordered. "Let nobody in."

Before long some of the men were burned and some half blinded, for the tank had not been altogether wrecked and the spirit, expanded by the heat, welled up from its lower part. The men not burned were breathless and nearly exhausted, but they labored on, until a few stopped for a moment when a bell clanged noisily in the street and somebody beat on the gate.

"Here's fire-engine; let her in!" a man outside shouted.

## THE SPIRIT TANK

"Water's nea use," Stayward replied. "They can play hose on hooses if they're keen on a job."

There were fresh shouts, the crowd in the street began an angry clamor, and the gate shook. It looked as if the firemen were resolved to come in, but the gate stood the battering and Stayward's men worked on. The fire was slowly dying out under the showers of sand and soil, and at length only spasmodic spurts of flame leaped up from the trench. Stayward threw down his shovel and lifted his hand.

"I reckon you have done a good job and I will not forget," he said. "Noo we must wait until she cools and you'll gan back to ovens."

They went off. It was not Stayward's rule to say too much, and he and Creighton went to the office. Creighton's hands and face smarted; Stayward's coat was riddled by holes. The sleeve of the young man's shirt was burned and his arm was stained by soot. He stopped for a moment by the door, with the light from a window opposite in his eyes, which hurt because he had been in the smoke.

"My nephew, Geoffrey Lisle; he has come down for a short holiday," Stayward remarked.

Lisle bowed to Creighton, whom he could not see distinctly. The office was small and Creighton sat in the shadow behind the open door.

"You have had bad luck this morning," said Lisle. "It will cost you something to re-plate the tank and I think a number of windows were broken when the top blew off. However, I must try to get rid of this soot and put on my jacket."

He went behind a partition where water and towels were kept and the others heard a splash. Then he resumed, speaking across the low partition: "Didn't you build the thing rather near the street?"

"We were cramped for room. The yard is small," Creighton replied.

"One doesn't want a tank of explosive spirit beside one's office, but there are rules about such things. How did you satisfy the local council?"

"I left that to your uncle. I don't know the arguments he used, but they seem to have had some weight. The important thing is, he didn't see a better site for the tank."

Lisle laughed. "Well, I admit he is rather hard to beat. However, since I've burned my arm I'll go and see if the engineer can give me some olive oil. I know my way about and expect you want to talk."

He went off by a door behind the partition, and Stayward said, "The lad has been at the works when you were away. He's employed by a good firm of mining engineers and, for a young man, his judgment's quick and sound. I expect you saw he spotted the worst trouble we're going to have?"

Creighton said he had noted this and Stayward, knitting his heavy brows, was silent for a minute or two. He was a big, rugged North-countryman, with steady eyes, a stern face, and touches of white in his hair. Although he had been to a famous school, he used the Cumbrian dialect when he was moved. The Staywards had long owned a belt of bleak hillside and had kept it after the small *statesmen*, driven by economic pressure, sold their farms. For the most part, they were frugal folk, and since the weather was inhospitable and the soil was poor, now and then invested money in mining ventures. There were useful minerals in the hills but the cost of extraction generally absorbed the profit.

Stayward's father, however, had sold much of the estate and lost the money on Liverpool shipping shares. Creighton imagined his partner's ambition was to buy back the land, and with this object he had mortgaged his diminished inheritance and built the coke ovens. Now it looked as if the last of the Stayward money was gone.

"What's damage going to cost us?" Stayward asked presently.

"It depends," said Creighton. "To begin with, if we're liable for the repairs to the houses——"

"We are liable. We put tank in wrong place and must pay."

"There was nowhere else it could be put."

"Weel I ken that," said Stayward. "I took the risk; when I built ovens it was all a risk. However, we'll say it costs five hundred pounds. Where's money coming from?"

Creighton tried to hide his disturbance. Stayward knew they were embarrassed, but Creighton hoped he did not know how bad the situation really was.

"Not from the bank, I think," he answered. "There's not much use in bothering Evans."

Somewhat to his relief, Stayward nodded. One danger was put off and something might happen that would ease the strain. Creighton had a hopeful temperament and never fronted trouble until he was forced. In this Stayward was different; he studied obstacles ahead and made his plans to move them from his path.

"I see a way," Stayward said. "Greenbank folk are blowing out a furnace and will not want their coke, but we have a stock of soft coal good enough to make foundry stuff. We'll put it in ovens and work off the foundry contract. They pay end of month for all deliveries."

Creighton got a bad jolt and the hope he had begun to indulge vanished. Stayward's plan looked good and Creighton could urge nothing against it but the convincing argument he durst not use. The coal that would make foundry coke was not theirs, because he had pawned it with the bank manager.

"I don't know," he said, as carelessly as possible. "We'll soon have to pay the colliery owners."

"Colliery must wait. Trade's slack, and we take a lot o' their coal; they must get their interest and mayhappen will not bother us much."

"But——" said Creighton and stopped, for Stayward gave him an impatient glance and got up.

"Have you no guts, man? Unless we take a bold line and keep it, there's nowt but ruin for us. Weel, I'll give foreman his orders to start on foundry coke in morning; and then I'll look at damage."

He jerked his powerful shoulders, frowned, and went off, while Creighton sat in a slack pose and gazed moodily in front. He durst not tell his partner the coal they were going to sell the foundry belonged to the bank. Moreover, this was not all; there was another irregularity he had used to persuade Evans, and Stayward was honest. Creighton would not think about it. After all, perhaps, Stayward need not know, and the coking of the inferior coal was enough to

# THE SPIRIT TANK

occupy Creighton. To sell goods one had already pawned was obviously dishonest, but Creighton wondered whether it was criminal fraud. Although he did not know the law about such things, he was afraid. However, Evans would not find out for some time, and Creighton went off to the laboratory.

## CHAPTER IV

### STAYWARD FINDS OUT

STAYWARD promised full satisfaction for the damage the bursting tank had caused. The promise was characteristic; Stayward was hard and exacted all that was his, but he paid his debts. Indeed, his stern honesty gave Creighton ground for anxious thought, because he knew they could not hold out long and he dreaded Stayward's anger when he found out how the reckoning had been put off.

Creighton began to see that his efforts were useless. Disaster was getting very near, and since he generally took the easiest line, the temptation to run away was strong. He did not go, partly because it demanded an effort he could not rouse himself to make, and party because he must give his wife some explanation before he went. Creighton shrank from enlightening Janet. He knew her well; she would be very bitter and would not see that she was to some extent accountable for his disgrace.

He waited, bracing himself with liquor in the morning before he started for the works, since he half expected to find when he arrived that Stayward knew. All the same, he kept their account books in the safe, where they would not catch Stayward's eye, and did not talk about their embarrassments.

For a time nothing disturbing happened, and then

one afternoon Creighton drove back moodily to the works from a neighboring mine. The strain he had borne was wearing him, and he was bothered by a letter from Ruth that arrived when he left home. She wrote bravely about her studies, but the effort she made was rather obvious. In fact, she said too much, and Creighton, understanding his daughter because he loved her, got a hint of disillusion and anxiety that he thought she meant to hide. He wondered whether Ruth was finding out that her talent for music was less than she had thought.

Creighton hoped not. Ruth had got her year at Munich, but this was all he could give her. One needed much talent to make one's mark, and if she had not enough her disappointment would be sharp. It was plain he could not help her to try again, and somehow one did not expect Ruth to make a good marriage. If she gave up her hope of a musical career, it looked as if she must resign to a life of dreary economy in the quiet dale. Creighton reflected with a touch of rather grim amusement that Janet might be forced to use stern economy soon.

When he stopped inside the big gate at the yard he felt a curious dislike for the works. A tall chimney of raw yellow brick poured out thick smoke, acrid fumes escaped from the ovens, and the yard smelt of soot and tar. The men's wet faces were blackened, their rough clothes were stained, and all one saw was marked by squalid ugliness. Creighton was something of an artist, and although, except for chemistry, he had no constructive talent, he could feel.

At the beginning, the ugliness had not jarred him much. For a time he was absorbed by his invention.

The study of the strange chemical combinations that took place in the tar was fascinating. With a proper plant, one could distill a remarkable number of useful essences from the sticky mess coke ovens had not long since wasted. For all that, when the object of one's experiments was strictly economical, the fascination wore off; Creighton admitted he had no industrial genius. He had gone on in order to earn the money Janet needed, and now he was tired of it all.

Stayward was not about the yard, and when the foreman said he had gone to the bank Creighton got a jar. He went to the office and his hand shook as he picked up some letters the afternoon post had brought. When he read the letters he knew why Stayward had gone to the bank and it was ominous that the safe, where they kept their books, was open. Creighton looked at his watch. It was nearly four o'clock. Stayward had been shut up with the manager for some time after the bank closed its doors and Creighton could imagine what they talked about.

Conquering an impulse to drive off before his partner's return, he sat down. The reckoning had come and there was nothing to be gained by putting off his interview with Stayward until the morning. He felt a strange dullness that rather blunted the suspense. At length Stayward came in, and sitting down, threw some documents on his desk. Although Creighton knew his nerve was good, he looked badly shaken. His glance wandered about the office, he moved once or twice with a curious jerkiness, and then his face went grim and he fixed his eyes on Creighton.

"I've seen Evans at the bank," he said.

## STAYWARD FINDS OUT

"Then I expect you got a nasty knock," said Creighton. "I'm sorry——"

Stayward stopped him with a scornful gesture.

"You're sorry? Man, have done with cant! Though I never quite trusted you or Janet, you have cheated me over long."

"I think we won't talk about Janet. The dispute is ours; it has nothing to do with her."

Stayward laughed, savagely. "Keep your smooth talk for your wife's smart friends; it will not go with me. There never was a Hassal ran quite straight, but Janet has made her man a thief."

"This line won't take us far," said Creighton, coloring. "Let's stick to the subject. I'm your partner and the refining plant is mine. The coke ovens do not pay. The Durham makers get a higher price for harder stuff; our profit's on the spirit and dyes we extract from the refuse. The process is my invention."

"Do you claim you invented the extraction of these products from waste tar? I imagined everybody knew a much better plant than ours has long been working in this country and Germany. Did we not lose the last large order because the German stuff cost less?"

"I'm not a fool. All I claim is, my process gives better results than others when you use our poor coal. Anyhow, nobody else has found a way of breaking up the particular chemical combinations that bother us. I have. You must use my plan or stop the ovens."

"We'll talk about this again," said Stayward, with a grim smile that disturbed Creighton. "In the meantime, you imagine the partnership justified your robbing me?"

"I haven't studied the law," said Creighton, whose

face got very red. "For all that, it is understood a partner is entitled to use the money he has helped to earn. His drawings are not limited to his share of the profit on the sum he invested."

"How much did you invest?"

"My invention."

The veins swelled on Stayward's forehead and his eyes sparkled, but with an effort he controlled his rage.

"You joined me when nobody else was willing to try your plan. Folks declared our coal wouldn't pay for coking; I said it would, if I could distill spirit in the tar. Well, I backed my judgment; how you ken. Sold land that belonged to Staywards for three hundred years, borrowed and mortgaged, and put into the venture aw I had——"

He stopped, as if for breath and resumed: "Noo where has it gone? While I labored, living plainer than my workmen, stinting myself and saving, your wife spent my money on her dinner parties and her London clothes."

"Oh, well," said Creighton, deprecatingly, "I imagine Janet did no more than her neighbors expected. In a way, she was forced to keep the rules of the people to whom she belonged."

Stayward let himself go. He sprang from sturdy yeoman stock and was proud of his ancestors. When angry, he was rude, like them, and used their dialect.

"The Hassals?" he said with scorn. "There are old standards who mind when t' Hassals first came to the dale. Spendthrift wastrels, weel-kent at betting clubs and small race meetings, where one was warned off. Folks you could trust to have a hand in the jobbery when land was sold above its value and rents

# STAYWARD FINDS OUT

were putten up. Walling off bits o' common and straining manor rights, so they could plant larches on fell-foot and let the shooting. I reckon that's aw t' Hassals did for countryside."

"I don't see what this has to do with our dispute," Creighton remarked in a languid voice.

"Then, I'll let you see! Staywards farmed their land; they worked and paid their debts. We were kenned and trusted lang before t' Hassals came. But you let Janet rule you and make me party to a theft!"

"Is it theft to borrow?"

"You pawned goods that were not ours, and when, kenning nothing o' this, I sold them, let me use the money that ought to have paid the loan. Noo we owe their value to the colliery and the bank. But you will not shame me again. I've done with your tricks. Our agreement breaks to-night."

Creighton pulled himself together. He had expected something like this, but he wondered whether Stayward knew all.

"An agreement is not easily broken, unless both parties consent."

Stayward smiled harshly and picked up a document from the bundle on his desk.

"Partnership's one thing and *per-procuration* another. I do not ken the law weel, but I reckon *this* is forgery. Although I have not denied my hand yet, I think Evans suspects."

Creighton's mouth opened loosely and his pose got slack. He leaned forward as if the strength to hold himself upright had gone. His curiosity was satisfied. When Stayward began to put the documents in the safe he got up.

"If you turn me out, my patent carries royalties——"

"We'll talk about patent in morning," said Stayward very grimly. "Noo you'll gan and leave me to grapple with the ruin you have made."

Creighton went and Stayward clenched his fist when he heard the throb of the car. For a time, he sat still, frowning. He was proud and reserved and it was long since he had said so much. In a sense, he had taken a ridiculous line; there was no use in lashing his feeble antagonist with savage talk. His business was to break the fellow and not to scold like an angry woman. This, however, was not important and he had got some satisfaction from letting himself go.

Presently he called his foreman, who had come from some coke ovens where another process for refining tar was used. Stayward talked to the man for a time and when he sent him away searched two or three iron boxes. At length, he found a document with the seal of the patent office, and thought it typical that Creighton had not bothered to take the thing away. Stayward spread out the parchment on his desk, and for two or three hours studied the patent, comparing the specification with some drawings Creighton had made and a sheet of chemical formulæ.

Stayward was not a chemist, but he was tenacious and very shrewd, and since he started the ovens had learned something about the actions and reactions that went on when they refined the tar. Moreover, he knew Creighton and presently found, as he had half expected, that some of the stated particulars were vague. In order that the holder may forbid anybody else to copy his invention, a patent must be precise,

## STAYWARD FINDS OUT

but Creighton, or his agent, had left an opening for dispute. Stayward, studying the carelessly-drawn specification, began to make some plans.

When he was satisfied the plans would work he locked the office and set off up the smoky street. His house was some distance off and he was not young, but on the whole he liked the walk. He had no other relaxation and thought it kept him fit. Sometimes he reflected with dry amusement that Creighton used a car.

Dusk was falling when he reached Nethercleugh, the last of his inheritance and recently mortgaged. The house had been built for farmers and had sheltered many generations of Staywards who knew nothing of luxury. The thick walls were rough-dressed slate, and rose, without ornament, from amidst a group of bent ash trees. A dry-stone dike surrounded the garden, where potatoes grew, for it was characteristic that there were no flowers. Behind the house, boggy fields rolled back to the moor, and, with a feeble blink of light from one window, Nethercleugh looked strangely desolate. The evening was dark and a dreary wind tossed the ash trees' groaning boughs.

Stayward opened the door in the porch and entered the slate-flagged kitchen. They used no rugs and carpets, the furniture was old, and the low ceiling rested on worm-eaten, crooked beams. Narrow windows pierced the thick walls and strangers thought Nethercleugh dark and cold. An old woman, knitting by the peat fire, turned her head when Stayward came in. Belle Ritson and a kitchen girl were all his household. He put his hat on the table and pulled up a chair.

"You must get rid of Nancy, Belle, and if you're wise, you'll look for another place at hiring fair," he said.

The old woman's face was lined and reddened by the winds that wailed about Nethercleugh. She scarcely looked up and her knitting needles clicked steadily.

"I was here when ye were born and I'm too oad to shift," she said.

"You'll not can manage when Nancy's gone. The hoose is big."

"I'll try 't. T' lass is young and feckless. I'll no' miss her."

"Then, I don't know about your wages and our food. I'll need to cut down the shopkeepers' bills."

"Wages can wait; I dinna spend much," said Belle, and stopping her knitting, quietly looked up. "Is coke ovens no running weel?"

"They're running all right. Trouble is, I don't know if they and Nethercleugh are mine."

"Then, your partner's takken your money to pleasure his lady wife? There's some good gentry, but aw t' Hassal lot is bad. Hooiver, ye're none easy robbed."

Stayward smiled, rather dryly. "All the same, money's gone and I've broken partnership. I may recover; I don't know yet, but it will be a long fight."

"Staywards is stubborn fratchers," Belle replied. "Weel, I alloo we'll mannish. Ye'll need somebody to tent ye and I'm past boddering aboot my meat. Noo ye'll gan to parlor and I'll bring ye yours."

"You're a leal soul, Belle," said Stayward, who was moved by her staunchness.

"I'm oad," she said. "I'm used with Nethercleugh and I'll not can bodder to try another place."

## CHAPTER V

### MRS. CREIGHTON REFUSES

AFTER his interview with Stayward, Creighton drove home, weighing gloomily a half-formed plan. It would be hard to tell Janet, but she must be told and, if possible, persuaded to agree. The situation needed a desperate cure, and he nerved himself to make a plunge. Janet could help; in spite of her extravagance, she was clever and resolute. If she supported him, they might make a fresh start; but he knew his wife and doubted.

At dinner Creighton said nothing about his embarrassments, although he noted that Mrs. Creighton now and then looked hard at him. After the meal was over they went out on the terrace and he leaned against the low wall, on which red geraniums flowered. Mrs. Creighton occupied a neighboring bench.

The evening was calm, and the light was going; a smell of flowers floated across the lawn and one heard lambs crying on the hill. The dark firs were losing their sharpness and a little mist began to creep about the crest of the moor. Creighton was conscious of a curious pang. The serenity and beauty of the spot appealed to his love of ease. He shrank from effort and struggle, but his weakness and Janet's folly had banished him from this quiet retreat. He must go out and front the storm, but he feared disaster if he went alone.

"You are moody," Mrs. Creighton remarked. "I suppose something has gone wrong at the works?"

"All has gone wrong," said Creighton. "Stayward has found me out."

Mrs. Creighton moved abruptly, but next moment resumed her quiet pose, although her glance was keen.

"You're ridiculous when you're theatrical," she said. "What has Stayward found out?"

"That we have squandered his money and he has not enough to keep the ovens going. As you know, I have none. He has broken our partnership."

"Ah!" said Mrs. Creighton and was silent for a moment or two. Then she resumed: "From the beginning I disliked John Stayward. He is not our sort, but I thought he could help you. Now it looks as if he had cheated us."

Creighton laughed harshly. "Stayward is persuaded I have cheated him and he has some grounds, but we'll let this go. He has turned me out and we cannot live at Iveghyll on your income."

The color came into Mrs. Creighton's hard, pale face and her eyes sparkled.

"I don't know if you cheated Stayward, but you cheated me. You were not poor when I married you; you had talent and an occupation. I thought you might go far."

"I buried my talent. You were fastidious about the use I made of it, and when at length I dug it up it had rusted. Hard wear keeps one's talents bright. But you look impatient and to philosophize won't help much."

## MRS. CREIGHTON REFUSES 43

"How do you mean to help? It wouldn't be strange if you had a useful plan."

"We won't quarrel," said Creighton, and there was an appeal in the look he gave her. "I've been slack and perhaps your reproaching me is justified. We'll leave it there. We must make a fresh start and I have a plan."

Mrs. Creighton said nothing for a few moments. She had got a hard knock, but she had pluck and the hurt braced her and made her savage. She thought she had borne much for her husband's sake, but now the ambitions to which she had stubbornly clung were altogether gone. She must give up the high place she had fought for, her neighbors would no longer own her rule, and nobody would give her the deference she felt she was entitled to claim. A bankrupt's wife had no social claims.

"Well?" she said, coolly.

Creighton pulled himself together. He doubted if he could persuade Janet, but he must try. This was a duty he owed both; she was his wife and for her sake he must submit to the rules of civilization and earn by irksome labor the means to live. After all, he was rather a good chemist, and although his occupation had lost its charm, there was nothing upon which he could fall back if he gave it up.

But he needed Janet's support.

"We must leave Iveghyll," he said. "Your friends will drop me when they hear Stayward's tale; it's possible they will drop you. Your money will not support us and I cannot be a burden on my wife. Very well. Suppose we make a plunge, trust our luck, and start again in a new country? One has chances of making good in, for example, South Africa or Canada."

"What do you think of doing in South Africa?" Mrs. Creighton asked, in an ironical voice.

"There are posts at the mines," said Creighton, vaguely. "I know something about the analysis and refining of precious metals and would keep the post I got. I think I have enough skill for this, and when you have no other resources you stick to your job. In fact, I feel we have come to a turning and the way we turn is important. I'm getting old and can't go back when I've taken the new path."

"I think that is so," Mrs. Creighton agreed and pondered. Then she asked: "Where does your new path lead?"

"Up hill, I must admit. I've come down rather fast, and it's plainly time to stop. There's a rough climb in front, perhaps the struggle will be long, but, if you help, I think we'll reach smooth ground."

"A long struggle, in a rude country! Oh, I know in some of the towns they have big hotels, handsome offices, and modern clubs; but where would you find the grace and refinement we value in England?"

"It's possible we value our surface refinement too high," Creighton remarked. Then he laughed. "If we leave out your friends and people of their sort, I don't know if we have much refinement in the North. Stayward, for example, is as rude a type as one would expect to meet on the back-veldt."

"The back-veldt! Some of the mines are there, long distances from even a squalid Boer town. Life at such a place would be impossible. I cannot see

## MRS. CREIGHTON REFUSES 45

myself keeping house in an iron shanty, with a savage Kaffir boy to help."

"No," said Creighton, smiling. "I cannot see you. Somehow, you don't fit into the picture. Well, it looks as if you don't like my plan. What is yours?"

"Mine provides for Ruth, whom I think you have forgotten," Mrs. Creighton replied. "She must stay in England and go on with her music. Perhaps she will be a famous player; it is possible she will make a good marriage. Since we are forced to give up Iveghyll, we will go to Beckfoot cottage. It ought to have been mine and I expect my cousin will let me have it for a very small rent. With a few alterations, Beckfoot might suit——"

She stopped and Creighton imagined she was thinking about enlargements and new furniture. It was obvious that she left him out of her plans, and on the whole he was resigned. Janet meant to go her way and he would go his. After all, he was something of a vagabond and had long chafed against conventional restraints and monotonous work. Perhaps he was not too old to taste adventure and indulge vague romantic longings he had controlled.

"Then there are your patent royalties. You must fight Stayward for your rights," Mrs. Creighton resumed.

"I'm going to see him in the morning. For all that, it wouldn't be prudent to reckon on the royalties."

"But we will need the money. You have none."

"I won't need much," said Creighton dryly. "Ruth must have her chance, and my stay in this country will embarrass you. Well, I think I'll try South Africa."

Mrs. Creighton looked hard at him and hesitated. Then she said thoughtfully: "Perhaps the plan has some advantages. After all, if you didn't get a good post, you could come back."

"That is so," Creighton agreed. "On the whole, I think the advantages outweigh the drawbacks."

He got up, lighted a cigarette, and strolled off across the grass with a feeling of half bitter amusement. Janet had chosen her path and he must take his alone. Well, she was not romantic and perhaps she was justified. For one thing, Ruth must have her chance. Creighton had never loved his wife as he loved his daughter. Yet it would be a pull to leave the dale and his thoughts were melancholy as he looked about.

The light had gone and the black moors cut against a pale green and orange sky. The firs had faded to dusky spires; moving sheep made blurred dots on the long slope of a hill, and the splash of the beck came drowsily across the evening calm. The calm soothed Creighton, although he knew he had enjoyed it too long. When he ought to have struggled he had loafed, and now the reckoning had come. One must pay for slackness and folly, but he did not mean to grumble. He could pay; his languid temperament made this easier. By and by he returned to the house and talked to Mrs. Creighton about altering Beckfoot cottage.

In the morning, she stated that she would go with him in the car to the mining village, and although Creighton did not know her object he agreed. It was about ten o'clock when she got down in the smoky street and Creighton drove to the office, where Stayward was waiting. The latter looked worn and stern and roughly signed Creighton to sit down.

## MRS. CREIGHTON REFUSES

"About your patent royalties," he said. "I see we have thirty pounds, in notes and gold, in the safe; it's all that you have left. If you will write me a receipt, I'll pay you the sum for the use of your invention."

"This is ridiculous!" Creighton exclaimed.

"Not at all. It's thirty pounds or nothing," said Stayward, who put a drawing on the desk, and Creighton noted that he used his ordinary colloquial English. When Stayward was cool and on his guard, he dropped the Cumbrian dialect. John was ominously cool now.

Creighton picked up the drawing and started, for he thought he saw the line Stayward meant to take. The plan showed some alterations to his distilling apparatus, and the new arrangement of the pipes would work.

"If I'd drawn that patent, I'd have made my specification tight," Stayward resumed. "I reckon yours wasn't worth the fees. Anyhow, I'm going to use it, and if you claim my modified process is an infringement, you can put your lawyers on my track." He paused and added with a grim smile: "Going to law's expensive. Perhaps you had better think before you begin."

Creighton durst not go to law, but the blood came to his face.

"It's robbery!" he declared.

"If we are going to talk about robbery, I have much to say," Stayward rejoined. "Better let it go! I'm getting old, but I've paid my debts since I began to work. I offer you thirty pounds for the use of a patent any man with brains can infringe. If our works had been larger and our stuff well known, somebody would have copied your plant before. Well, I'm ready to fight. Are you?"

It was obvious that Stayward could not be moved. Creighton knew he was just, as far as he saw, but very hard, and there was no use in begging for mercy that would be refused. Besides, unless he asked Janet for money, he would need the thirty pounds.

"You know I'm in your power," he said. "I'll take the money."

"Then write a clean receipt, giving me full use of the invention until the patent runs out."

Creighton did so, and Stayward, who examined the document carefully, counted out the sum. Then he got up, as if to indicate that the interview was over.

"That's done with and I've done with you," he said. "If there's anything you're not satisfied about, send your lawyers. The foreman will not let you through the gate again."

Creighton went out and found Mrs. Creighton waiting by the car. He saw she carried a small handbag.

"Where have you been?" he asked.

"I went to the bank," Mrs. Creighton replied. "I wanted to get there when it opened. You see, I had not used all the sum you gave me some time since."

"And you thought it prudent to draw the rest?"

"Of course," said Mrs. Creighton. "I imagined Stayward might be spiteful since you had quarreled. I meant to get to the bank first."

Creighton laughed. Janet's caution was typical, and she did not need him. One could trust Janet to secure all she thought was hers.

## CHAPTER VI

#### RUTH IS MOVED TO ANGER

CREIGHTON had been neraly a year in Africa when Ruth came home, and on the evening of her arrival she sat with her mother in the cottage drawing-room. The ornaments and some of the pictures she had known at Iveghyll had gone, but the small room had been expensively decorated and Ruth thought it held too much furniture. She sat by an open window and, looking out on the garden, owned that Beckfoot had charm.

A copper beech spread its branches across the narrow lawn, flowers filled the borders by the clipped hedge, and in the distance the high fells lifted their rugged tops above the sweep of moor. Mountain-ashes dotted a ravine where a beck splashed in the fern, moisture trickled down the bright-green creeper on the wall, and although there were gleams of sunshine, gentle rain was falling. It was a typical evening in the misty North.

Ruth liked the smell of wet soil and the soothing murmur of the beck. She had come home hurt and disillusioned, but she loved the fells. So far, she had not given Mrs. Creighton all her confidence and she studied her quietly. Her mother looked tired and dissatisfied; her face was thin and her eyes were hard. One felt she was getting old sooner than she ought, but Ruth could account for this. Her father was in South Africa and her mother did not bear poverty well, although the poverty was not very marked. Ruth was sorry she had no comfort to bring but rather an extra load.

In the meantime, Mrs. Creighton saw her daughter had developed since she left home. She had not thought her beautiful; Ruth had not the charm that commands quick admiration, although her figure was graceful and her carriage was good. Her face was grave, her eyes were too calm and contemplative, and she had not much color. People had sometimes thought her dull. Now she had got a touch of dignity and although she was quiet, her smile was easy. Mrs. Creighton felt that the girl had, so to speak, awakened and become human. She had been absorbed by her music before.

"It must have hurt to leave Iveghyll, but I like Beckfoot," Ruth said presently. "I want you to tell me about father's quarrel with Mr. Stayward. You know I would have come home before he sailed, but you urged me to stay."

"His wish was you should get your year for study," Mrs. Creighton replied. "Then there was no time. He went by the first steamer after he resolved to go."

She mused for a few moments. To give up Iveghyll and own that she was poor had hurt much; moreover, she knew people blamed her husband for her poverty. She had not indulged Creighton while he was at home, but now she was his stanch and resolute defender. He had written to her, from Johannesburg, and again from a Boer dorp farther west on the Rand, but he did not tell her much, except that

## RUTH IS MOVED TO ANGER

he had found employment for pay that met his needs.

"I will get you his last letter," she said.

Ruth studied the letter. It was careless, but she understood her father and thought his carelessness was forced. Things were not going very well with him, although she doubted if Mrs. Creighton knew, and hesitated to disturb her.

"Why did he quarrel with Stayward?" she asked.

Mrs. Creighton told her a moving tale. Enforced economy was hard, she missed her husband more than she had thought, and she blamed Stayward on both accounts. She was an obstinate woman with some skill for argument and by long brooding over her misfortunes had almost persuaded herself that Creighton was his partner's victim. It was a relief to pour her hatred into Ruth's sympathetic ears. The tale, however, was not altogether false. Mrs. Creighton saw when she must avoid exaggeration and when frankness helped plausibility. Studying her daughter, she saw the girl's eyes sparkle and the color come to her skin. Ruth, in fact, was getting angry, but wanted to be just.

"In a sense, the money we used was Stayward's," she remarked.

"No," said Mrs. Creighton firmly, "it belonged to the house, in which, of course, your father was a partner. This justified his using the money he needed, particularly since there was no stipulation that he must not do so. Then it's important that but for your father's invention Stayward could not have started the ovens; his patent enabled them to carry on the business. Making coke did not pay; they earned their profit by refining the tar."

Ruth was young and Mrs. Creighton's argument looked plausible. She allowed it to persuade her, but there was much she wanted to know, because she doubted if her mother would be frank again.

"The invention was father's," she agreed. "Why did he not make Stayward pay for using it after they broke the agreement?"

Mrs. Creighton saw her opportunity. She was on firm ground now.

"Ah," she said, "this is where one sees Stayward in his proper light. Your father trusted him and his patent was not very carefully worded. Stayward is unscrupulous and saw how he could copy the pipes and retorts."

"But could we not have stopped him if we had gone to law?"

"Going to law is expensive, particularly in a dispute about a patent. One must engage clever lawyers and get famous engineers to prove your antagonist's plan is an infringement of your rights. If we had been able to do so, we might have won, but Stayward knew your father had no money."

"So he robbed him because he was poor!" Ruth remarked in a hard voice.

"Yes," said Mrs. Creighton. "Something like that."

Ruth's eyes sparkled and her face got hot. She hated injustice and was moved to anger because her father, whom she loved, had suffered wrong.

"Stayward is a cruel, unscrupulous man. If we could punish him——" she said.

"I'm afraid he cannot be punished. He is very cunning and your father was careless," Mrs. Creighton replied.

## RUTH IS MOVED TO ANGER 53

Ruth said nothing for a few moments. Creighton's gay carelessness had long had a charm for her. She thought him trustful and generous, and to feel he had been victimized by his calculating partner hurt. But she wanted to know more.

"Why did father go away?" she asked, and hesitated. "Did Stayward try to prejudice people? I mean, did he tell them father ought not to have used his money?"

Mrs. Creighton pondered. So far as she knew, Stayward had said nothing about his grounds for breaking the partnership and she was puzzled by his reserve, but she did not want to talk about this. She meant to work on the girl's feelings until Ruth saw Stayward from her point of view.

"I think he durst not, and people would not have believed his statements," she replied. "After he stole the patent, we were poor. My small income would not meet our needs, but your father was resolved you should not give up your studies. He declared you must have your chance of making a career."

"Then, he really went away in order that I need not come home?" said Ruth, and tears came to her eyes. "But I knew he would do something like this. He was very generous. It hurts; you know how he loved the dale! Yet he went, for my sake——"

She paused and turned her head. When she turned again her look was strained.

"Mother," she said, with forced calm, "it's horrible to feel he gave up all he had—for nothing."

"Ah!" exclaimed Mrs. Creighton. "Why do you say *for nothing?*"

Ruth's face was very pale and the touch of red in

her thick, brown hair emphasized the whiteness of her skin. Her gray eyes were wet and shone with changing lights as she struggled with confused emotion; pity for her father and pity for her much-tried mother, who must get another knock. There was not much pity for herself, because Ruth had pluck.

"I rather dreaded telling you, but you must be told," she said. "Well, you know my ambition. At Munich I found I could get mechanical cleverness, but I knew before I went this was not enough. I hoped I had the power that makes one's music live——"

She paused and with an effort forced herself to go on. "At the beginning, I was satisfied. I worked hopefully at painful exercises that stretch the finger muscles; I got control of the violin on the awkward shifts. My hands and ear were trained. I could feel the delicate shades of sound we call the *nuances*. Then I began to doubt. To stop the notes exactly true and give the strings the smooth vibration that thrills the wood and makes it sing is something, but after all it is not much. One can get this by study, but perseverance is not genius. Sometimes my masters looked thoughtful when I played and I got anxious and disturbed. However, perhaps what I mean's not very plain and I'm boring you?"

"No, I must try to understand."

"Well, I could develop pure tone and mark the rhythm, but I could not seize and reproduce the passion of a theme. Somehow it eluded me. I could not strike the spark that gives music fire. Mine was mechanical and cold. All the same, it was long before I would own the truth. I fought for my ambition; if I had not genius, I had resolve. I thought it might

# RUTH IS MOVED TO ANGER

be possible to win the gift I wanted by stubborn work."

Ruth stopped for a moment and smiled, a brave but melancholy smile.

"It was all no use. If talent is not given you, you must go without, and at length I was forced to see. There was another girl; her hands were not trained, her muscles were weak, and her playing was marked by faults, but she had power. I knew work would take her where it would not take me. Then I went to the master and told him to be frank. He said I had taste and skill, but when I urged he owned that this was all."

"Ah!" said Mrs. Creighton dully. "Then, your study has been wasted? You cannot be a musician?"

"I can teach beginners. Perhaps I play well enough to get engagements for second-class concerts. Since I have no other occupation and mean to help you, I must try to be satisfied."

Mrs. Creighton was moved. She knew Ruth's tenacity and pictured her obstinate struggle and the bitterness of her disappointment. Mrs. Creighton, herself, found the disappointment hard to bear, because they were poor and she had hoped much from the girl's talent. All the same, she had, since Creighton went away, begun to see that her cold selfishness had gradually separated them, and she thought he left her without a pang. In a sense, she had lost her husband, but she did not mean to lose her daughter. One could not altogether go without love.

"My dear!" she said, beckoning, and when Ruth advanced drew her down and took her in her arms.

Ruth's forced calm gave way and resting her head

on her mother's neck, she indulged in healing tears. After a time she got up and resolutely dried her eyes.

"You have helped me much; I wanted help," she said. "Now I must brace up, but it's hard. Father's going away haunts me." She crossed the floor and opened the long window. "The rain is stopping. I think I'll go out."

A few minutes later she crossed the lawn and went up the wet road. She had told her story and her mother had been kind. Ruth admitted, with a feeling of shame, that she had hardly hoped for this; somehow she had not expected Mrs. Creighton to sympathize. Well, the confession she had dreaded was done with, and she thought about her father with mournful tenderness. It hurt to feel his efforts to help her had been thrown away. Indeed, the futility of his sacrifice tempered her pity with a sense of humiliation. He was marked by a strange futility; he failed at all he tried, and so, she owned, did she.

Ruth, however, durst not dwell long on this, and it was a relief to weigh Stayward's part in their troubles and give her anger rein. Her father had, perhaps, been careless, but his partner had profited by his generous trust. She hated Stayward for his cunning and greed. Love for his victim had made her hard, but she did not know her mother had meant to work upon her grief and pity. Mrs. Creighton had, in fact, talked better than she knew.

After a time, Ruth tried to banish her anger. She must be practical. Since Stayward had robbed them, she must earn some money, and if she had no talent for music, she had skill. By and by she would look

# RUTH IS MOVED TO ANGER

for pupils and small concert engagements, but not just yet. Keen disappointment had shaken her and left her dull; she must rest and gather strength to begin another struggle. Ruth was not beaten yet and meant to fight. Although she could not hope for high triumph, something might be won.

## CHAPTER VII

#### RUTH'S ADVENTURE

THE sun was low, the wind had dropped, and it was very hot. The moor shone red and purple, and the long, straight road reflected dazzling light. In the distance, rugged fells cut, faint and blue, against the serene sky. There were no walls and the dust that trailed behind Geoffrey Lisle's throbbing bicycle streaked the parched grass and heather. Geoffrey drove fast, because a tire was slack and he wanted to reach Nethercleugh before it collapsed; besides, he had traveled far and was hot and tired. He was alone, and the side-car carried his thick nailed boots, a Burberry jacket, and a few other things he needed for a climbing holiday. One could reach the high rocks from Nethercleugh and climbing was the only relaxation in which he indulged.

Geoffrey was practical and had concentrated on fitting himself for his occupation. His father and mother were dead, and the small inheritance by which he had lived while he worked off his apprenticeship to a house of mining engineers was nearly exhausted. In order to gain further experience, he had stayed another year for very small pay, but in a month or two he must look for a post and he knew well-paid mining posts were not given to beginners. Although he was not clever he was tenacious and honest and his employers trusted him. Geoffrey wondered whether they meant to offer him an engagement, and thought he would like to stay. So far, however, they had said nothing about their plans.

When he got a holiday he went to Nethercleugh. For one thing nobody bothered him there; he could start at daybreak for the fells and come back when he liked. It was characteristic that when Geoffrey took a climbing holiday he meant to climb and not to loaf and talk. For all that, in the evening, when he was tired, he got some satisfaction from his uncle's society. Stayward did not talk much, but his remarks were shrewd and generally touched by ironical humor. Geoffrey did not know what Stayward thought about him. The old fellow was reserved, but so long as they agreed while he was at Nethercleugh, Geoffrey was satisfied.

By and by the bicycle crossed the top of a hill and Geoffrey saw a girl some distance in front. There was nobody else on the wide sweep of moor and because she broke its loneliness he gave her a careless glance. She carried a violin case and walked on the short grass by the road. She was tall and although the grass was rough, he thought she moved with an athletic grace. It was curious, because the particular grace rather marked mountaineers and running men than girls. Yet she was going slowly, and, if she were tired, he could not see her object for keeping the broken and boggy edge of the moor.

For a few moments her figure was outlined against the sky, and then was lost in the purple heath as the bicycle sped down into a hollow where the road crossed a noisy beck. When he climbed the hill on the other side Geoffrey saw her sitting in the dusty grass, and stopped the engine. The bicycle rolled on for a few yards and when he pulled up in front of the girl he wondered, half embarrassed, whether he ought to have done so.

Now the draught that had whipped his skin had gone, it was very hot; the girl's face was rather white, and she looked tired. Turning her head quietly, she gave him a level glance and he noted that her gray eyes were calm. There was something dignified about her. He thought she was too proud to hint at her surprise.

"I saw you in front," he said. "Then I missed you and when I saw you sitting down I wondered whether you were faint. The hill's pretty steep and the sun's scorching."

"I am not at all faint," she replied and added with a twinkle: "It's a nail in my boot."

"That's awkward," Geoffrey remarked feelingly. "I know something about it. Last time I was in the neighborhood and went over Rough Screes, a sharp clamp-nail worked through. Anyhow, it's not a day to walk and carry a load, even if your foot were all right. How far are you going?"

Ruth studied him, for she saw where his question led. He looked frank and sympathetic, and she was satisfied he had stopped because he thought she needed help. Besides, she had been a student and for the most part her musical friends laughed at conventions.

"I am going up the dale a short distance from Newlands village," he replied.

"That's three or four miles," said Geoffrey. "Since the car's not occupied, wouldn't it be ridiculous if you

## RUTH'S ADVENTURE

walked. All the same, I'd better warn you a tire's getting flat; but if it does go down before we get to Newlands, you'll be some way farther on."

Ruth got into the car, Geoffrey started the engine, and the bicycle ran, rather jerkily, down the hill. When they climbed the next rise the jolting was marked. The extra weight had told upon the leaky tire and Geoffrey pulled up.

"I'm sorry; afraid we'll have to stop," he said. "It's too far to run to Newlands on the rim, but I'll get the tube out in a few minutes."

He removed the double-ended tube while Ruth found a seat on the roadside bank. When he joined her, carrying the tube, he frowned.

"The hole is pretty big; thought I felt the thing stick to the cover and I expect it's torn," he said. "I hope you don't mind waiting."

Ruth did not mind. Her foot hurt worse since she had rested and she doubted if she could walk to the village. Moreover, she was amused by Geoffrey's honest frown. It was obvious he did not want to stop. When he had smeared the tube and a large patch with a smelling solution he remarked:

"You can't make a good job in a hurry and perhaps we had better wait until the stuff is properly set. I don't want the tire to let us down again, and I must make an early start in the morning. I want to climb Scarp Fell and cross the Pinnacle ridge."

"Do you know the Pinnacle?" Ruth asked with some interest, for she was a mountaineer.

"I have been up. I went by Black-ghyll, but had some trouble at the chock-stone and think I'll try the buttress to-morrow."

"Were you alone?"

Geoffrey said he was and Ruth gave him a keen glance. She saw he was not boasting; it looked as if he did not know his getting over the chock-stone was something of an exploit.

"The gully is generally climbed by two or three people who use a rope," she said. "When they come to the stone, the second man lifts the leader, who afterwards pulls him up."

"It is rather an awkward spot," Geoffrey agreed, and Ruth studied him while he examined the tube.

He looked strong and one got a hint of resolution. His glance was frank; she thought him sincere and perhaps unsophisticated but not dull. On the whole, she approved him. Then she smiled and thought about something else. They would resume the journey in a few minutes and after he put her down at Newlands they would not meet again.

"I'm afraid the solution's not ready yet. Perhaps the heat stops it hardening," he remarked apologetically. "Sorry to keep you! Have you walked far?"

"From Carnthwaite."

"Oh, yes," said Geoffrey, glancing at the violin case. "They had a charity entertainment at the hall. I saw something about it in a newpaper. Tableaux and music on the lawn! No doubt, you were playing; but why——"

He stopped and Ruth understood his touch of embarrassment; he was going to ask why they had not driven her home. Indeed, she had felt rather hurt about this. The Latimers of Carnthwaite were her mother's friends and Ruth had hesitated when, using some tact, they had offered her a fee for playing.

# RUTH'S ADVENTURE

She needed money and conquered her fastidiousness, but she had noted a subtle difference in her hosts' manner and had left Carnthwaite, feeling sore and angry. Although she told herself it was foolish, their neglect hurt.

"Music is my occupation, you see," she said. "Then the cars were occupied."

Geoffrey's glance was sympathetic and she wondered whether she had weakly indulged her bitterness. All the same, she had seen one car roll away with a load of girls who had not far to go, and another start with two or three fat country gentlemen, for whom she thought a little exercise would be good.

"Anyhow, it was too far to let you walk in the sun," Geoffrey declared. "It's curious, but some people think when you earn a fee you oughtn't to get tired. I'm sorry you went."

"A professional player cannot refuse an engagement."

"I expect that is so," Geoffrey agreed. "I'm an engineer and must look for an engagement soon. The trouble is, engagements one would like don't seem numerous. I suppose most of us must be satisfied with the other kind."

Ruth smiled, for she approved his naïve philosophy, and he picked up the tube.

"Not hard yet! I mixed the stuff myself and I thought the tube was bad," he resumed. "Looks as if economy doesn't always pay. However, the solution *will* get hard and you are in the shade."

A thorn tree threw a shadow across the road and Ruth was satisfied to rest. A little beck bubbled in the grass and, leaping out, splashed in sparkling threads down the bank. The noise it made was soothing and in the distance the rugged fells cut against the sky. Ruth looked up at a sweep of broken crags.

"Since you have come to climb, I suppose you like the fells."

"Of course. If you want space and freedom and to try your strength, I don't think England has anything grander. One must own the North is often bleak and dark, but sometimes it does not rain, and if you stand on the high crags when the sun shines through the mist, you get glimpses of a beauty you can hardly grasp. However, since you live in the neighborhood, I expect you know how the wet rocks shine and the moving beams light up the green of the mossy belts, though they don't pierce the wonderful blue at the bottom of the dales."

"I do know," Ruth said quietly, for, when one loved the fells, his enthusiasm was not extravagant. "Perhaps," she added, "its charm is its elusiveness. Outline and color change and melt. Nothing is harshly distinct."

Geoffrey nodded. "The beauty's dazzling; you feel it ought to be veiled. Sometimes the veil's half lifted, and then the mist rolls down again and all is dark. But you don't mind; you remember the glimpse you got and are satisfied. Well, I expect great music moves you like that?"

"Yes," said Ruth, thoughtfully, "when a master plays! Even then, you feel the strange elusiveness—!" She paused and resumed: "I think your notion about the veil is good. Sometimes it's thin, but it is not lifted altogether. One's imagination reaches out to seize

# RUTH'S ADVENTURE

what lies behind. Still one can never reach far enough."

Then she smiled. "Well, you are going to climb the Pinnacle to-morrow by the buttress line. If you go alone, be careful when you come to the smooth slab on the traverse. The fine weather will hold, I think. How long have you got?"

"Three days. Then I must go back and draw mining pumps, reckon the cost of pit-props, and occupy myself with things like that. No doubt, they're useful things, but they're sometimes dreary."

"Useful things are dreary now and then," Ruth agreed. "However, I expect the solution is getting dry."

Geoffrey picked up the tube and stuck on the patch. Then he stood upon it and afterwards put a big stone on the spot.

"We must give it another minute or two," he remarked. "Perhaps I've bored you, but one does not meet many people who know the fells. People who look up at the rocks from the tourists' paths don't know them at all. For all that, it's not my habit to philosophize——"

Ruth imagined he meant to apologize for his extravagance and not to hint that she had made him talk; he was not subtle enough for this. She wondered why some men hated to be thought romantic when the romance was good. All the same, she knew she had made him talk and did not see her object for doing so. Perhaps it was because they were strangers with a common hobby and would not meet again. There was something melancholy about this.

He put back the tube and she noted that he had

strong hands and a workman's firm touch. Then he helped her into the car, the engine rattled, and a cool wind whipped their faces as the bicycle climbed the hill. When they ran down from the moor ragged hedges streamed back, pastures and small, bent trees rolled by, and presently the bicycle sped through a white village where a beck flowed between the houses and the road. Geoffrey stopped at a guide-post that marked a corner.

"If you like, I'll drive you to your house," he said.

Ruth hesitated for a moment. Her foot hurt, but her arrival in the side-car would excite Mrs. Creighton's curiosity. She did not know her helper and her mother was conventional. Mrs. Creighton would, no doubt, sooner have stayed on the moor all night than allow a stranger to bring her home.

"No," she said, "thank you. I have not far to go."

She got down and, moved by some impulse, gave Geoffrey her hand.

"You have been very kind. I hope you will have a good holiday!"

Geoffrey drove on to Nethercleugh and after the frugal evening meal was over sat in the slate porch, lazily smoking and talking to Stayward. He thought his uncle looked old and worn, for since Creighton left him Stayward had made a desperate up-hill struggle. Running daunting risks, he had somehow carried on his business, but he was making progress and hoped he had conquered the worst of his difficulties. He did not talk about them and, for the most part, listened to his nephew, whom he was glad to see. As a rule, Geoffrey and Stayward agreed. In some respects, their temperaments were alike, and

## RUTH'S ADVENTURE 67

when they differed each, so to speak, tolerated the other's idiosyncrasies.

The evening was calm and the bent ash trees round the house were still. The long fields that rolled down hill looked cold and darkly green, and the smoke of the furnaces by the coast floated in long gray smears across the pale-red sky. The porch was getting cool and there was something that braced one in the air. Geoffrey liked Nethercleugh. He had inherited a vein of the Stayward austerity and the bleak sternness of the old house rather appealed to him.

"Do you know a music-teacher in the neighborhood?" he asked.

"I do not," said Stayward. "Man or woman?"

"A girl, and rather young."

"Pretty?" Stayward suggested. "Where d' you meet her?"

"On the moor. I don't know if she was pretty or not," Geoffrey replied thoughtfully and mused.

Although the girl's eyes were good and he liked the warm glow in her hair, he did not think her charm was physical. Yet she had charm and he admitted that he would like to meet her again. There was something about her manner; frankness tempered by a hint of dignity and pride. One felt she was proud, but she looked tired and had let him help. Geoffrey was curious and pitiful.

"I really don't know if she was a teacher; she said music was her occupation," he resumed. "She had been playing at Carnthwaite and they let her walk back. Her boot hurt and I picked her up. That's all."

"Oh, well," said Stayward. "It's something to be young, but if you're a canny lad, you will leave music-teachers alone and think about your job. Your apprenticeship runs out soon, doesn't it?"

Geoffrey said it did and Stayward pondered. "I doubt if I'd have much use for you at the ovens yet."

"I don't know if I'd like to come," Geoffrey rejoined, smiling. "We're both obstinate, and somehow one obeys orders easier when they're not given by a relation."

Stayward nodded. "You're as stubborn as the rest of us; one can see you're Margaret's son. We'll let it go, but if your masters do not offer you a post, you can talk to me again."

"Thanks!" said Geoffrey. "You hinted that the ovens might soon be busier."

"It's possible. Looks as if the trade in the new dye might be a big thing. Cost me much, altering plant, to give my customers the stuff they wanted, but I'm getting it right."

"I suppose you make the dye by Creighton's process?"

"Not altogether. Creighton's patent helped, but it did not take me far enough. I mind when we once talked about trying the new stuff, he said it could not be made. Tom was a clever chemist, but he did not see where his invention led. His kind are easy satisfied and stop too soon. When you feel you're on the right road, you need to trust your luck and gan forrad."

Geoffrey nodded. To push forward was the Stayward plan.

"Where is Creighton now?" he asked.

"He went abroad. It's all I ken," Stayward replied.

"Tom was soft and shiftless; his foolish wife ruined him."

Something in Stayward's voice indicated that there was no more to be said, but Geoffrey pondered. He had heard it hinted that Stayward had dealt unjustly with his partner, and although he doubted this, he sometimes wondered why Stayward did not deny the tale. All the same, Geoffrey thought he liked his stern reserve. He began to talk about something else and when he had smoked out his pipe they went into the house.

## CHAPTER VIII

#### MRS. CREIGHTON'S JEALOUSY

RUTH had gone with Mrs. Creighton to the colliery village and while she waited for her, looked about. A winding-engine rattled as a cage came up a neighboring pit and an ungainly tank-locomotive pushed a row of clanking trucks across the street. Tired horses stood, with drooping heads, beneath the wooden loading stage, and a cloud of smoke dimmed the sunshine that made the blackened houses look uglier. Coal dust blew about and acrid fumes came from Stayward's coke ovens. The smoke and steam indicated that trade was brisk and Ruth noted the group of men waiting at the big gate. Since a paper was fixed to a post, she imagined Stayward was engaging fresh hands.

Mrs. Creighton was occupied in the general store, and Ruth, knowing why she had been left outside, felt sympathetic but amused. Her mother hated buying groceries and could not resign herself to traveling by the public wagonette that ran between the village and the dale. Ruth owned that when one had used a comfortable car it jarred to crowd into the slow vehicle with fat countrywomen who carried heavy baskets. For all that, since Mrs. Creighton's orders were small and her payments irregular, tact was needed to get supplies of superior quality at the lowest price. Mrs.

## MRS. CREIGHTON'S JEALOUSY 71

Creighton had some talent for doing so, but Ruth surmised she did not want her to note the arts she used.

By and by she came out, carrying a number of parcels, while an untidy boy with a larger load went up the street. Her face was hot and when she gave some of the parcels to Ruth she looked angry.

"Thwaites is getting insufferable," she remarked. "I'm sorry now we stopped dealing with the stores in town, although, of course, their writing to me as they did about the last bill could not be borne."

"But how has Thwaites vexed you?" Ruth asked. "I have not found him rude."

"My dear, I hope you do not imagine a grocer would be rude to me! One resents the fellow's greed and independence. I do not think I am remarkably fastidious, but the bacon I buy must be good and Thwaites has sold the piece I like to Stayward. It was the same with the butter; he knows I only use Danish, and yet he let Stayward have the keg. I really have some grounds for being annoyed."

Ruth tried not to smile. She knew poverty had not destroyed Mrs. Creighton's sense of her importance.

"Why does Stayward need so much food?" she asked.

"To feed his navvies!" Mrs. Creighton replied, with a theatrical gesture. "Men like that must have the best while we go without! The thing is ridiculous and it gave me some satisfaction to tell Thwaites so. He turned to get some wrapping paper, but I suspected he wanted to laugh. Of course, I did not actually see him laugh, or I should have been forced——"

She stopped, as if to leave the grocer's punishment to Ruth's imagination.

"After all, we owe him rather a long bill," Ruth remarked. "Besides, Stayward does not employ navvies."

"His advertisement asked for navvies. Thwaites told me about it," Mrs. Creighton rejoined. "It seems Stayward is going to level that old brickfield and enlarge his works; he has got some important orders and is buying new machinery. There is no room for the men at the village so he boards them in a shed. Thwaites says he pays them extra wages to work at night, because the business for which he wants the new machinery is going to be large. You can, without much effort, understand my feelings about this."

Ruth understood and, to some extent, sympathized. Mrs. Creighton had come to hate John Stayward and had watched his recent progress with bitter jealousy. It was, in a sense, ridiculous, but Ruth imagined his buying the bacon and butter her mother liked would aggravate her sense of injury.

"It looks as if father broke the partnership too soon," Ruth said in a thoughtful voice. "One feels it more because he was often too late. Well, I expect to seize the proper time for doing things is hard, and I'm like father. When I found out I had no real talent for music, he had sacrificed himself for me and gone."

"Stayward broke the partnership; he cheated your father," Mrs. Creighton declared. "I think he knew about the dyeworks' orders and wanted all the profit. He is very cunning, and trustful people are at the mercy of men like that. It hurts to see him prosper by using what is ours."

Ruth said nothing. She imagined she must not indulge her mother too much. Her jealousy might be-

## MRS. CREIGHTON'S JEALOUSY

come dangerous to herself; she brooded about her injury oftener than she ought. Ruth was relieved when they reached the wagonette and Mrs. Creighton, packed between two countrywomen with large baskets, could not talk.

The other passengers were not silent and when the jolting vehicle rolled slowly up the hill Ruth noted their remarks. She knew what her mother thought about Stayward and in the main agreed, but now she heard the views of others whose judgment was free from prejudice, her curiosity was excited.

"Eggs is up," said one. "Thwaites paid me twopence a dozen mair this week. Sims as if 't new men at coke ovens is taking aw t' stuff he can get, and Jim tell me they want mair hands at pit. Weel, it's good for countryside when a man like Stayward sets things moving."

"They'll gan fast noo Stayward's getten started," another replied. "He's no' the kind to let grass grow under 's feet when he taks the road. Oad stannard and a canny dalesman. Good luck 't him!"

"Ovens was in varra low water no' lang sin," said a third, who put a roll of oilcloth on her and Mrs. Creighton's knees. Then she turned to the latter and remarked: "I reckon your man gave up over soon. Mayhappen it was bad luck, but some folks is like that. If Mr. Creighton had hodden oot, you'd be riding home in the lile green car noo. No' that I'm fond o' cars; raising clouds o' stour and running over hens."

Mrs. Creighton said nothing, but Ruth saw her outraged look and imagined her feelings. It was some relief when one of the others broke in:—

"I mind John Stayward's coming to see my man. 'I want your teams, David, to lead firebricks fra Greyrigg but I canna promise when you'll get paid,' he says; just like that.

"'Tak' horses; I'se wait,' says David, and before lang money com't. David kenned his man. Mayhappen John has a tight fist, but you'll can trust him. Neabody can say different. Staywards awiss pays."

Ruth mused. It was something to be trusted, for people to know one paid one's debts. She admitted, that, as a rule, the Creightons paid when they were forced. The countrywomen's view of Stayward's character clashed with hers, but they knew him. He was a dalesman and, so to speak, belonged to them. Ruth was just and tried to be logical. She argued that one does not trust a thief, but when the passengers began to talk about sheep and farm-servants' wages she banished her thoughts. After all, Stayward had cheated her father, and her mother's bitterness, although perhaps unhealthy and extravagant, was grounded well. Moreover, Ruth had something else to ponder, because she had got a letter at the post office.

When the wagonette stopped at the white village Mrs. Creighton and Ruth got down and set off up the dale. The hills shut off the wind, and the sun was hot in the deep hollow. The road was steep and rough, and Mrs. Creighton's boots were thin. After a time she stopped where a big stone lay beneath a sycamore.

"It's shady and I am tired," she said. "Arguing with Thwaites and traveling in that horrible wagonette

## MRS. CREIGHTON'S JEALOUSY 75

has exhausted me. I think we will rest for a few minutes."

Ruth agreed, with a touch of amusement. She was sympathetic, but there was something humorous about Mrs. Creighton's sitting by the roadside. The parcels of groceries and her dusty boots did not harmonize with her clothes and look of ruffled dignity. For herself, Ruth was content. She liked to sit in the shadow and look out on the sunny hills. The long slopes had gone yellow, except where threads of shining water came down and the mossy belts were luminous green. In the background, broken crags rose above the edge of the moor. Sometimes the sycamore's broad leaves rustled, and then all was still. Ruth loved the quiet dale and sighed when she took her letter.

"I have been idle for some time and Maud Chisholm makes a useful suggestion," she said. "I think I told you she had started some music classes at Rainsfield. Well, she is getting pupils and wants me to join her."

"The girl you met at Munich? You know nothing about her relations?"

"I know Maud," said Ruth. "I don't think her relations are numerous. Besides, I am not going to live with them."

Mrs. Creighton looked thoughtful. "One runs a risk by making a friend of a girl whose people one does not know. Then Rainsfield is a dreadful town; all shabby streets and factories, and the people are uncouth."

"Rainsfield is ugly. I don't know if I like the people, but perhaps that is because I have only seen them in the streets. However, it looks as if they were prosperous. Maud says the fees they pay are good and she could get more pupils if she taught the violin. Although I cannot play really well, I think I could teach. Then we owe much and I must earn some money."

"It is certainly desirable," Mrs. Creighton agreed. "If I had met Miss Chisholm's friends, I might have felt less doubtful about letting you go. After all, it is not necessary that you should go. Suppose we wait——"

Ruth hesitated, for she had been arguing against herself. She was fastidious, and in Germany had got numerous jars that her ambition helped her to bear. Now ambition had gone and she knew music meant dreary toil without much reward. She did not want to leave the quiet dale, but saw she ought.

"We cannot wait," she answered firmly. "Maud declares she must know at once because she can let the room she meant for me. It is hard to go, mother, but I feel I must. If you think for a moment——"

"I do not like it," said Mrs. Creighton in a resigned voice. "All the same, since you are resolved, I suppose I must agree. If, as I expect, you find you cannot stay with Miss Chisholm, you'll be satisfied to come back."

Ruth smiled. Although it was very possible she would get some rude knocks, she did not think she would come back. Then Mrs. Creighton got up and when they resumed their walk her eyes were very hard.

"If Stayward had not stolen the patent, you need not have gone," she said. "Now, while we have nothing, he gets rich by theft."

She indulged her morbid jealousy, and Ruth let her talk. When Mrs. Creighton concentrated on her grievance, she forgot all else, and Ruth did not want to satisfy her curiosity about Maud Chisholm. Maud's point of view was not Mrs. Creighton's, and she hated conventional rules. For all that, she had some rules, which she kept staunchly. When they got home, Ruth wrote a short note and a few days afterwards left Beckfoot.

In the evening the train stopped at a big grimy station and when Ruth got down a girl pushed through the crowd on the platform. Maud was tall and thin, and her clothes were rather shabby. Her face was flushed, as if by speed, but it was pinched and she looked jaded. She did not kiss Ruth; it was not Maud's habit to kiss her friends. She put her hand on the other's arm and held her back for a moment or two.

"You're not exactly pretty, but you look very fresh and calm," she said. "Puritanically, or perhaps I mean ascetically, calm! However, I expect the freshness will soon wear off, and marked prettiness is a drawback for a job like ours. Then you have brought flowers. A truly rustic touch!"

Ruth laughed. "I don't feel calm; in fact, I'm excited. I wondered whether you would forget to come to the station; you do forget things. But people are looking at us. Where can we get a taxi?"

"A taxi!" Maud exclaimed. "Would you squander the cost of three or four meals on a drive? If you booked your luggage as I directed, we will get a tram. They're cheap and not remarkably slow. Come along."

She pushed Ruth forward, and crossing the station as fast as she could walk, stopped outside until a noisy tramcar rolled up. The evening was hot and they went on top. When the car lurched down the street Maud took and smelled Ruth's flowers.

"Beautiful things!" she remarked. "They talk about clean skies and cool green lawns where people whose life goes smoothly lounge in the shade, but beauty of form and color strikes a foreign note at Rainsfield. It's lucky devouring industry has left us beauty of sound.

Ruth agreed. The clouds were low and the smoke of mills and forges hung, thick and yellow, about the roofs. The car ran through a long, mean street, past rows of little shops with sooty fronts. One saw stale vegetables, torn newspaper posters, and discolored signs, and now and then from an open window there floated a smell of fish and meat. The people on the pavement had white faces and walked slackly, some with shoulders bent.

"Nature made England beautiful; modern commercialism made Rainsfield what it is," said Maud. "The people take the color of their surroundings. They look sad, but when you know them you find they are not. Their eyes are dimmed by the smoke, but their ears are good and nobody loves music better than the people of our ugly Northern towns. The old English spirit's in them and they have hope. England was merry England once and may be again. Some day these folks will see, and then towns like Rainsfield will be swept away."

"And if it happens soon, you will help them to build on better lines?"

"Oh, no! An artist is not a bricklayer. His job is to teach the harmonies of form and color and sound.

When the others grasp them they will build on a firm foundation, but it may be long and one gets tired. Now let's be practical! I must call at this shop."

They got down and Ruth followed Maud into a hot and dusty shop where swarms of flies buzzed and nothing looked fresh. Maud bought some food and gave Ruth a greasy parcel.

"I forgot to bring a basket," she remarked. "Davies will use old newspapers for wrapping, probably because they're cheap. Up town you get nice greaseproof stuff, but they charge you a penny more."

"I think I'd sooner pay the extra penny," said Ruth, glancing at her stained gloves.

"You haven't taught music at Rainsfield," Maud rejoined. "When you have been with me for a few weeks, you will lost your fastidiousness."

Ruth thought it possible, but was not comforted, and she looked about rather drearily as they went up the street. Not far off, a row of tall chimneys poured out smoke that floated above the roofs in a dingy cloud. One heard big hammers and felt the throb of ponderous rolls. Then there was a break in the houses and Ruth, looking through an open gate, saw a black river roll between banks of mud. A grimy building with lattice windows stood by the water's edge and the smell proclaimed it a tannery. Farther on, rows of small red houses straggled across a field with broken fences of colliery rope.

"Our parish!" said Maud. "You will find our flock is rather mixed and sometimes hard to lead, but it's growing."

She turned up a side street behind the tannery and stopped in front of a small house. There was a yard on one side of the building, but part of the space was occupied by an iron shed. Maud unlocked the door of the shed and they went through to a dark, untidy kitchen. There was no fire, but a tin kettle boiled on a ring of gas-jets that made a horrible smell.

"Florrie has remembered the kettle," Maud said with some surprise. "The ring smells because she spilt some grease on it and I haven't cleaned the holes. You can go to your room while I make tea. First door at the top of the stairs, and if it's not all you like, we'll alter things to-morrow."

Ruth went upstairs and sat down on the shabby iron bed. The room was very small and dusty curtains flapped in the draught at the open window. One smelt the river and the tannery, and when Ruth looked out her heart sank. On one side were chimneys, roofs, and soot-stained walls; in front, fields from which the grass was worn, foul ditches, and lines of rusty iron rope. Farther off, a railway bank, gaunt coalpit towers, and another smoke cloud.

The contrast between the dreary view and the green hillslopes at Beckfoot was marked. Ruth was highly strung and tired, and for a few minutes her courage melted. She felt daunted and tears came to her eyes. Then she pulled herself together, washed off the grime of her journey, and went down to the kitchen where Maud was frying bacon in a black and battered pan.

## CHAPTER IX

#### RUTH GETS TO WORK

IN the morning Ruth breakfasted on stale bread, bacon, and thick coffee. When the meal was over Maud pushed back the greasy plates and smoked a cigarette while she informed Ruth about her housekeeping. For the most part, she lived on bacon, because it was easily cooked; the drawback was, the plates were hard to wash. One must economize on hot water when the supply of gas was controlled by the pennies one put in the slot.

The iron shed was the music-room and had been occupied by a sculptor of funeral monuments. Maud was forced to rent the house with the shed, but let the rooms she did not need. Florrie and Gertie, who used them, generally paid their rent. One girl kept a draper's books; the other did something at the tannery. They were good sorts, but had not much imagination. Some of Maud's pupils paid, and some did not.

"I did not know you lived like this," Ruth said, hesitatingly. "If you had gone to a larger house farther out, would you not have got on faster?"

Maud laughed. "My business is not to get on; I teach people who want to learn. Then you don't know the plaster villas—they will call them villas—along the tramline, and their dreadfully respectable occupants.

I do; I belonged to these people until I broke away. Their code is all, *You mustn't,* and is founded on, *What would the neighbors think?*"

"I have known people like that," Ruth replied, with feeling. "One tries to take the proper line, but hates to find it drawn by another's rule. To be free is worth something."

"All the same, you must pay for freedom," Maud remarked and threw away her cigarette. "However, you might put things straight and then come to the music-room."

Ruth washed the plates, in a very small quantity of water, folded the dirty tablecloth, and when she had as far as possible satisfied her feeling for neatness sat down for a few moments and pondered. She liked Maud, but did not approve her household management. Although freedom was good, it did not necessarily mean bad food and general disorder. Then Maud was strangely thin, and when she talked her face flushed. Her movements were restless; it looked as if her fiery enthusiasm burned her up. Yet Maud was sometimes shrewd and always sincere. Moreover, she could play and had refused some good engagements in order to teach. Perhaps it was extravagant, but if Maud did not altogether feel her mission was to proclaim the gospel of beauty where things were ugliest, Ruth imagined she felt something like this.

Then Ruth got up and went to the iron shed. Bright sunshine shone down through the long window in the roof, and the quivering beams searched out the dust on the floor and the cracks in the walls. Maud occupied the music stool, turning from the piano, on which she now and then struck a note. Her hair was rough,

## RUTH GETS TO WORK

and in the strong light one saw stains on her dress that suggested careless cooking.

A man sat opposite, his violoncello resting on the floor. His clothes were rather shabby, his shoulders were bent, and his face was pale. Ruth saw his hands were hard and rough, and his hair was touched by white. He looked puzzled, but while she studied him he put his bow on the strings.

"Noo, Miss, we'll try 't again," he said.

Maud struck a few chords and the man began to play. He stopped the notes true, and Ruth thought the tone was good, but he had no feeling for rhythm, and after a few minutes he put down his bow and frowned.

"No," he said, "it willunt do! When the rests comes I'm late in starting."

"A little late, Jimmy," Maud agreed. "Don't watch the score this time. Try to *feel* when you ought to play."

"I canna," he said dejectedly, and they began again.

Ruth sat down and listened. The music was a great composer's, but not difficult except for the broken time. Jimmy labored through it doggedly, with his mouth set firm, and Ruth felt sympathetic when he missed the beat. Maud was very patient, and now and then encouraged him with a smile. They played for half an hour, and then he got up.

"Thank you, Miss. Gans better, don't you think?" he said. "If I can keep 't up, mayhappen bandmaster will let me in."

"I think he ought," Maud declared. "When will you come back for another practice?"

Jimmy hesitated. "I'm takkin' your time. It's not in bargain."

"We won't bother about that," Maud said, smiling. "You must satisfy the bandmaster. Come to-morrow afternoon."

He thanked her and when he went out she turned to Ruth.

"Well?" she said. "What do you think about him? The strings are your department."

"His intonation's good, but he has no sense of time. Then his hands! I suppose heavy work has stiffened them like that. Of course, he will never play much."

"Is this all?"

"No," said Ruth thoughtfully. "You feel he's extraordinarily keen and obstinate. He doesn't mean to be beaten. In a way, it's moving!"

Maud nodded. "It is moving. He works all night and gives up to music much of the time he needs for sleep. His one ambition is to join the tannery band. Perhaps it's his way of escape from crushing dreariness. He's paid well, but he must live near the fires he watches, and, except at the fair holiday, they never go out. Well, your job's to help him into the band and perhaps this is worth some trouble."

She went to the door when somebody knocked, and a man came in with a little girl who carried a violin case. His clothes were rather smart and his manner was urbane.

"I expect you're Miss Chisholm?" he said to Maud. "Mrs. Green told me about you; said you was painstaking. Amelia has a talent for music. Goes in the family—I play the cornet, by ear. Thought she'd better learn the notes, so I've brought her to you."

# RUTH GETS TO WORK

Maud beckoned the child, and taking her violin from the case plucked a string.

"To begin with, it's a dreadful fiddle," she said. "Tune the thing, if you can, Ruth," she resumed, and presently gave the child a smile. "Now take your fiddle and try to play this with me."

She began a well-known air, and after a time looked at Ruth.

"She stopped the half-tones correctly. I think her ear is good," said Ruth.

"Very well," Maud remarked, turning to the man. "I won't teach your daughter pretty pieces, but perhaps I can teach her music, if she studies hard. If this is what you want, take her to Johnston's in the Foregate and get her a fiddle. He doesn't keep the German kind. Then you can burn the other thing."

The man looked annoyed, and hesitated. "There's the question of hours and fees."

"Fees?" said Maud, giving him a printed card. "You'll find all about them here. The important thing is, the child may learn to play."

He went off with the little girl, and soon afterwards a shabby woman came in. Maud indicated a chair and asked. "Why has Tommy stayed away for the last two weeks?"

"That's what I've come about," the woman replied. "His brother George has lost his job, and Lena's on half time; work's slack at mill. Tommy'd begun new quarter, but I thowt——"

"You thought I would let him off the rest?" Maud interposed. "Well, I won't. Don't you know your boy loves music and will make a player?"

"But t' money——" the woman began, and Maud stopped her.

"You have no sense of values. I mean money's nothing, and giving the lad a chance to use his talent is all. If you don't send him back, I'll come for him. I expect you'll pay me some time, and if not I won't grumble much."

The woman's hard, lined face softened, but she looked embarrassed and nervously twisted a fold of her dress.

"Weel!" she said and glanced about the room. "Mayhappen I might come in noo and then and wash up place a bit. Looks as if it needed a scrub."

"It's possible," Maud agreed. "We'll talk about this again. Sorry I must turn you out. My class is waiting."

The woman went away with a grateful look, half a dozen small children came in, and until they stopped for lunch Ruth was busily occupied. The lunch was bad, the iron shed got very hot in the afternoon, and Ruth felt jaded, but she held out until Maud sent off her last pupil at four o'clock.

"Saturday is hardest; the children are not at school," she said. "You had better rest for the evening, but I must go out and play for a mill band."

When the time came Ruth let her go, and then began to put the kitchen in order. Maud was a splendid teacher, giving with royal generosity all the gifts she had, but her notions about the common needs of life were rude. Ruth shrank from the blackened pots, the greasy sink, and the litter of dirty plates and cups. She did not think she had much talent for household work, but if she could not manage better than Maud,

## RUTH GETS TO WORK

they must presently give up. Food that was sometimes raw and sometimes burned would not support one long; and although hot water was not altogther cheap, Ruth rolled up her sleeves and got to work. When she had finished, Maud returned and laughed as she looked about the room.

"You don't like untidiness; you have a practical vein," she said. "All the same, I don't imagine your reforming mood will last. Cleaning up is, no doubt, a novelty, but it soon gets monotonous. I have tried. One does meet musicians who are sometimes methodical. It's the steady strain that tells."

Ruth smiled, rather sadly. "I don't know if I'm a musician or not, and I've grounds to doubt. For all that, beauty is order. Rhythm's important in music. You must have the measured beat."

"Oh, well!" said Maud. "You must tell me later why you wanted to teach. The occupation has some drawbacks, but we won't bother about it just now. One gets horribly languid on Saturday evening, and I think I'll rest."

She picked up a book, Ruth mused, and they presently went to bed.

In the morning, Maud declared she needed fresh air. She said they would picnic in some woods and perhaps get tea at an inn, and after breakfast they set off, Maud carrying a straw basket of food. While they waited for a car, a young clergyman came up, and glancing at the basket, gave Maud a friendly smile.

"I expect we shall not see you this morning."

"No," said Maud. "We are going to loaf in the woods. Wouldn't you like to come?"

"I would like," he admitted. "All the same, it's not expedient."

"It's not obvious that you and the vicar put expediency very high," Maud rejoined with a laugh. "The last Easter procession that nearly led to a riot, for example! You had been warned that a number of your flock who don't come to church would show their righteous disapproval. Perhaps you would have been just a little disappointed had they not done so."

She beckoned Ruth and when they turned away resumed: "They're human at St. Margaret's, and one rather admires them for their obstinacy. When I opened the school, there were grounds for imagining the vicar was disturbed and tactful inquiries were made. Now, however, I think he's satisfied and to some extent we are allies. In their fight with dirt and dreariness, they use any help they can get."

"I liked the curate's face, although he looked rather haggard. Then I thought he stooped in his walk."

"One soon gets haggard at Rainsfield," Maud replied. "Nature gave him a weak body, and a sensitive refinement I think he finds a burden. For all that, he has a fiery pluck that will either break him or carry him far. Something of an example of the spirit of conquering the flesh. The trouble is, the beaten flesh wears——"

She stopped, for a street car rolled up, and getting on board, they ran past long rows of houses with little gardens, green railings, and sooty plaster fronts. Cars went by, throwing up thick dust; young men and women on bicycles toiled in the sun up the long hill. Smoke stained the sky; the air was hot and stale. By and by the houses vanished and the iron posts led

# RUTH GETS TO WORK

on across scorched pasture where the hedges were blackened, and streaked by dust. In the valley below, the river wound in loops that shone like silver and then faded to oily black where the shade of alders lay. Its banks made an inky smear across the fields.

When the car stopped, Maud took a lane that turned up hill and the country got greener. She walked fast, with something of the energy that marked her talk, and when she stopped her face was hot and she breathed hard. Ruth, who had climbed the rugged fells, was cool and for a few moments looked about.

Dark firs rolled up the hillside; below was a belt of plain where white farmsteads stood among squares of pasture and yellow fields of corn. Then there was a long slope, dotted by the red gashes of claypits, and from the fold beyond the top a hazy cloud of smoke spread across the sky. The thin vapor dimmed the ridges behind, but Ruth thought she saw chimneys and colliery towers.

"The view's wide," said Maud. "I don't know if it's beautiful, but after the streets, it rests one's eyes and Rainsfield has nothing better. Now I'll take you to my favorite spot."

They plunged into the wood and presently stopped at a bank by its other edge. They lunched there and afterwards lounged among the fern, talking and looking out across the plain. In places, slanting sunbeams touched the straight red trunks, and there was a sweet resinous smell, and it was cool in the shade.

"This is all I know of rural England," Maud said by and by. "Some day you must show me your high peaks and mountain lakes."

Ruth's eyes got wistful. "I should love that, but I

hardly durst think about it yet. One could not stop at Rainsfield if one's mind dwelt on the dales. Next year, perhaps, when the crabapple and wild cherry bloom, we will go to Beckfoot and walk all day in the wind that sweeps the moors. You shall have a room that looks up the ghyll where the water twists like shining threads among the stones."

"I think not. We will stop at country inns, a different place every night. You see, I'm something of a vagabond. Then Beckfoot is your mother's, and I doubt if she would approve of me."

"You don't know her," Ruth rejoined, although she felt Maud's remark was, perhaps, justified.

"You have talked about her. Anyhow, I wouldn't like to strain your mother's hospitality, and I know where I belong. If we're rich enough to be extravagant, we'll take a walking holiday in Spring. Now tell me why you left the fells. You haven't been very frank about it yet."

"The story's long," Ruth said hesitatingly.

"We have nothing to do all afternoon and I'll try to be sympathetic," Maud replied.

Ruth told her. She trusted Maud and wanted her to understand. Besides, Maud was shrewd and Ruth felt she would like her support for the view she took of Creighton's wrongs. When she stopped she looked up, rather anxiously.

"I think you made a wise choice when you left Beckfoot, but I'm not sure you wanted to satisfy me about this," Maud observed. "You meant to plead your father's cause, and you plead it well, although I doubt if all the arguments are really yours. Tell me more about the man who cheated him."

## RUTH GETS TO WORK

Ruth did so and Maud mused. "One feels you drew your father better than you knew," she said presently. "It's obvious that he loved you and you owe him much. I don't know about the other man. His portrait's not lifelike. There are touches that don't agree."

"Ah," said Ruth, "you haven't met Stayward."

"I have been trying to see him from your point of view, but must own it's hard."

Ruth colored and was silent for some moments. She was honest and admitted that her point of view was her mother's. Sometimes, indeed, she had vaguely doubted, but she banished her doubts and tried to be stauncher afterwards. Stayward had broken the partnership, stolen her father's patent, and driven him away. This was obvious, and it was much.

"He is hard and cruel. I hate him!" she exclaimed.

"I think he is hard," Maud agreed. "For all that, you have not heard his story, and a sense of injury doesn't help one to be just. Wait and reserve your judgment. Some day, perhaps, all will be clearer. Now we'll let it go and talk about something else."

She talked about music and her pupils until Ruth forgot her bitterness, and when the shadows got longer they went to an inn and drank tea in an arbor in the garden. Then they started down hill for the trolley line, and the gas lamps were burning in the hot streets when they reached the town.

## CHAPTER X

#### GEOFFREY'S NEW POST

STAYWARD sat in the porch at Nethercleugh and quietly smoked his pipe while Geoffrey lounged on the slate bench opposite. The sun was low, but its level beams pierced the ragged trees about the house. Sometimes the leaves rustled, and then the soft patter died away and all was quiet. It was typical that the men lingered outside while the evening got cold. They sprang from a rude stock and their ancestors had long braved the savage winds that swept the moors. Bodily comfort did not appeal to them, and on summer evenings, when the peat fire in the kitchen burned low, the old house was dreary. Geoffrey, who had been on the hills since morning, was satisfied with the hard slate bench.

"You go back on Monday?" Stayward remarked.

"I must start at five o'clock. It will be eight when I get to the office and I want to work out some plans by noon. I told the chief I'd have them ready, and I go down a pit with a colliery manager after lunch. Some trouble about ventilation, and I expect we'll have to find a cure before we come up."

Stayward nodded. It did not strike him that to drive a motor bicycle across England, over the high Pennine mountains, was a strenuous preparation for a long day's work. Work had never daunted the

## GEOFFREY'S NEW POST

Staywards, and when he was young he had done things like that, although he had used a horse and not a bicycle. Now machinery ruled, it had turned his restless activity into fresh channels and given him greater power. This was all.

"Have they said anything about a new job for you?" he asked.

"Not yet. I'm rather puzzled. Of course, they're not obliged to give me a post, but the chief seemed satisfied and there's only a few weeks to go. In fact, I've been studying the advertisements in the engineering newspapers. So far, I see nothing to suit."

"They're cautious folk on the North-East coast," Stayward remarked. "Mayhappen I could get you a job in Canada, if it's worth your while."

"I have not much money and mustn't be fastidious."

"Weel, you ken the Redbank Hilliards? Jim, who went to Canada, was my friend, and some time since he wrote about a silver vein in North Ontario. I had a little money by me then and sent him some. They opened the mine; it's small and Jim and I hold a number of the shares. The ore's about paid expenses, but that's aw; we never got a dividend, and when I started the ovens I tried to sell. I got a bid of five shillings for the five-dollar shares and told Jim I'd hold. Noo the manager's going and I reckon Jim Hilliard would give you the job."

Geoffrey asked about the pay and pondered when Stayward stated it. For Canada, the sum was small, and one gained nothing in reputation by managing an unprofitable mine. All the same, he would have control and adventure called. In the meantime, Geoffrey thought Stayward studied him with dry amusement.

"If I can get the post, I'll take it. I'll start as soon as I'm free," he said.

"Then, I'll tell you what we'll do," Stayward replied. "If you earn me a dividend, we'll share what I get." He paused and resumed with a twinkle: "I reckon the offer will not cost me much. Anyhow, I'll write to Jim in the morning."

He filled his pipe and smoked quietly for some minutes. Then he asked: "Did you see the music teacher you talked about again?"

"I did not. It's strange, but nobody seemed to know her. I was told there was not a music teacher in the dale."

"Looks as if you had been inquiring," Stayward observed.

"I have inquired," said Geoffrey, giving him a level glance. "The girl was attractive. I've thought about her since."

Stayward's face was inscrutable, but Geoffrey imagined he pondered. Indeed, he had a strange feeling that his uncle knew something he did not mean to tell.

"It will be lang before you can support a wife."

"That is so," Geoffrey agreed. "All the same, if I were rich enough to marry, I think the music teacher is the kind of girl I'd choose. However, since I haven't yet earned your dividend, we can let it go."

Stayward said nothing. As a rule, they did not talk much, but their half-conscious understanding of each other made for harmony. Both were firm and, to some extent, frank. When they did not agree they did not dispute; they knew argument would not help. If Geoffrey had not known this, he would have urged

# GEOFFREY'S NEW POST

Stayward to talk about the girl with the violin case.

"You're busy at the ovens now?" he said.

"We're throng. I cannot give dyeworks all the stuff they're asking for, and there's a new product I'm putting on market other folks want. It's not standardized yet, and when I'm experimenting, I cannot mind the works. If you were a chemist, I'd give you a good post."

"I don't know if it's unlucky I'm not a chemist; but you are not," Geoffrey replied. "In fact, it's rather hard to see how you make the dyes. The fellow you have got in the laboratory doesn't look clever."

"He kens his job. That's all I want. When I get on the track of a new combination, I tell him what's needed and let him work 't oot. The man can analyze; he cannot invent."

Geoffrey knew his uncle could invent. Stayward had brains, but Creighton had taught him all the chemistry he knew, and Geoffrey sometimes wondered how much he owed to instinctive skill, and how much to rude tenacity. Not long since he had grimly fronted ruin; now he was prosperous and breaking new ground. If his labors did not wear him out, he would reap the harvest, and Geoffrey knew the Staywards wore well.

"If you had kept Creighton, it would have helped," he said.

"I think not," Stayward replied. "Tom married a foolish woman. I could not keep him unless I kept his wife. I needed a working partner; Janet wanted a master of otter hounds and mayhappen a Lord Lieutenant. She's ambitious and varra obstinate, but it was not my plan to earn the money she would use to put her man high. She pushed him on until he clashed with me; and then Tom got broke."

He mused for a time, with knitted brows, and Geoffrey said nothing. When Stayward looked like that, it was not hard to picture his antagonist's defeat. Geoffrey knew his stubbornness and something about the woman who had rashly opposed her plans to his. Yet he did not know all; Stayward kept his stern reserve and would not tell the tale.

By and by Stayward got up and knocked out his pipe. "I'll write Jim Hilliard and let him know you'll come. Weel, you have had a long day on the fells and better gan t' bed."

Geoffrey went off to his room under the flagged roof and took off his clothes by the fading light. Old Belle was parsimonious about candles and ruled Nethercleugh with stern frugality. Geoffrey rather imagined his uncle was getting rich, but he had obviously not given up his Spartan code. This was not because he was greedy. Old habits were strong and the Staywards were primitive folk.

Geoffrey got into bed and heard the ash-leaves rustle while he recaptured drowsily the thrills of his scramble among the crags. Then the high rocks and dark gullies faded and his imagination pictured another scene; a long white road that crossed a belt of crimson moor. A girl with a violin case toiled up a hill, and as she crossed the top her figure cut against the sky. The picture was fixed on Geoffrey's brain; he saw it in his dreams, and sometimes when he smoked his pipe and mused. It began to melt, however, and when the ash-leaves rustled again he had gone to sleep.

## GEOFFREY'S NEW POST                97

On the Monday he left Nethercleugh, and a few days afterwards the head of his employers called him to his private office.

"Your engagement terminates this month, and perhaps you have wondered whether we meant to offer you a post," he said.

Geoffrey admitted that he had done so, and stopped. He knew when he had said enough.

"We had an object for waiting," his employer resumed. "We wanted to keep you, if you were willing, but did not see how we could best make use of you. Now the thing is plainer. I expect you have heard about the new colliery and coke-makers combine?"

"I have heard about it," Geoffrey replied.

"Very well. We have been appointed the Combine's consulting engineers, and I thought your help might be useful in the new business we are going to undertake. My partner agrees and we have decided to offer you a three-years' engagement. There are a few stipulations, which I'll state——"

Geoffrey listened with close attention and afterwards pondered. The pay was good, and he imagined he could carry out his duties. The post would help him to make better progress than he was likely to make in Canada, and he would earn more money. On the whole, he thought Stayward would release him, because his object for suggesting Geoffrey should go to the silver mine was probably to find him employment. All the same, since he had promised to go, Geoffrey hesitated about asking for his release.

"Well?" said his employer.

"The thing needs some thought. To begin with, I expect my job would be to consider plans for economies in getting coal; improved haulage, lighting, and machinery?"

"Not altogether. It looks as if we shall have most to do with new refining plant for treating the waste tar from the coke ovens. I imagine you know this industry is extending fast, and economical coking now depends upon the skilful use of the by-products. The Combine will spend a large sum on experiments, and there is, in particular, a rather unstable product they are anxious to make. If they can get over some difficulties caused by the chemical reactions, they can supply the dyeworks with a new fast color that will command a very good price."

Geoffrey said nothing for a few moments. His uncle had talked about the new color and had made a small quantity. Geoffrey knew he had long worked at the problem, and had some hope of finding out how to get the needed chemical stability.

"I'm sorry I must let your offer go," he replied. "For one thing, I'm not a chemist."

"We are not chemists. Your work will be mechanical; planning retorts and condensers."

"All the same," said Geoffrey, "I must leave it alone."

The other looked at him with some surprise. "May I ask why?"

"I'm the nephew of a man who is working on the Combine's line. He's something of a pioneer and has spent money and labor breaking new ground. I can't help people with a bigger capital to rob him of his reward."

"You mean Stayward? I had forgotten he was

## GEOFFREY'S NEW POST

your relation. Anyhow, he works in a very small way."

"That's the trouble. With its command of money, the Combine may beat him," Geoffrey rejoined.

His employer smiled. "I don't suppose you imagine your help would turn the scale? Besides, there's a large and growing demand for all the colors and spirits one can extract from tar. I expect Stayward will get his share of the business."

"It's possible," Geoffrey agreed, but his glance was steady and his mouth was firm. "I don't imagine my help's worth much and I'd have liked your job. For all that, I'm not going to back up people who are against my uncle."

"You're staunch," the other remarked. "Well, I'm sorry; we wanted to keep you. But perhaps we can come to an agreement that would prevent your interests and Stayward's clashing."

"I think not. If the Combine gets hold of the dye business, Stayward and the other small men must let it go. It's plain I cannot work for his antagonists. There's another thing; I ought to warn him the Combine is on his track."

The other smiled. "Then, you needn't hesitate. The Combine's plans are not secret, and they'll presently be stated in engineering newspapers. However, since you won't stop with us, can we help you get another post?"

Geoffrey thanked him and told him about the Canadian mine. "If I could have taken your job, I'd have let the other go," he added. "Still you see, the thing's impossible."

"I don't know if I do see, but I respect your

scruples. Well, I expect there's no use in trying to persuade you they're extravagant, although they hint you are the kind of man we ought to keep. Since you are resolved to go, I wish you good luck."

Geoffrey went out, and when he had finished his work returned moodily to his lodgings across the town. He thought his duty was obvious, but was sorry it had been forced on him. In this matter, his luck was certainly not good. He had refused a post that ought to give him an opportunity of winning some professional reputation and might lead to something better. His engagement in Ontario would probably lead to nothing; people who controlled big companies were not keen about employing a man from a small, unprofitable claim.

Moreover, he must work with rude appliances to which he was not used, and handle men of a new type, and no doubt bear numerous disappointments. If the mine were closed, he would have lost valuable time when he ought to have been making progress, and would, so to speak, be stamped unfit for another post. He frowned as he weighed this, but he did not hesitate. He had taken his line and must keep it. Although it might cost him something, there was no other plan. Stayward was his nearest relation and had been kind, and Geoffrey could not reward his kindness by joining his antagonists. One could not do a shabby thing like that; there was no more to be said.

# PART II
## THE RIDEAU MINE

# CHAPTER I

### THE BUSH

THERE were delays about Geoffrey's appointment that kept him for some time at Montreal, and winter had begun when he stood, one evening, outside a wooden hotel in North Ontario. The sun had set and a red glow shone behind the pines, and Geoffrey, who had not yet got used to the Canadian frost, shivered in his new furs. He had arrived at the desolate spot in the afternoon, but had since been occupied and he now looked about with some curiosity.

The pines were small and ragged, and rolled back, in somber, straggling rows, far to the North. Beyond them lay a wilderness nobody but fur-traders and adventurous prospectors had penetrated. For the most part of the year, the wilds were frozen and not many of the prospectors had found minerals worth exploiting. The land-agents who had tried to boom the district round the settlement had lost their money, and where a Canadian land-agent is beaten the neighborhood has very few advantages.

For all that, a handful of settlers, with the indomitable optimism that marks their kind, had built their homes by the track, which ran out from the forest and plunged again into the trees. Three or four shiplap stores and houses, roofed with shingles, and a post office, covered with painted iron, stood near the rails, and the hotel, farther back, was an ambitious frame building of two stories. In the clearing, sawn-off stumps, blackened by fire, stood in broken rows among round, outcropping rocks. The ground was frozen deep under the thin snow, and all was very quiet. Indeed, Geoffrey wondered whether the brooding quietness was ever broken, except when the great freight trains roared past, and twice a day the passenger cars stopped. He imagined the latter stopped because a water-tank stood near the agent's shack, and not because somebody wanted to get down.

The spot was dreary, but it was characterized by something Geoffrey had not known in England. To begin with, the air was strangely clear; the pines stood out from the background, sharply distinct. Then the wooden houses and split-rail fences that ran in zig-zags looked very new. The houses were well-built, with stoops and verandas, and the contrast between their smooth neatness and the rugged bush was marked. Put down, as they were, in virgin forest, one felt they proclaimed man's challenge to the wilds. The square clearing and the ugly rubbish dumps indicated that the settlers were stern utilitarians and had no thought for beauty. The landscape was grim, but Geoffrey rather felt it bracing than forbidding. This country was for the resolute and young.

The evening, however, was very cold and Geoffrey did not philosophize. He must, if possible, resume his journey in the morning, and this threatened to be difficult. The mine was some distance to the North, and so far as he could learn, nobody was going there. In summer, communication was by canoe; in winter, but not often, sledges came and went across the snow.

Now the rivers were frozen and the snow had hardly begun to fall.

He went back to the hotel and after supper sat by the big globular stove. Two or three other men occupied chairs, which they tilted up, and put their feet on the pile of cordwood. They were big fellows, with hard brown faces, and were marked by a ruminative calm. There was no carpet; the floor was dirty and rough. A nickeled lamp hung near the stove, but its light did not travel far and the end of the big room was shadowy. One smelt hot iron and unseasoned lumber.

Presently the landlord joined the others, and rolling a cigarette, got a light with a splinter of pine. Geoffrey smiled as he watched him, for he sprang from a frugal stock and thought the thing was typical. It looked as if one did not buy cigarettes and use unnecessary matches in the bush.

"Is there no way of getting to Whitefish Forks?" he asked the landlord.

"If you can wait a week, I reckon some of the Rideau boys may come down for grub."

Geoffrey said he did not want to wait and the landlord indicated a man whose head was bent as if he were asleep.

"Jake allows he's going up with his wagon, and if he hustles, he might make it before the snow comes. Anyhow, you can wake him; he'll fall off that chair."

The man opened his eyes when Geoffrey touched him, and when he heard what he wanted asked: "Where are you going?"

"To the Rideau mine."

"What are you going to do there?"

"I'm going to take control."

"The new boss!" said the other. "Then, you can't go with me."

He shut his eyes and when he went to sleep again Geoffrey looked at the landlord, who smiled.

"I guess you've got to let it go at that. Jake's freighter for the Forks Company; he sure won't take you."

"The Forks claim adjoins ours, I think," Geoffrey remarked. "What has this to do with his not taking me?"

"There was some trouble about your frontage on the mineral lode, and when the mining office allowed your claim the Forks gang got mad. The Rideau boys told me the last boss and Pelton of the Forks used to watch each other all the time. Your man allowed Pelton meant to tunnel under him."

Geoffrey knew nothing about this. "I can't see why they wanted to tunnel under us," he said. "You probably know the Rideau ore hardly pays for smelting. Is theirs worse?"

"I reckon it's pretty low-grade dirt, and can't figure why the Forks Company hold on. All the same, they're spending money on development, and so far they pay their bills."

"In the meantime, it's not important," Geoffrey replied. "I've got to reach the mine soon. Is there nobody who can take me?"

The landlord smiled. "You came in on the afternoon train. I reckon you've been around and made inquiries."

Geoffrey said he had been round and found two of the settlers had teams. He added that it was strange both declared their horses were engaged.

# THE BUSH

"Then, it looks as if you'd got to wait until some of the Rideau gang comes along."

"I can't wait," Geoffrey declared. "I'll start soon, if I'm forced to walk."

The other saw he was resolute, and glancing at the freighter, decided he was asleep.

"Trouble is, you'll have to camp two or three nights on the trail, and it's freezing pretty fierce," he said. "You'll want a tent, blankets, and cooking truck, and a tenderfoot like you couldn't pack them all." He lowered his voice. "Say, suppose you wait two or three days? Then, if the snow comes, I might find you a hand-sled and an outfit. You'll make it easier if the snow packs good."

Geoffrey thanked him and began to talk about something else. On the whole, he thought he could trust the landlord, although he imagined others had plotted to delay his reaching the mine. He resolved to wait a few days and then start if the snow came or not.

The snow came before morning and blew about the hotel all day. Geoffrey, trying to conquer his impatience, sat by the stove and sometimes read old newspapers, and sometimes smoked and thought. He was puzzled. Hilliard at Montreal had not told him much about the Forks Mining Company, and Geoffrey doubted if he knew much. The company was small, but it had obviously some power at the settlement. Perhaps this was because it spent money there, but one could not see why people who had money to spend bothered about a mine that turned out worse ore than the Rideau. The Rideau had not paid its shareholders, and they held on because nobody would buy the stock.

The thing was puzzling, and when Geoffrey tried to get some light from the landlord his remarks were guarded.

"I keep a hotel and don't reckon I'm a mining expert," he said. "It's possible the Fork gang are playing a clever game, but you can't count on that. Everybody knows when you open up a mineral lode you have got to trust your luck. You may go on, piling up a dump of rock that doesn't pay to smelt, and then, perhaps, one day you bottom on rich dirt. Needn't be very rich, anyhow. If it's good enough to sell the mine to a sucker, you get your money back."

Geoffrey thought the suggestion plausible. Rather than face a certain loss, a small company might go on working, in the hope that good luck would help them to recover the capital they had spent. Then there were sometimes disputes about the frontage of adjoining mines, and if the manager of the Forks had tried to tap somewhat better ore in the Rideau block, this would account for much antagonism. Geoffrey resolved to think no more about it, and the day passed drearily.

Stinging draughts swept the big room, which but for a table and a row of hard chairs was as empty as a barn. The shiplap walls creaked in the icy blast and clouds of snow blew about the clearing. The water froze in the tin basins that occupied a shelf in the passage, and when Geoffrey broke the ice before dinner he found the solitary small towel as hard as a board. Two or three railroad hands came in, shaking off the snow, and sat down at table with grimy faces. One told Geoffrey a sensible man had no use for washing in a frost like that.

The meal occupied about ten minutes, and Geoffrey's appetite was not satisfied when the others got up and a haughty waitress made it plain that she expected him to do so. So far as he could see, his companions had no English characteristics. Their talk was direct and their frankness remarkable. Everybody's ideas were clean-cut, and nobody deferred to his neighbor's. Geoffrey thought their habit was to concentrate; they had certainly concentrated on their dinner. These were not men who hesitated or bothered about refinements. Geoffrey imagined they did things roughly, but did much. On the whole, he approved. His ancestors were rude, and he had inherited something of their simplicity. Moreover, he was young and felt one needed only a few plain rules and to fix one's eyes on one's object. One made progress that way, along a straight path.

There was not much to interest him after the men went out. The West-bound train rolled into the station, headed by a giant plow that threw off waves of snow. The engines stopped at the water-tank, where fires burned, and then vanished, with the long, white cars, into the forest. After a time, a freight came up from the West, laboring hard. One heard no snorting; the blizzards drowned the explosive beat of the exhaust and the snow dulled the noise of wheels. Streaming black smoke and showers of sparks alone indicated strain. The wheat-cars rocked, white and ghostlike, across the switches, a plume of smoke whirled about a gap in the trees, and the train was gone.

Geoffrey shivered and went back to the stove, feeling the strange sense of contrast one often gets in Canada. Fifty yards in front of him, man's modern inventions rolled along the track that linked far East and West. Fifty yards behind the hotel, one plunged into virgin bush, where, because the Laurentian rocks are the oldest in the world, the tangled pines had grown since the beginning.

Soon after dark Geoffrey went to bed, and when he got up loafed away a day of glittering, stinging frost. In the afternoon, the landlord stated he could get him a hand-sledge.

"If you're going, you had better pull out while the snow's pretty good," he advised. "I reckon you ought to make it in about three days, and, if you watch out, you can't get off the trail. Now I'll tell you what you ought to take."

Geoffrey bought the things at the store across the clearing and was surprised by their cost. One of the guests helped him to load the sledge and fix the traces, and soon after daybreak he set off. The other men had gone to work, and there was nobody about but the landlord, who wished him good luck. Geoffrey felt dull and lonely as he crossed the clearing. After all, with the thermometer below zero, it was something of an adventure on which he had embarked, and the start was strangely flat.

At the edge of the trees he wanted to look back, but did not. The cluster of wooden houses, the track, and water-tank, stood for civilization, and he did not know the wilds. Until he left the hotel a few minutes since, he was, so to speak, in touch with familiar things, and the way back to the cities was open. Now all in front was strange. Yet he was young, adventure called, and setting his mouth firm, he plunged into the bush.

## THE BUSH

The sun rose, red and dim, in a frosty haze. The slanting beams that touched the slender trunks had no warmth, and his breath went up like steam in the nipping air. He thought thin vapor floated round his body. At first, there was no feeling in his hands, which looked monstrous in his stuffed mittens, and although he breathed hard as he hauled the sled he was not conscious of the traces on his shoulder. He had climbed English hills in winter, but he had not known or imagined cold like this.

Then the bush seemed dead. There was no wind, the ragged pine branches were motionless, his feet and the sledge-runners were silent on the snow. One could not see an animal or bird. It looked as if everything that could travel had gone South.

On the whole, Geoffrey was glad the sledge was heavy. Effort braced him and banished daunting thoughts, and after a time a little warmth crept through his body. He looked about, but there was not much to see. A few gray clouds floated overhead. In front, the bush rolled back as if it rolled on for ever. The pines were all alike; small, stunted, and sometimes leaning awkwardly. The trail was rough and in places cumbered by new growth, but where it was needful trees had been chopped, and one could follow the sinuous line.

Geoffrey had walked far in England, over rougher ground, and resolved he would not stop for lunch. He was anxious to shorten the distance to the mine and wanted to make a good first day's march. Besides, he doubted if, without a fire, he could stand the frost. Although the trace began to gall his shoulders and his legs to ache, he pushed on.

## CHAPTER II

### GEOFFREY ENGAGES A COOK

IT was getting dark on Geoffrey's second evening in the bush, and as he pushed on up the frozen river he looked rather anxiously ahead. The trail he had left at noon was rough, and he had been directed at the settlement to follow the river until he joined the track again by a lake. Now he looked for a spot to camp, because one needed thick bush for shelter from the biting wind, dry wood for fuel, and a patch of level ground, if possible behind a rock. On his first night out, Geoffrey had tried to sleep in the tent, but wakening nearly frozen, he pulled it down and stretching the cloth windward of his fire, used it for a screen. For all that, he had not slept much, and now he was very cold and tired.

The river banks were steep; the trees were small and scattered. Those on the western ridge cut against a dim red glow that shone behind the trunks. Those in front melted into a vague blue mass that thinned and opened up as Geoffrey advanced. He saw no shelter and was getting disturbed. For one thing, he could not go on very long, and to pitch camp in the dark would be awkward. Unless he could get warm and sleep, he doubted if he could start again in the morning. Although the sledge ran smoothly, his shoulders ached from the strain of the trace, and his foot was galled. The snow made walking hard.

# GEOFFREY ENGAGES A COOK    113

Except for the dreary sighing of the pines all was very quiet; in fact, there was something in the quietness that daunted one. The river was nearly straight, Geoffrey could see some distance ahead, and the snow-covered ice ran, smooth and level, into the gloom. It looked like a dusty highway, and Geoffrey thought about the road that came down across the moor to Nethercleugh.

He began to dwell upon the summer evening when his bicycle climbed the hills. The reflected light had hurt his eyes, as the fading snow-blink hurt them now. He pictured the long white road running on in front, with darker belts that marked the hollows. It looked as if fatigue and cold had sharpened his imagination, for the picture got strangely distinct, and he saw a lonely figure against the sky on the crest of a hill. He had seen it often, but never quite so clear, and he recaptured without an effort the hollow where he and the girl had waited by a beck that bubbled in the brass, her gracious calm, her soft voice, and all that she had said. A lark was singing, and in the distance circling plover called. Somehow he could not forget her; in quiet moments she haunted him, and the haunting had charm.

Geoffrey stumbled and getting his balance, pulled himself together. He was very cold, and must find a spot to camp. His hands were numbed and unless he reached shelter soon he might not be able to make a fire. On the first night this had bothered him. By and by the river widened and although the light had nearly gone a blurred mass loomed ahead. It looked like a wooded hill, and something at its foot caught

Geoffrey's eye. A small red spark twinkled in the gloom, went out, and began to twinkle again.

He pushed on and the spark got bright. It was a fire; somebody had camped among the trees. Geoffrey's weariness vanished and he began to run. To find he was not alone was strangely comforting. Some minutes afterwards he dragged his sledge between the trees and stopped. A snapping fire threw red reflections on a ledge of rock and the straight pine trunks, and a man, sitting on some branches, looked up. A blue Hudson Bay blanket covered his shoulders, the hair had come off his skin cap, and his face was lined and brown.

"Hallo!" he said. "I guess you saw my fire?"

"I was remarkably glad to see it," Geoffrey owned. "The bush gets lonely after dark. I'd like to camp here, if you don't mind."

"Not at all," said the other, and Geoffrey noted he had a cultivated voice. "Your coming's pretty good luck, particularly if you have brought some food."

Geoffrey saw the blackened can and tin plate by the fire was empty and began to unload his sledge. When he had thrown off his tent and blankets he opened a bag of provisions.

"I'll make supper when I've thawed a bit," he said.

"Unless you're a cook, you had better leave it to me. I know something about the job," the other remarked.

Geoffrey was glad to let him cook, and sat down by the fire. The rocks and trunks kept off the wind, and the hollow behind the ledge was warm. Moreover, he saw the man could cook, and the hot ban-

# GEOFFREY ENGAGES A COOK

nock and fried pork and beans he presently turned out of the pan looked appetizing.

"You'll join me, of course," he said. "You have earned a share."

The other filled his plate and ate. Then he brewed some strong, sweet tea from Geoffrey's pack, and when he had cleaned and put back the tins began to scrape an old pipe.

"My pipe's frozen," said Geoffrey, taking out his cigarette case. "See if you like these."

They smoked for a time and Geoffrey imagined his companion was studying him. He was not curious about the other. All he wanted was human society.

"Which way are you going?" he asked.

"North, to Whitefish Forks. I started from Indian Lake six days ago, and since my grub is finished, it looks as if my luck was good. I ought to make some distance on a supper like this."

"Why didn't you take more food?"

"For one thing, at the bush settlements food is dear. Then the blizzard held me up and after that the going was slow."

Geoffrey thought the others' luck had not been good recently. His lined face and ragged coat indicated this. Moreover, he was getting old, and Canada is a country for the young.

"The Forks is a pretty lonely spot and hard to reach," Geoffrey remarked. "I suppose you have some business there?"

The man laughed. "Why, yes! Just now my occupation is looking for a job, and it has brought me across from the Pacific slope by broken stages. I belong to the army of deadbeats that's moving East.

Since trade got bad in British Columbia the tide that generally runs West has turned, but the nearer we get to the Atlantic, the worse things look."

He occupied himself about the fire and Geoffrey lighted another cigarette. Supper had revived him, and the warmth was coming back to his numbed body. The branches his companion had arranged made a springy seat, and after a long day's march it was strangely pleasant to loaf with his back to the rock and his feet to the snapping fire. Thin smoke blew about, and now and then the blaze leaped up, driving back the shadows that closed in again when it sank. Rows of small trunks caught the reflections, and for a few moments stood out against the gloom. Geoffrey was young and liked to feel he had well used his muscles.

He mused about his companion. The fellow talked like an Englishman, and Geoffrey imagined he had heard his voice before. This, however, was improbable, because his face was strange. On the whole, he liked the man and felt vaguely sorry for him. He wondered how far he might venture to indulge his curiosity without being impertinent, and reflected that in Canada one could go some distance.

"What particular job do you expect to get?" he asked.

"I heard the Rideau manager had advertised for a cook and thought I'd try for the post."

"It looks as if you could cook. Supper was pretty good."

"Since I hadn't eaten much for two days, I'll own I made an effort. All the same, I believe I can cook rather better than I do anything else. When they

## GEOFFREY ENGAGES A COOK 117

broke up the gang at the construction camp, the boss gave me some compliments. Other employers, and I've had a number, did not."

"As a rule, employers use a cautious reserve," Geoffrey observed. "Had you cooked before you went to the camp?"

"I helped in a steamer's galley, in return for my passage; that's all. Canada's a good country for developing talents you didn't know you'd got."

Geoffrey resolved to offer the man the post. He liked his careless humor and, since the fellow had run some risk of starving, thought it indicated a philosophic temperament. He, however, wanted to satisfy his curiosity.

"England is the only country I know much about. I imagine you are luckier," he replied.

"The luck's not very obvious; all the countries I have tried are hard. In South Africa—I was on the Rand, and afterwards went North—malaria knocked me out. In West Australia I got hurt at a mining accident. Somebody stole my wad at a California opium joint. Men who could not get work were demonstrating in B.C., and I pushed on East across the plains. Now, since I have no money to buy food for the back trail, I expect the long trek will end at Whitefish Fork unless I get the job."

"I'll give you the job," said Geoffrey.

The other looked at him with surprise. "Is it yours to give?"

"I imagine so. I'm the new manager."

"Well," said the other, laughing, "it's some relief to know I'm hired, although I've got the post in a rather unusual way. I began by eating your supper and expect you noted my extravagance. Because all the food I carry wouldn't make one good meal, I thought I'd better seize the chance to get some nourishment at another's cost. In fact, I doubt if I'd have reached the mine had you not come along."

Geoffrey thought he did not exaggerate. One needs food to make a long march in the Canadian frost. When one's body is exhausted by toiling across the snow, nothing but plentiful nourishment will keep up the vital warmth. Yet he remarked the other's carelessness; the fellow had not been daunted by the risk he ran. Geoffrey wondered whether much disappointment accounted for his philosophy, but he had not made good.

"Oh, well," he replied. "We'll finish the journey together and the stuff in my pack ought to see us out. My name's Lisle; I don't know yours."

The other did not hesitate, but his eyes twinkled, and Geoffrey thought he understood his smile.

"Carson, Thomas Carson. As a rule, the boys call me old Tom."

He threw fresh wood on the fire, and after arranging his branch bed lay down.

"I don't expect the cold will waken us for some time, and I was too hungry last night to sleep much," he said.

Geoffrey lay down, but did not immediately go to sleep. It was not long since supper, and he imagined the warm food and the talk had stimulated his brain. He watched the smoke drift across the trunks and the shadows creep back and close again about the camp. The fire snapped and he heard the wind in the pine-tops. Sometimes he thought about his companion,

## GEOFFREY ENGAGES A COOK

who was now asleep, and sometimes about Nethercleugh. Perhaps it was strange, but he felt Carson had given his thoughts this turn. He had not seen the fellow at Nethercleugh, and did not imagine he had seen him at all. Yet there was a note in his voice he ought to know. One sometimes remembered voices long. For all that, Geoffrey could not remember Carson's, and after a time the rows of pine-trunks melted and the fire got dim. He pulled his blanket tight and went to sleep.

When he awoke it was dark and bitterly cold. The fire had sunk and one could see the sky. In places, a few stars twinkled with a hard, steely brightness Geoffrey had not known in England, but for the most part black clouds rolled by above the trees. He heard the wind in the branches, and a white dust that he thought was fine, dry snow blew about the trunks. With some trouble, for his hands were numbed, he pulled out his watch. It marked six o'clock, and he took his mittens and moccasins from a branch by the fire. They were dry, and he could put them on without risk of frostbite. When he had done so he threw off his blanket and got up.

Although the camp was sheltered, the cold pierced him like a knife. He gasped, as if he had plunged into icy water, and his legs shook. His flesh shrank from the Arctic frost, but by a stern effort he conquered his longing to creep back under the blanket. It was six o'clock, the days were short, and he must, if possible, reach the mine by dark. He did not mean to spend another night in the frozen wilds. His hip-joints ached, and the thick mittens bunched his fingers together awkwardly, but he began to move about.

The fire must be replenished and snow melted before one could make flapjack and coffee. The pork Carson had cut for breakfast looked like marble and broke when Geoffrey threw it into the pan. He noted that there was not much left, but if it lasted for another meal this would meet his needs. When he was mixing flour and hot water Carson got up and took the tin from him.

"You can roll up the blankets. Cooking's my job," he said.

The man looked older than Geoffrey had thought, his furs were ragged, and, standing with his shoulders bent, he shivered. Geoffrey had not meant to rouse him yet and felt pitiful.

"I think it's mine this morning. Your new duties haven't begun."

Carson smiled. "All the same, we'll both travel better after a breakfast one can digest. Mixing flapjacks is rather harder than it looks, and if you stay in Canada long enough, you'll find you won't make good time on a meal of half-raw dough."

Geoffrey let him have the tin and breakfast was soon ready. The flapjacks were crisp and light, the pork brown and firm, and Geoffrey thought he had enjoyed no drink like the hot sweet tea that tasted of wood smoke. The meal gave him warmth and energy, but for some minutes afterwards he fought a hard battle with his animal instincts. He revolted from the effort to leave the fire and front the dark and cold. Twice he took out his watch and persuaded himself he need not start just yet. Then he saw Carson was watching him with a sympathetic smile.

"You're new to the trail," the latter remarked.

# GEOFFREY ENGAGES A COOK

"Pulling out in the morning will come easier by and by."

"I'll own it comes hard," said Geoffrey and got up with a jerk. "To put off things doesn't help much. We'll pull out now."

He threw the sledge trace over his shoulder and they set off. The hard strap had galled his skin, and for some minutes it hurt him cruelly. The smart got less as he warmed to his work, and when day broke they were some distance up the river. There was no brightness in the East and leaden clouds covered the sky. The stiff pines were dim and a dreary wind wailed in their tops. Geoffrey stopped for a moment and looked about.

"I expect the point in front is where we ought to leave the ice and rejoin the trail," he said. "The fellow who told me about it declared one could reach the mine in about eight hours."

"Something depends on the snow," said Carson dryly. "I doubt if we'll find the going good until dark."

Geoffrey glanced at the gloomy sky and nodded, and leaving the ice, they plunged into the bush.

## CHAPTER III

#### SNOW

AT noon Geoffrey had not found the trail. The clouds were thick and the light was dim. He was crossing broken country where small ridges obstructed his view, and the landscape was strangely desolate, without a hint of life. By and by the trees in the background faded and snow began to fall.

Geoffrey took the sledge from Carson, who had followed the trail he broke but was dropping behind. His shoulder began to bleed where the trace galled, and all his muscles ached, but he pushed on with savage obstinacy. He began to doubt if they would reach the mine, but he durst not weigh the chances. The main thing was to keep going. To stop was to own defeat and in the North, Nature is merciless. Anyhow, although Carson was flagging, he meant to struggle forward until they found the trail. He must not admit that they were lost.

When the light was going Carson found the trail. There was not much to mark it, but some big stones had been rolled down a bank, branches had been chopped, and a short distance farther on there was a gap in a thicker row of pines. The signs of human effort were strangely comforting and to follow the broken line would bring one to shelter from frost and storm, but Geoffrey knitted his brows. He could not go much farther and Carson was exhausted. For a very short distance, blurred rocks and pines loomed in the snow, and then tossing flakes closed the dreary view.

Geoffrey pondered the situation, for although Carson was older and had been longer in the country, Geoffrey felt that he himself must take control. This was not because he was manager; now both risked frostbite and starvation, they were equal partners in a desperate undertaking, but he knew he had qualities his companion had not. On the whole he thought it rash to push on. They could not go far and had better pitch camp before it got dark.

"We'll stop as soon as we can find a sheltered spot," he said and they set off again.

The light had nearly gone when they reached a hollow by a frozen creek, and Geoffrey took an axe from the sledge. The cold that numbed his tired body dulled his brain and he shrank from the effort he knew he must make. Indeed, while he stayed in Canada he hated the labor of making camp after a long day's march. Yet, with the thermometer below zero, the man who shirks this task must freeze. One must cut thin branches for a bed, build a snow bank or a screen of logs, chop wood, and gather resinous chips for kindling. Then the beginner whose hands have lost their grip and sense of touch often struggles long to get his sullen fire to burn.

Geoffrey knew little about the use of the axe, but he was young and obstinate. Moreover, he knew it was a battle for his life between him and Nature, and he did not mean to be beaten. In this fight temperament counted for much. Somehow he brought down three or four small trees and hacked off their branches.

He cut the trunks and laboriously built a wall on three sides of a square. The tent, propped by branches, made a faulty roof and in front he made his fire. He did not know what Carson did, although he saw his indistinct figure moving about. Nothing was important but the splitting of enough wood to last the night. At length, supper was ready and Geoffrey looked at Carson when he saw the meal was good.

"There's something left for breakfast," said the other, meaningly, and Geoffrey nodded.

In the morning he must make a stern choice, but much depended on the weather and the choice must wait. Geoffrey did not talk. He was dull and worn out, and for a time sat with his back against the logs. The tent flapped and strained and a cloud of tossing flakes blew across its top, whirled about the fire, and vanished in the streaming smoke. The light did not travel far and when it sank the wavering white curtain drew in. By and by Geoffrey, slipping down on the branches, pulled his blanket over his head and went to sleep.

When he woke in the morning, snow blew about the fire. The tent flapped, but the deep note the tossing pines struck was softer. They had roared like the sea; now the noise was like the beat of languid surf on a gravel beach. Carson had got out the cooking tins and turned to Geoffrey when he saw he was awake.

"You're boss," he said. "Just now I'm satisfied to be cook. We have enough food for a good breakfast, but that's all."

Geoffrey knitted his brows and said nothing for a minute or two. He was boss, because he was young and resolute and he suspected that Carson was resigned and weak. Yet he felt his responsibility. His life and another's depended on the choice he made and he did not know the chances against him. To begin with, he did not know how far off they were from Whitefish Forks. Although he thought they must reach the mine by dark or freeze, he hesitated.

His mother was a Stayward and he was rather like her than his father. The Staywards were stubborn and cautious, but they could run risks where risks were needful and it looked as if he must take a bold line now. To husband food and start hungry meant a slower march and speed was important. Yet if speed did not save them, there would be no food left.

"The thing's a gamble," he remarked.

Carson nodded. "We know the stakes and if we lose we pay. Well, I've been something of a gambler for long."

"If we are forced to camp again, a few morsels of food wouldn't be of much use," Geoffrey resumed. "On the whole, I think we'll reach the Forks to-night or not get there at all. Very well. You had better cook all the stuff. We'll make the plunge."

"There's another thing," said Carson, after he put the last of the pork in the pan. "The sled's a drag; hauling the load keeps us back."

Geoffrey frowned. He did not know how long he could keep going, but if he left the sledge with the tent and blankets he would freeze soon after he stopped. Yet, although the risk was desperate, to travel light meant to travel fast. In the meantime, Carson waited and Geoffrey thought he began to understand the fellow. Carson had pluck, but it was negative, apathetic pluck; he bore things philosophically when perhaps they need not be borne. Geoffrey saw he must choose for both.

"I reckon we couldn't keep the trail in the dark and this means we must finish the march while we can see," he said. "Well, since it's a race, we won't start carrying weight."

Carson agreed and in a few minutes they set off, and almost forgot the cold when they plunged into a drift. The fine dry snow rolled like waves in the wind, sometimes to their knees and sometimes to their waists. They were breathless when they struggled through, and Carson looked at Geoffrey, who understood him although neither spoke. If drifts like this were numerous, they would not reach the Forks.

A faint light pierced the storm clouds and for a time the trail was better. One could follow the line, for in places a prominent tree was blazed. Somebody had chopped a branch or sliced off a slab of bark. For all that, their labor was heavy and about twelve o'clock Geoffrey stopped to let Carson come up. He felt slack and his muscles ached, but he was conscious that he was not quite doing his best. The trouble was that although he had some power in reserve Carson had none. In a few moments Carson joined him and, breathing hard, leaned against a tree.

"The custom is to noon for an hour on a long hike," he said.

Geoffrey laughed, a hoarse laugh. They were crossing a thinly-wooded tableland and the snow blew in a white cloud between the scattered trees. Close by, a big drift tossed behind a rock. There was no shelter and as Geoffrey braced himself against the wind another drift began to gather about his legs.

"If we stop, I expect we'll stop for good," he said. "We'll get on while we can."

"You go too fast," Carson grumbled. "I doubt if I can keep up."

Geoffrey gave him an impatient glance. Carson's back was against the tree, but his head leaned forward and his eyes were half shut. He looked spiritless and very limp.

"You must keep up," said Geoffrey, roughly.

"I don't see the advantage; I'm stopping you. If you go on, I can follow the trail you break, at the pace that suits me best, and you can send back some of the miners to look for me."

Geoffrey hesitated. Since he had stopped he felt half frozen, and the snow was getting worse. Speed alone could help him to escape and Carson's suggestion was plausible. He thought the fellow wanted to give him a chance to finish the journey, but perhaps he shrank from the stern effort to keep up. The temptation to agree was strong, but Geoffrey would not. He felt if he gave way now he would always be ashamed.

"You are coming along," he said in a hard voice. "When you can't keep up I'll drag you."

He imagined afterwards he had struck the proper note. Carson meant well, but as a rule, was satisfied with this; if his plans did not work, he languidly acquiesced. When Geoffrey knew his story, he understood his fall. All the same, he liked the fellow.

They set off and Geoffrey broke the trail. He did not remember much about the afternoon. His brain was dull, his eyes were dazzled, and he concentrated on getting forward. As they advanced, blurred rows of trees moved back out of the tossing snow. Sometimes the broken line they tried to keep bent round projecting rocks. Sometimes they stumbled down steep pitches and struggled with straining muscles up the other slope. They never got a long view and nothing broke the sense of desolation. But the trail led on and they knew where it stopped men sat by cheerful fires.

At length, when Geoffrey was exhausted, the tossing pines got dim. He realized half consciously that he was pulling Carson along, but could not remember when he began to do so. Indeed, he remembered nothing; his rough calculations about speed and distance had faded from his brain. All he knew was it was getting dark and he must keep Carson on his feet. They would soon be unable to see the trail, but he was strangely undisturbed by this. Conscious hope and fear had gone; blind instinct urged him to continue the struggle.

They stopped at the bottom of a rise and Carson leaned against Geoffrey. Billowing drifts crossed the uphill track, the pitch was very steep, and Carson, moving off a yard or two, sat down in the snow.

"This hill will baffle us. I wonder whether it's the last," he said and laughed hoarsely. "Luck plays strange tricks. When I was at Vancouver I helped search for a man who had strolled away from a picnic in the bush and got lost. We found him, a week after, lying about fifty yards from a trail he couldn't see. I remember he looked calm. Perhaps there's a point of exhaustion at which one no longer feels much and weakness deadens pain. It looks as if we'd soon find out——"

Geoffrey seized his arm. "Stop this drivel! Get up!"

He jerked Carson to his feet, shook him and pushed him forward, and they began the laborious climb. Now and then they stuck for some minutes in a drift, and before they reached the top the light had altogether gone. Geoffrey did not know if he had kept the trail. The wood was thin and one could not see the trunks a few yards off. Since they might be heading away from the Forks, he doubted if there was much use in going on, but he struggled forward, pulling Carson, until as they crossed the summit the latter fell.

Geoffrey left him alone and tried to get his breath. His heart beat, his head swam, and for a few moments he was conscious of nothing but the cold and an overwhelming fatigue. Then he thought in one place there was a glimmer in the snow. He went forward and saw it plainer. There was a light, not far off, and the light was steady. It was not the trembling reflection a campfire threw. Pulling himself together, he went back for Carson.

"Get up," he said. "We have made the Forks."

Carson was dazed and slow, and Geoffrey used the little force he had left. The light might vanish and leave them without a guide. To run a risk now was unthinkable, and he pushed Carson forward savagely. The light got brighter and grew into a square patch of illumination. Then the dark bulk of a house loomed ahead and Geoffrey struck a log wall. He followed the wall until he felt a door and when he could not find the latch beat upon the boards.

The door opened and he plunged into a long room. A stove twinkled in the middle, and Geoffrey got a vague impression of light and warmth and tobacco smoke. His frozen flesh began to tingle and the blood came to his head. The floor rocked, and, letting Carson go, he made for a bench. He thought he heard somebody fall, but he did not stop. The physical reaction from the Arctic cold thrilled him with pain and he must reach the bench.

"Look after the other fellow," he said and, sitting down, leaned against the wall and shut his eyes.

## CHAPTER IV

### THE MINE

THE morning was keen, but Geoffrey stopped for a few moments outside the log-house and glanced about. One end of the rude building was his office and bedroom; the men occupied the rest of the house. Fifty yards away, a small shack covered the pumping engine and winding gear at the top of the shaft; then a rounded mass of rock cut off the view. A rusty chimney stack behind the rock marked the neighboring mineral property, the Whitefish Forks. Rows of small pine-stumps, four or five feet high, surrounded the shaft, but the snow had covered the ugly ore-dump.

On one side, the forest was pierced by a shallow valley, through which the Whitefish flowed, and abreast of the mine a tributary plunged over a high ledge. The fall was sheeted in ice, and frozen spray hung about its front in fantastic patterns like filmy draperies. Geoffrey thought the likeness was marked when the water covered the rocks with a wavering embroidery of foam. No doubt the mine had been called the Rideau after a famous curtain fall.

There was no wind. A clear sky, luminously blue, overhung the wide sweep of snow. For the most part, the pines were white. They looked strangely stiff and formal, but here and there a raw-green pyramid stood out from their glittering ranks. Below the fall, where the savage current broke the ice, the water was black as ink, and thin mist floated above the open channel. The mist looked blue against the snow, but where the beams of the red sun pierced it, took rainbow hues.

Geoffrey shivered and moved on. His overalls, slickers, and rubber boots did not keep him warm, but he felt invigorated and confident. He was young, and in Canada the young soon get a careless optimism. Moreover, although the mine was not important, in a sense it was his. He meant to remodel its arrangements, cut down the working costs, and following the vein by scientific rule, get out better ore. In fact, he was going to make the undertaking a success and win recognition for himself. There were difficulties, and he had studied some, but, if one was resolute, difficulties could be conquered.

He nodded to Carson, who was chopping cordwood. The fellow used the axe well and his cooking satisfied the men. Carson was making good and Geoffrey felt he had not been rash when he engaged him. One liked to know one's judgment was sound. Besides, he had saved the fellow from freezing. One did not dwell on things like this and exaggerate their importance, but, after all, if he had not come along, Carson could not have reached the Forks. He felt well-disposed to Carson and meant if possible to help him on. In the meantime, however, he had something else to think about.

When he reached the shaft he did not bother about the winding gear but went down a rope. Descending this way was easier than climbing the gullies in the Cumbrian crags, and he did not mind the miners re-

## THE MINE

marking his nerve and confidence. Men rather liked a boss whose physical strength was as good as theirs. Passing the mouth of a dark tunnel, he went down to the end of the rope and his mood changed when he entered an inclined gallery. Geoffrey had youthful weaknesses he now and then indulged, but he was a miner and in his occupation was practical and sometimes clever.

The tunnel was strongly timbered and heavy beams held up the fissured roof. Some bent and Geoffrey gave these a thoughtful glance and weighed the need for fresh support. It was something to feel he was accountable for the safety of his men and could drive the tunnel where he would. Water trickled from a number of the cracks, although the frost stopped the surface drainage. He saw that to keep the mine dry after the thaw began would be something of an undertaking.

By and by he stopped at the working face. His hat was wet, but the pit-lamp on its brim had not gone out. Men were throwing broken rock into a wheeled tub, and candles stuck about the walls gave a dim light. A man controlled a jarring machine and Geoffrey heard its cutters bite the rock. At Montreal he had urged that the new borer should be sent and he was satisfied to note the thing was running well. He meant to urge the spending of larger sums on up-to-date machinery, but he must wait. The expense would have to be justified; directors asked for results.

He ordered the man to try a new adjustment of the cutters, and except for the clink of a spanner and the thud of stone in the tub there was silence when the machine stopped. Then Geoffrey thought he heard a muffled knocking behind the wall of rock. He beckoned the foreman and sat down on a heap of props.

"The Forks people, I suppose?" he said. "Looks as if they were working close to the boundary."

"Pretty close," the foreman agreed. "They've been cutting rock there for some time."

The noise got louder and Geoffrey listened carefully.

"*Above us,* I think," he remarked.

"That's where they are."

"It's strange. The vein dips, and carries better metal the lower one gets. I understand the stuff you raised when you pushed the top heading back the other way to the outcrop was not worth bringing up?"

"Mean dirt," said the other. "Anyhow, I reckon the Forks crowd have got a plan. They're not suckers."

Geoffrey knitted his brows. "Then, I don't know why they try the top when the pay-dirt is underneath. They're suspiciously near our front. I'd like to look at their workings."

"The last boss tried," the foreman remarked with a grin. "When he got back he wore a bandage for a week, but there wasn't so much bad feeling then. I allow they might shoot you up."

"Bad feeling?" said Geoffrey. "D'you mean the men, so to speak, take sides. The dispute's not theirs."

"You give our crowd a chance and see. Treat them fair and if you want them I reckon they'll back you good. This is a white man's country; white men made it, but the Forks gang run their show with foreign trash. I allow they don't make trouble about a crooked job."

Geoffrey pondered. At Montreal, Hilliard had told

# THE MINE

him Ross was honest and Geoffrey approved the fellow. Feeling his youth and the strangeness of the country, he had half expected some opposition when he took control but had encountered none. The opposition might, however, have risen had he not made it plain unconciously that he was just and firm.

"They've stopped," he said presently when the dull knocking ceased. "Drilling for a shot, I think."

Ross nodded. "Looks like that, but they haven't used much powder at our end of the tunnel. The stuff we're cutting through won't stand for it."

They waited for a few minutes and then Geoffrey started. The rock shook and some of the candles went out. He rather felt a dull concussion than heard a report, but it was not the shock that brought him to his feet. A crack opened above the boring machine, a beam bent, and the roof bulged down. Then a big stone began to work out from the crack.

"Get from under!" Geoffrey shouted and pushed back the man at the machine.

Next moment the stone fell and smashed on the rock beneath. Water dripped on Geoffrey's head, he missed the light of the pit-lamp, and, putting up his hand, found his hat had gone. The man he pushed was uninjured, but it was obvious that the roof was coming down.

"Another beam!" he shouted and picked up a prop.

Two men brought the beam and he jammed the prop beneath one end while somebody fixed another prop at the opposite side of the tunnel. The props were cut a little too long and ran obliquely between the roof and floor, in order that when the bottom end was driven forward they would wedge up the beam. It was plain that speed was needful. The roof bulged, the walls worked, and water poured from the opening cracks. Unless the timbers were fixed in the next few moments, the gallery would fill up and all who stayed there would be buried.

Geoffrey saw this half-consciously, for his action was rather instinctive than reasoned. To weigh the risk was to court defeat, and he was driven by a reckless savageness. The roof must not come down and the costly rock-borer must not be smashed. He was going to prevent it; the trouble was that the time at his disposal was very short.

He did not doubt the men. Although the risk was theirs but not the profit, they would follow a bold lead, and he was leader. A plain command went some way; example went farther. While the roof cracked, he threw himself upon the prop, using the weight of his body to help his msucles, and somebody struck its foot with a heavy maul. Across the tunnel, men struggled to place the second prop. Their bent figures were indistinct, for half the lights had gone out. One heard their labored breath and their feet shuffle in the mud.

In a sense, the struggle was unequal. Overhead, a crushing load of rock obeyed the law of gravity; below, in the collapsing tunnel, without proper room to move, flesh and blood, strung to desperate tension, strove to resist. For a time, the men, like their leader, labored with unthinking primitive fury. The new beam bent in the middle, but it was not long, and if they could wedge the props tight, it might not break. There was not room to swing the heavy hammers and the men crouched in ungainly attitudes to get their arms back. Then their bent bodies lurched forward to deliver the blow. Other men, straining and gasping, steadied the posts while small stones and water rained down.

Geoffrey was conscious that the struggle could not last. Unless they won in the next few moments, all would be crushed. Yet this did not daunt him and it did not daunt the rest. They were miners and had at other times matched their indomitable stubbornness against Nature's powers.

A stone fell and a man's face got red with blood, but he swung his maul as if he did not know. The prop he struck straightened and Geoffrey, laboring with beating heart and the veins on his forehead swelling, forced back the post he held. Somebody struck its foot a smashing blow, the timber groaned and stood upright. The beam was wedged; he thought it would stand until he got another across. He had won the time he needed and could use his brain. Now he must study where the worst pressure came and where fresh supports ought to be put.

Half an hour afterward he picked his trampled hat out of the mud, and sitting down on some props, lighted his pipe. The candles were burning and the men had resumed their work. Their figures cut against the uncertain light that touched the nearest timbers and emphasized the shadows between. Farther off, beams and props closed upon each other until it looked as if the tunnel were lined with solid wood.

Geoffrey did not know if he was physically tired, but he felt slack, for now and then it costs a leader something to front his responsibility and lead. On the whole, Geoffrey was satisfied. He had saved the tunnel, and although he had not consciously used much thought, his brain, working mechanically on the studies he had made in English mines, had well guided him. This, however, was not all. Mining was a scientific business; one measured depths and calculated pressures, in order to work in harmony with Nature's laws, but a time sometimes came when one must trust human pluck and muscle. He had stood the strain and an important consequence was that the men would own his rule. They had seen he was not a drawing-office critic and exacting paymaster, but flesh and blood like themselves and willing to share their risks.

By and by Ross, who had supported him nobly, came up. Geoffrey had liked Ross before, but now imagined the man looked at him differently.

"We cannot allow the Forks people to shake up our heading like this," he said. "I'll send a note across, telling them we'll hold them accountable for the damage."

Ross grinned. "Well, I allow it's the proper plan!"

"But you don't think it will lead to much? I don't know your Canadian laws, but I imagine the Forks Company is accountable."

"Unless your wad is pretty big, you want to leave the law alone when you're up against a crowd like our neighbors. Arguing before a judge costs a pile."

"You imply the Forks lot are rich?"

"Well," said Ross, dryly. "They've money behind them. They're spending some and it's a sure thing they don't get much from the mine."

"It looks like that," Geoffrey agreed. "Anyhow, I'll send a note. Suppose this leads to nothing, will you come with me some night and try to get into the mine?"

The foreman gave him a glance in which Geoffrey thought there was an approval he had not remarked before.

"Why, yes," he said. "When you want me I'll certainly come along."

## CHAPTER V

### GEOFFREY TRESPASSES

GEOFFREY sent a note to the Forks manager and got a curt reply. The fellow stated he had used a very small quantity of powder and was not accountable for the damage. If the roof was weak, it was the Rideau Company's business to put up proper timbers. Geoffrey frowned when he read the note. Pelton was plainly working along the Rideau's frontage and had perhaps cut into their block, although since the ore was poor, his object was hard to see. Anyhow, since he had gained nothing by argument, Geoffrey resolved to get into the mine and investigate.

About eleven o'clock one night Ross knocked at his door and Geoffrey shivered as he dressed. The night was dark and very cold. A biting wind wailed about the shack and fine snow fell. Geoffrey shrank from the frost, and the snow would make it awkward to find the Forks shaft. For all that, the darkness had some advantages, because to go when the night was clear and calm might lead to his getting caught.

He put on his furs, although he knew they would embarrass him in the mine. One could not bear the cold without some protection. Then he hooked a pit-lamp on his hat, and trying to banish his doubts, set off. One could not see six yards in front and he could not find the Forks boundary post. It was with diffi-

## GEOFFREY TRESPASSES

culty he kept clear of the stumps that covered the clearing and he got something of a jar when the foreman touched him and a shadowy building loomed close by.

"The Forks bunkhouse," Ross remarked.

Geoffrey stopped. It was obvious that he had lost his way, and had he fallen over a stump the miners might have heard the noise. The bunk house was only a few yards off, but it was dark. Geoffrey knew all the work was done by a day shift and imagined the men were in bed. Still the sparks and luminous vapor that streamed from the stove-pipe on the roof indicated that somebody had not long since thrown on fresh wood.

"Where's the shaft?" he asked.

"East from the house," said Ross.

"Where's east?"

"On our left, if we're looking the way I reckon."

Geoffrey signed agreement and they went off. He doubted if they could find the shaft, but he meant to try and knew the snow would cover their tracks. After a time his foot struck something and he plunged into the snow. He felt branches crack, and getting up breathlessly, began to look about. At first he could see nothing, but presently distinguished two or three tall white objects and a hazy mass in the background.

"I fell on branches. We have run into the slashing," he said. "I see the bush behind the belt they've cut. If we headed east, the shaft's another way."

"I sure don't know where she is," Ross admitted. "I wouldn't bet much I could find the Rideau."

"Oh, well," said Geoffrey. "If we ramble about much longer, we'll freeze. Let's try again."

They left the edge of the bush and presently Ross stopped at the bottom of a rough white bank.

"The ore-dump, though I don't know how we got here," he remarked. "If we cross the top, I reckon we'll hit the shaft."

Geoffrey grumbled while they climbed the bank. Some of the broken rock was small and slipped down under his feet; some was large and the snow had not solidly filled the holes. He broke through the treacherous covering and was surprised he had not hurt his legs. There seemed to be no end to the stones, he could not tell if he was going straight, and it was some relief to find he did not cross his tracks. He fell once or twice and thought he made an alarming noise, but at length Ross indicated a large, indistinct object in the blowing snow. It looked like a building and for a few moments they stopped and listened.

They had grounds for imagining the miners were asleep in the bunkhouse, but this was not certain. At the Rideau extra timbers were sometimes put up at night, in order not to interfere with the work of the day shift. One could not take it for granted nobody was below and to be caught might have awkward consequences. All the same, Geoffrey was resolved to go down.

He beckoned Ross and went cautiously into the house built over the shaft. It was very dark but all was quiet, and with numbed hands he awkwardly lighted his pit-lamp and then gave Ross the match. The feeble illumination touched the rough beams and the wheels overhead, flickered about the rocky floor, and rested on the mouth of a dark hole. Geoffrey saw

## GEOFFREY TRESPASSES 143

the top of a rude ladder, hooked to a log that guarded the shaft.

"I wish I'd got slickers," he remarked. "A long, thick coat's awkward in a tunnel, but if I leave it here, I'll probably get wet. I don't know if one man could work their ore-skip."

"I'm not going to try," said Ross. "If you're going down, I'm coming along."

Geoffrey meant to go, but admitted that his resolve was perhaps ridiculous. He was trespassing, and if the Forks people treated him roughly they would be justified. Then he did not know if he expected to find out anything important, and the dark hole looked forbidding. However, since the adventure would not stand calm reflection, he had better start.

The ladder shook and when he had gone down some distance the cross-pieces were wet and slippery, but the shaft was not deep, and when he got off at the bottom he threw the light on a compass he had brought and noted the bearing of the tunnel he entered. Counting his steps, he went forward cautiously and came to an opening where the ore was worked. There was nothing remarkable. The rock was like the Rideau rock, but he picked up some small pieces and filled his pocket.

He could do nothing more. When he went up he must try to reckon the height he climbed and afterwards, in the daylight, get the compass bearing of the shaft from two objects whose distance apart one could measure. Then he could make some useful calculations. In the meantime, he must get out of the mine as soon as possible. Ross went first, and Geoffrey measured with his hand the gaps between two or three cross-pieces on the ladder.

"Count your steps as you go up," he said, and waited for Ross to give him room to climb.

It was some relief to feel that in a few moments he would reach the clearing. Perhaps he had run some risk, and he was getting impatient, although nothing indicated any ground for alarm. Ross was very slow, but Geoffrey understood why he was cautious when he came to a spot where the ladder was greasy with water and mud. The wood cracked and shook, and he could see nothing but the faint glimmer round the foreman's head and his heavy boots slipping on the cross-pieces where the light of Geoffrey's pit-lamp fell. He counted the pieces and wondered with growing impatience when Ross would get to the top. At length the other stopped and the light on his hat moved suddenly forward.

"Wait until I get a holt; I'm at the ledge," he said.

It looked as if he stumbled when he got up, for there was a jar in the dark and his boots scuffled on the rock. Geoffrey wondered why he made so much noise, and feeling for the ledge, got his feet on the last cross-piece. When he lifted his body across the timber the movement threw the faint beam of his lamp forward, but except for this the shafthouse was dark. The brim of his hat confined his view to the ground and he saw somebody's legs.

"Find the door and get it open, Ross," he said.

The foreman did not answer, but somebody seized Geoffrey's arm and pulled him across the ledge. Next moment his hat was knocked off and the light went out. It was obvious the legs he had seen did not belong to Ross, and Geoffrey grappled with the man. He threw him back and heard him fall, but another

## GEOFFREY TRESPASSES 145

came on and it was plain that he had two or three antagonists. The shaft-house was very dark and he could not see how many there were. For all that, he was not going to be captured.

He struck and the other man let go. For a moment nobody seemed to be in front and he tried to find the door. He could not, and he durst not move much for fear of falling down the shaft. Then, while he waited, highly strung, trying to pierce the dark, his antagonists closed with him. He got a blow home, but this was all. He was surrounded, buffeted, and pulled to and fro, until he and two or three of the others went down.

A heavy man fell upon him and he struck his head against the rock. He was exhausted, and could not resist when the others dragged him up and pushed him through the door. Somebody pulled his arms behind his back and urged him forward with a kick. It was plain there was no use in struggling and he let the men lead him away. Geoffrey imagined they had seized Ross as he climbed across the ledge and had perhaps thrown a coat over his head so that he could not shout. The fellows had found out trespassers were in the mine.

After a few minutes Geoffrey saw the bunk house and one of his captors knocked at a door. The door opened, a beam of light touched the snow, and the miners who held Geoffrey's arms pushed him forward. He stumbled and when he got his balance the door was shut. He stood, confused by his struggle and the change from dark to light, in a small room with log walls and a stove in a corner. After the cold outside, the room felt intolerably hot.

"Sit down," said somebody and Geoffrey saw a young man occupied a chair by the stove.

Geoffrey pulled up another chair and looked dully at the man, whom he had not yet met. The fellow's keen glance and commanding voice indicated that he was in control.

"I suppose you're Mr. Pelton, the manager?" Geoffrey remarked. "You, no doubt, know me. Where's my foreman?"

"I am Pelton. Your man's in the bunk house, and since the boys are quiet I reckon he's resigned. If he makes no trouble, they'll leave him alone."

Geoffrey pondered. He felt savage and humiliated, but there was no use in indulging his rage. He was caught and the advantage was with his antagonist. It was plain Pelton was not a rude prospector; his voice and easy manner indicated some cultivation.

"You knew we had gone down your shaft?" Geoffrey resumed.

"Why yes. One of the boys heard somebody outside the bunk house; another declared it was snow slipping down the roof. If they'd argued about it longer, the snow might have covered your tracks, but when they went to the door your steps were not wiped out. We reckoned to wait until you came up. Well, I expect I've satisfied your curiosity."

"Not altogether. I don't quite see what you're going to do about it now."

Pelton smiled. "To begin with, I must inform my employers; their lawyers will tell them how to get after yours. However, I won't get their instructions for some time and thought about holding you and the foreman for a guarantee against fresh trespassing."

## GEOFFREY TRESPASSES       147

"I doubt if you could hold us."

"I could try," said Pelton coolly. "The boys are a pretty hard crowd and are rather up against your men. Our lot won't join the proper labor unions or something like that. We employ foreigners because they're cheap, and get a number of political freaks and anarchists, who kick against all organized rule. One fellow suggested that the best plan to fix you was to unhook the ladder while you were climbing up. In the bush, men who go outside the law in a mining dispute now and then get hurt."

Geoffrey thought he had run some risk, but he did not mean to be kept a prisoner. For one thing, it would persuade Hilliard and the other directors that he was not fit for his post. He imagined Pelton understood his embarrassment, because he looked amused. While Geoffrey pondered his reply a noise began in the adjoining bunk house and he laughed.

"I rather think your fellows are having some trouble to hold my foreman," he remarked.

Pelton listened, and then got up when somebody came to the door. A beam of light shone out and Geoffrey saw one of the Forks miners and Carson. The cook gave him a twinkling smile, and Pelton said, sharply, "Well?"

"I bring a message from the Rideau boys," Carson replied. "I reckon they sent me because nobody was keen to go, but one hinted that if I was held up it wouldn't weaken the garrison much."

"Your message?" Pelton snapped.

"The boys are bothered about the boss's stopping so long. If he's not back pretty soon, they're coming across to pull up your bunk house and fire the pieces down the shaft."

"Thank you, Tom," said Geoffrey, who looked at Pelton. "However, I don't expect they'll be forced to meddle."

"Tell the boys your boss and the foreman will arrive in about half-an-hour," Pelton replied. "That's all. Get out."

Carson turned to Geoffrey, who nodded. "You can go, Tom."

When Carson had gone Pelton smiled. "You have won. There are some toughs among my crowd, but yours is stronger and the boys are white. After all, I'm a Canadian, and perhaps we've hit the best way out. Well, that's done with. S'pose you take a cigar and let's talk."

Geoffrey lighted a cigar and Pelton resumed: "Your pocket looks pretty bulky. I expect you're taking some specimens of our ore along. What d' you think about the rock?"

"So far as I can see, it's very like ours."

"Poorer, on the whole?"

"I imagine so," Geoffrey replied.

"Then, I reckon you see why we're working close up to your front?" Pelton remarked in a careless voice, but Geoffrey imagined his carelessness was forced.

"I really wanted to find out if you had bored beyond our front."

"Were you satisfied?"

"My calculations are not made and we didn't take a measuring chain," said Geoffrey. "All the same, I was puzzled; the vein dips, but your shaft's not deep."

# GEOFFREY TRESPASSES

Pelton looked at him rather hard. "I expect you noted how far we had gone down. You imply we'd have struck richer dirt at the bottom of the lode?"

"Something like that. You know, of course, that none of the ore is rich."

"That is so," Pelton agreed and was silent for a few moments. Then he resumed: "Managing a mine like the Rideau is not a well-paid job and you were hired in the Old Country, where wages are low. Well, I allow you're out for money, or you'd have stayed at home. Suppose I made you a proposition?"

"I'd think about it," said Geoffrey cautiously.

"Very well. You went down our mine without leave and were caught. When my employers get after yours, I reckon they won't approve your rashness. Now I'm willing to promise they'll do nothing about the thing and to pay you five hundred dollars if you'll let me look over the Rideau block."

Geoffrey knitted his brows. He was honest, but he saw Pelton was keen. This was obvious, since the other must know his offering five hundred dollars was significant. Pelton expected to get value for the money, although Geoffrey could not see how he meant to do so. For all that, it was plain that if he took the bribe he would be in the other fellow's power and must agree to his next demand. He weighed the possibility of his leading Pelton on until he found out his plan, but admitted that he was not clever enough for the part.

"I must refuse," he said. "My employers treat me justly and I want to keep my job."

Pelton studied him and then observed with rather marked carelessness: "It looks as if they were lucky!

Anyhow, I won't try to persuade you. Five hundred dollars is a good sum; I doubt if I'd get it back."

"We'll let it go," said Geoffrey, smiling. "I must get off. If I stop much longer, the boys may come for me."

He went, but when he reached his room at the mine he sat for some time by the stove, smoking and thinking hard.

## CHAPTER VI

### CARSON EXPERIMENTS

SOME time after his visit to the Forks mine, Geoffrey came up one evening from the Rideau shaft, where he had stopped to make some measurements when the men left work. As a rule, he ate with the others in the bunk house, but, expecting to be late, he had told Carson to bring his supper to the office. Since he had not been occupied as long as he had thought, he wondered whether he must wait for the meal.

When he opened the door he stopped with surprise. Carson sat in front of the table, but he was not getting supper ready. He held Geoffrey's powerful magnifying glass, small pieces of stone were scattered about and a delicate balance stood beside an uncorked bottle of acid. While Geoffrey noted this Carson turned with a start.

"I didn't expect you yet," he said awkwardly.

"It looks like that," Geoffrey rejoined. "What are you doing with those things? You seem to know their use."

Carson was obviously embarrassed, but Geoffrey thought his eyes twinkled. Shutting the door, he sat down and waited with some curiosity for the other's reply. To find his cook engaged in scientific experiment was strange and perhaps suspicious. After a moment or two, Carson pulled round his chair and fronted him.

"I have worked in a laboratory. The specimens you brought from the Forks were lying on the shelf. I thought I'd like to examine them, although it's not my job."

"That's obvious," Geoffrey remarked and pondered.

He was a mining engineer, not an analyst, although he knew enough about chemistry to make simple tests. If Carson was a chemist, his skill might be useful. For all that, since the mining laws were rather complicated and one's title to a mineral claim was sometimes disputed, the fellow's curiosity might indicate that he had been bribed. Geoffrey, however, rejected this supposition. The Forks people would not bribe a man to analyze their ore. Then he thought Carson honest and was generally ready to trust his judgment.

"What do you think about the specimens?" he resumed.

"I can't make a proper test; one needs apparatus you haven't got. All the same, the percentage of silver's low."

"Lower than ours?"

"I'm the cook and don't know how much metal you get."

Geoffrey thought for a moment, and then crossing the floor took a paper from a box.

"Here's our last assay report."

Carson studied the analysis and presently remarked: "The samples came from the bottom of the lode?"

"Yes," said Geoffrey and Carson knitted his brows.

"Well," he said, "the ore you brought from the

Forks won't assay like this. I imagine it carries less silver and won't pay for the refining. Then the acid gives a hint of a curious reaction I don't think your rock would show. Is their shaft as deep as yours?"

"No," said Geoffrey. "Pelton is following the top of the vein."

He lighted his pipe because he wanted to think. To begin with, it was rather strange he felt his giving his confidence to his cook, about whom he did not know much, was justified. Carson, however, had now dropped the Western colloquialism he used with the miners; he talked like an educated man and his easy frankness struck the right note.

"The thing's puzzling," Carson remarked. "You had better send the specimens off for assay, although I doubt if you'll get much light then." He paused for a few moments and added: "If I could use a good laboratory for a week—— But I ought to get your supper."

"We'll let supper wait. Do you know much about chemistry?"

"I can make a working analysis, when the job only needs mechanical accuracy. To solve a problem that demands imagination and instinctive feeling, is another thing. Once I could use both, but that power is gone. Well, you got a hint of my story the night we camped in the snow. It's not for nothing I'm a miner's cook!"

Geoffrey mused, for the other had said enough. In Canada, one met men who had wasted precious talents and lived by rude toil. The strange thing was, he felt he had met Carson somewhere else. His voice roused puzzling memories; Geoffrey had felt it do so before. For a few moments he thought about Nethercleugh, the coke ovens, and the road across the heath, but he pulled himself up. Carson had nothing to do with Nethercleugh.

"If the company would send us proper apparatus, it might be useful now and then to know how much silver the ore carries," he said. "Although I don't think they'll do so, you might tell me what you want."

Carson told him and Geoffrey made some notes. Then the other cleared the table and put some plates by the stove.

"I guess you want your supper, boss," he remarked.

When the meal was over Geoffrey packed up the specimens ready to send off, and wrote to Hilliard, asking for the chemical appliances. A few days afterwards, a freighter, returning to the settlement, took the letter, but when the reply arrived it threw no light on the Forks Company's plans. Hilliard stated he thought they wanted the mine, and if he could get a just price, he would probably sell, but the Forks people had not given him a serious offer. He doubted if it would be worth while to buy the rather expensive apparatus for which Geoffrey had asked, but he would talk about it to the other directors.

Geoffrey found the winter dreary. In North Ontario the frost is often Arctic and there were days when he shrank from crossing the open space between his room and the shaft. Snow as dry and fine as dust blew about and touched one's skin with the sting of intolerable cold, and it was a relief to plunge into the mine. Perhaps the calm nights were worse. All was strangely quiet, except when a pine branch split; water froze a few yards off the red-hot stove, and

Geoffrey, wrapped in furs and blankets, shivered in his bed.

Now and then he heard wolves, the savage Northern timber wolves, but they did not come near the house and he wondered what they ate. He had not seen an animal since he reached the Forks and the rifle he sent for had not been used. He had practised walking on snow-shoes, but when he went out the silence and desolation of the frozen wilds daunted him.

The miners felt the loneliness and strain, for they now and then asked a week's leave and went off with the freighter to the settlement. Moreover, one or two did not return but sent word they had had enough. On the whole, their deserting did not embarrass Geoffrey. Wages were high, and since the frost stopped surface work, it was sometimes difficult to keep the men usefully occupied. All the same, he did not want more of them to go. Winter was getting over, and when the ice broke the ore they had raised must be sent off and work that had waited since the snow fell must be resumed.

Coming up from the mine one evening, Geoffrey went to the river bank. After the dry biting cold that had ruled for long, he liked to feel the damp air on his skin. There had been a shower and the snow stuck to his long boots. Although the snow had hardly begun to melt and the frost would, no doubt, come back for a time, spring was not far off and he rejoiced with half-conscious gladness that winter was going.

He stopped opposite the Curtain fall and looked about. The light was fading and a belt of smoky red shone behind the pines, which had shaken off the snow and rose, darkly green and rigid, against the band of color. The snow on the ice had lost something of its dazzling whiteness; it looked dull and wrinkled, as if it had shrunk. Then the delicate hoarfrost had melted from the frozen spray that covered the front of the fall. The ice was ribbed, in strange harsh patterns, where it had not long since looked like soft drapery. There were deep cracks and Geoffrey heard the cascade roar beneath its covering. The channel below the fall was open and loose floes shocked on the angry, dark stream. Geoffrey had not yet seen the ice break up, but he imagined it would be an impressive spectacle. By and by Ross joined him.

"She'll break soon and make trouble for us," the foreman remarked, indicating the river.

"I expect a big flood would bring the water near the shaft," Geoffrey agreed. "The rock we're boring is loose; no doubt there'll be some leakage through the fissures. Then we must reckon on the drainage from the smelting soil. I asked for a larger pump some time since, but it has not arrived."

"I don't reckon much on leakage. We'll fix that," Ross replied. "The flood may pile up an ice-dam in the narrows below the pool, and you can't figure how high a dam will go. Depends on the way the big blocks come down; sometimes they climb out on the rocks and standing ice; sometimes they drive clear. Trouble's surely coming to us, but as I wasn't at the mine when she broke last spring, I don't know how much."

Geoffrey studied the ground. He hardly thought the gorge below the pool would fill with ice, but if it did so, the flood would reach the mine. Glancing at

## CARSON EXPERIMENTS 157

the Forks chimney stack behind the rocks, he remembered that although their block ran down to the narrows, the buildings stood on higher ground than his.

"Well," he said, "I suppose we can do nothing until the ice does break. Can you cut a dam with powder?"

"You'd want some grit," Ross replied. "Might be done; depends on how the floes pile up. If the big stuff below gets away first, the jam mayn't be bad." Then he exclaimed angrily: *"Two* of the boys coming back from the settlement!"

Geoffrey looked across the clearing and saw two figures move out from the bush. One went in front, walking in snow-shoes with a dragging gait; the other was bent and laboriously hauled a sledge. Geoffrey and the foreman went to meet them and the others stopped. They looked moody and slack.

"You have come back; three or four days late!" Ross remarked. "Money all gone and you allowed we couldn't run the mine unless you helped? Why, I've seen liver men than you full of dope at an opium joint! Where's the rest of the bum crowd?"

"Aw, cut it out!" growled the miner. "I was full up all right when I hit the trail and my head's that sore now I want somebody to give me bad talk. Last jag I got on, I threw a dandy foreman down the ore-dump. Anyhow, the other boys aren't coming. Guess you made them tired and they've struck a softer job."

"Go off and sleep; I'll talk to you in the morning," Ross rejoined and turned to Carson, who had sat down on the sledge. "Is your head sore?"

"It was sore," said Carson, with a feeble grin. "Just now the trouble's in my back and legs. However, since I'm not as big and young as Allen, we won't swap compliments. Reckon I'll make the bunkhouse and see if my substitute has poisoned the boys."

He went off with the sledge and the foreman laughed.

"They'll be bright in the morning and I'm glad to see them back, although it's blame awkward we've lost the rest. Allen's a pretty good man and old Tom can surely cook."

Geoffrey smiled as he went to his office. Carson was cultivated and knew something about chemistry, and yet, in Canada, his strongest recommendation was that he could cook. The thing was ironically humorous. For all that, Geoffrey was disturbed because the others had not returned. Help would be needed badly when the thaw began. He was rather surprised that Carson brought him his supper and when he came for the plates sent for Ross and put out some cigarettes. Geoffrey was firm when this was needful, but he did not urge his authority.

"I want to know what happened at the settlement, Tom," he said.

Carson smiled. "I expect you know what does happen when men who have been in the woods for months make the settlements. Well, there wasn't much variety of amusement; we played pool and shook for drinks. The drinks were pretty numerous and in two or three days our money had gone; but when we thought about starting a stranger arrived. Said he'd struck it lucky over a mining deal, and he liked a good card game, and had money to burn."

"I reckon the boys helped him!" Ross observed.

"They did," said Carson. "The fellow was generous and not lucky at cards. He burned his wad all

## CARSON EXPERIMENTS

right, but when the jag had got started I imagined the liquor wasn't very good." Carson paused and smiled. "I was a judge of liquor once. All the same, the stuff was liquor and the boys were not fastidious. A prudent landlord doesn't give his best to men who have been tanking for some time. I thought that accounted——"

"Come off!" Ross interrupted. "I reckon the crowd was crazy drunk and you were drunker than the rest."

"It's possible," said Carson. "I'd been sober for long. For all that, the symptoms were puzzling. There was not the familiar exhilaration, and though the boys broke some things in the pool room they soon got dull. One felt languid——"

"I guess you knew you were doped, but didn't mean to stop."

"Something like that," Carson agreed. "The boys thought they could hold out as long as the stranger's wad, and by and by he began to talk about a new job. It was a soft job; a mine in the West, where the Chinook winds stopped the frost, and they were all to be bosses of a sort. I can't remember if they agreed to go, but in the morning the stranger and another fellow loaded them on the cars and they didn't argue. When the train was pulling out Allen jumped off."

"Why did Allen jump off?" Geoffrey asked.

"He *said* there was a cross-eyed foreman at the Rideau who'd once told him he couldn't fix a prop. He was going back to show the sucker. Besides, he'd forgot his pipe."

Ross grinned. "Allen's pretty good at props. Some day I'll put him in the river, and then he'll mebbe make a useful man. But, say, why did you come back?"

"For one thing, I don't trust plausible strangers. Then I felt myself responsible for Mr. Lisle's health and yours. The hash the other fellow cooks is worse than dope."

"Get out with your plates," said Ross. "The boss and I have got to talk."

Carson went off and Ross looked thoughtful. "The boys were doped," he remarked. "Six of them and Carson! I expect it cost that stranger high. Why'd he burn his money?"

"Perhaps he badly needed men."

"He'd have got them cheaper from a labor agent. Trade's not good now."

"Then it looks as if he wanted to get them away from us. I don't see his object."

"I don't see it," Ross agreed. "Well, I've put you as wise as I am. We've got to watch out. Somebody's playing a crooked game."

He went off and Geoffrey lighted a fresh cigarette. The men's leaving would embarrass him, because he doubted if he could engage fresh hands for some time. They, however, had not gone to Pelton, and seeing no light, he presently went to bed.

# CHAPTER VII

### THE DAM

HEAVY rain swept the bush and beat upon the bunk house roof. The noise the tossing pines made was like the roar of the sea, but Geoffrey did not think this had wakened him. He imagined he had heard another noise. When he lifted his head from his pillow all was dark. Since the thermometer had gone up, he had not given the stove much draught and the iron was black. He could hardly see the window.

Then he started, for the noise that had disturbed his sleep began again. A detonating crackle, like huge sheets of glass breaking, came out of the dark; there was a crash that shook the house, and he thought he heard men jump from their beds. Then he was conscious of nothing but an appalling roar that hurt his ears and jarred his brain. For a few moments the din unnerved him, but he knew what it was now; the river had burst its chains, the ice was breaking.

Geoffrey sprang to the door. The snow had not all gone, and while the rain beat upon him he saw against the faint glimmer the figures of men who had run out of the house. Then he heard Ross shout: "Nothing doing to-night, boys! You can come right back!"

Then men vanished and Geoffrey returned to his

bunk, but it was some time before he slept. The solid log building trembled, and confused echoes rolled across the woods. A tremendous noise came from the river; he heard giant floes shock and smash, and some rend to splinters on the rocks. By degrees, however, he got used to the din and went to sleep.

Going out at daybreak, he saw the channel was, for the most part, open. The ice had broken away from the fall and a muddy flood leaped across the ledge. Big floes drove down with the current, tilted their ends out of the water, and, plunging down the fall, vanished for a few moments in the angry pool below. Then, shooting out from the spray, they swept round the rocky basin, until the tail rapid seized them and flung them down the gorge.

Geoffrey thought a shelving rock at the top of the rapid was the danger point. So long as the floes that broke their edges on the stone swung round and drove on, he had not much to fear, but if they stuck and jammed, the savage current would throw the blocks that came behind on top and the pressure would squeeze all into a solid mass. He thought the mass would grow until it formed a dam that would hold back the flood. The river was obviously rising fast. The floes, however, drove past the shelf, and when Carson waved to him from the bunk house he went to breakfast.

After breakfast, Geoffrey went down the shaft and although he came up now and then saw no grounds for disturbance. He was short of men and now the thaw had come work must be pushed on. His habit was to concentrate and by degrees his occupation absorbed him. Sending for food when the men went up for dinner, he stopped below to adjust a boring ma-

# THE DAM

chine, and the afternoon had nearly gone when Ross touched his arm.

"I reckon we're wanted on top," the foreman said. "River's risen two feet in the last hour and the ice is packing."

They went up and Geoffrey frowned when they stopped on the rocks above the pool. The fall roared with hoarse fury and the spray blew across the woods. Sometimes for a few moments the tossing cloud got thin and Geoffrey saw that a white mass blocked the rapid. The ice had stuck and was piling up, for the current pressed down the pack and threw fresh blocks on top. Great floes leaped the fall and, shocking in the whirlpool, swept down and hurled themselves against the barrier. It was plain that the ice on some distant reach had broken and set free another flood.

Geoffrey saw he must face a crisis for which his studies in English mines had not prepared him. There one worked by rule with the help of powerful machines, but now the rules did not apply and he had no machines. He had some native resolution, his wits, and muscular strength. This was all; he felt he was matched unequally against savage Nature. Yet he must trust his luck and try to make good. If he were beaten, he might not get another chance to prove he was fit for a manager's post.

"Can we break the dam with giant-powder?" he asked Ross.

"We can try," said the foreman. "'S far's I can see, the rock at the end of the point is holding her up. If we can drill the holes, we might fire a few shots, but you want to get busy now."

This was obvious. Rain was falling, the light would not last long, and there was much to be done.

"I'll go for the boys and the powder," Ross resumed and vanished.

Geoffrey stopped and his thoughts were gloomy. Hilliard had not warned him that he might have trouble when the ice broke, but perhaps he ought to have seen this for himself and made some effort to guard against the flood. He might have thrown up a bank to protect the shaft; the ore last raised was not frozen and the surface of the ground was getting soft. Still the work would have cost much labor and men were short. It was strange somebody had bribed a number to desert when they were needed most. There was, however, not much comfort in thinking about this. Geoffrey had done nothing, and now it was, perhaps, too late.

He braced himself and climbed down the rocks to examine the end of the shelf where the floes had lodged. Something might be done there. The rocks were wet and slippery and in places fell straight to the angry pool. Caution was needed and it was some time before he got down to the water-level. When he stopped he saw Pelton, in shining wet slickers, sitting on a ledge.

"Flood's pretty fierce and rising," Pelton observed. "Looks as if she'd top the highest-water mark. Did you come along to look at the ice?"

"I did not. I want to see the end of the shelf."

"Where the rock's holding up the jam? What d'you mean to do there?"

"We thought we'd try to cut the ledge by a blasting shot."

## THE DAM

"Can't be done," said Pelton. "You're on the Forks block and we can't allow you to prospect our claim."

"You're ridiculous!" Geoffrey exclaimed. "You know we're not prospecting! If it's possible to break the shore end of the jam, the ice may drive away."

"We'll allow that's so," Pelton replied with an ironical smile. "I don't care if she drives away or not. If she holds and backs up the water, it won't touch the Forks."

Geoffrey understood and tried for control. "Do you imagine you can prevent my making an effort to save our mine?"

"You haven't got me," Pelton rejoined. "I don't want to prevent you. You can't start blasting on our claim; that's all." He paused and looked hard at Geoffrey when he resumed: "You see, I'm obstinate and don't like to be beat. Last time we met, you'd gone over the Forks mine but wouldn't let me see yours."

Geoffrey pondered. He thought the other had two objects; he wanted to explain his refusal to let Geoffrey break the dam, and to hint that he was willing to bargain. It was obvious Pelton had some grounds for his keenness to examine the Rideau workings. The explanation, however, was not plausible and Geoffrey did not mean to bargain. Then a dislodged stone rolled down the bank and looking up he saw Ross and some others in the spray. When he noted that one carried an iron box he saw a plan. The plan was rather theatrical, but it ought to work.

"Come along with the magazine," he shouted and turned to Pelton. "If you claim we're infringing the

Forks Company's rights, you can see your lawyers. Anyhow, we mean to fire the shot."

"I reckon we'll put you off the property," Pelton replied and climbed the bank.

"Your best driller, Ross," said Geoffrey, and Allen came forward with a hammer and a steel bar. "What about the dynamite and the fuses?"

"I fixed the detonators in a few sticks at the shack. It's damp-proof fuse."

Geoffrey nodded, and indicating a spot in the ledge some feet from the ice, said to Allen:

"Get to work. Five dollars if you sink a hole that will take a stick before the Forks gang arrive!"

Allen threw the bar to another man and glanced at the rock. "You want the hole *right there?*"

"Yes," said Geoffrey, who knew the spot was not the best for cutting the ledge. "Don't talk. Get busy!"

Allen swung his hammer and sparks flew from the end of the drill. His helper turned the tool and there was a sharp crunch when the hammer fell again. Geoffrey hoped the frost had gone out of the stone, for the thaw had not long begun. He looked about and to some extent was satisfied. The short, steeply-sloped ledge ran for a few yards from the main wall of rock and then sank into the ice. It would be hard for Peltons' men to get at his party unless they crossed the ledge. The situation had some drawbacks, but he need not bother about these yet. In the meantime, Allen and the other struck and turned the drill, and by and by the first, standing upright, stretched his arms.

# THE DAM

"I guess I've earned five dollars! Where's your powder?"

Geoffrey gave him a stick of dynamite that looked rather like yellow candle with a piece of black cord running from it instead of a wick. Allen carefully pressed the stick into the hole and closed the top with soil and bits of stone. Then Geoffrey took the end of the fuse and a mechanical lighter, and looking up saw Pelton and a number of others scramble down the rock.

"Pick your place for the next shot; it must take two sticks," he said to Allen. "If I shout, drop your tools and get back."

He saw Ross and the men were puzzled, but they must wait for enlightenment, and he held up his hand as Pelton's party advanced.

"Stop!" he said sharply. "Do you see what I've got?"

The light was going and spray blew about. Pelton stopped and stared, and the two groups of men stood, silent and curious, between the rock and the ice. Then it looked as if Pelton saw a light.

"Oh, shucks!" he said with a forced laugh. "You're not playing for a movie show."

"I promised I'd fire the shot," Geoffrey rejoined. He pressed the spring of the mechanical lighter and a spark leaped out. "When the first of your lot climbs the ledge I'll make good."

"Take my dare," said Pelton. "You haven't sand enough to touch her off. I'm coming now!"

Geoffrey stood very straight, his mouth set hard and his eyes fixed on the other. Perhaps it was theatrical, but in the wilds men are primitive; Pelton had declared he would put him off the claim and the Forks gang had no doubt been promised a reward. Geoffrey did not mean to go. Pelton advanced a few steps, slowly and then stopped. A hoarse laugh came from the Rideau men.

"He's beat! You've got him, boss!" cried one.

Geoffrey thrilled. The shock of a dynamite explosion does not spread far, but the fuse was short and although his men might have got away he imagined he would not. The thing was a stern test of nerve and he had won. He had persuaded his antagonist he meant to fire the shot that might destroy both. Afterwards he wondered.

He pulled himself together. Pelton was beaten, but the struggle with the flood had not begun, and Geoffrey told Ross to get the men to work. Allen, up to his knees in water, was trying to sink a hole for a heavy charge in the ledge, but frozen rock is hard to cut and Geoffrey doubted if the stone had thawed enough to yield to the tool. The rotten ice, however, was soft, and men with bars and hammers labored on the cracking mass.

The dam shook and worked. Wide fissures opened and shut with sharp reports, and there were deafening crashes when the current hurled fresh blocks against the barrier. Some leaped on top, some drove underneath and jammed, and now and then a foaming wave swept the broken surface. The ice struck high piercing notes that harmonized strangely with the measured roar of the flood. It was obvious that the job was horribly risky, but it must be carried out and Geoffrey waited until he thought his voice would reach the men.

# THE DAM

"A week's pay for all if we break the dam!" he shouted.

He did not know if they heard him, but they were working savagely and he looked about. The light had nearly gone and the spray was thick. The figures on the ice were indistinct. Pelton had vanished, but his party was the stronger and Geoffrey, remembering something, called Ross.

"All the boys are not here," he said. "Send a message to the mine. Two must stop and watch the shaft; the rest must come along."

Ross nodded, and Geoffrey, finding some shelter behind a stone, sat down. He did not think he had done with Pelton and wondered where the fellow would make his next attack. Geoffrey imagined the Forks gang must be reckoned on. For one thing, they were foreigners, and all immigrants did not make good citizens. Political refugees, turned fanatics by injustice, and criminals hating all authority, came across. As a rule, these did not join the labor unions, unless it was where they could lead a revolutionary section. They were fierce, illogical individualists, whose creed was destruction.

Geoffrey did not wait long. A stone crashed upon the ledge, and looking up, he saw blurred figures on the cliff. He moved quickly and another heavy stone fell at his feet. A minute or two afterwards a man was hit and dropped his drill. Then the stones came down in a shower and another man cried out. Geoffrey stopped in the gloom by the ledge and thought.

It was dark and spray rolled about the ice, but the Forks gang did not need to aim. The crest of the rock commanded the dam, big stones were dangerous, and if they were flung down freely, somebody must be hit. The work on the ice was dangerous and Geoffrey did not mean his men to run another risk. Signing to Ross, he collected all who could be spared and led them up the gorge. He did not think they could be seen from above and imagined the others were ignorant of his arrival when he reached the top. They were occupied, gathering and throwing stones, a short distance off, and Geoffrey's group crept quietly forward.

When they were near enough, they charged and for a few mad moments Geoffrey let himself go. It was something to be young and feel his strength; besides, he had borne much and Pelton had appealed to force. The Forks gang outnumbered his, but they had not expected an attack and hardly got together before the Rideau men came up. There was a shock, a short, confused struggle, and the others broke. They vanished in the dark, and Geoffrey went back, triumphant, with his head bruised and blood on his face.

Soon after he reached the ice, Ross said the job was finished and for a few minutes Geoffrey and the foreman were occupied with the fuses. Then they went off, as fast as possible, and while they climbed the bank a flash pierced the spray. A report shook the rock, other flashes sprang up, and echoes rolled along the gorge. Broken ice crashed upon the stones, and then a big white wave rose, shook its crest, and vanished.

"She's gone!" Ross gasped and Geoffrey's heart beat.

He waited, exhilarated by his victory, for a minute or two, while the broken floes shocked with tremendous

## THE DAM

noises on the flood that swept the wreck away. Then the crashes got faint and the roar of the river rose in a hoarse, triumphant note. Geoffrey roused himself and seeing the others had vanished made for the bunkhouse. He was tired and his head hurt.

## CHAPTER VIII

### CARSON RESUMES HIS OCCUPATION

GEOFFREY awoke late in the morning. His head ached and his face was cut, but as soon as breakfast was over he went down the shaft. There was much to be done, because he must try to improve the drainage before the water the thaw released reached the workings, and his new pump had not arrived. Then he must send off a large quantity of ore when the floods sank and the river was open for canoe transport.

Pelton's attempt to prevent his breaking the dam puzzled him. He wanted to think about it, but was occupied all day by mechanical problems that forced him to wait until he left the mine. After supper he pulled a chair to the stove, put his feet on a box, and lighted his pipe. Nobody would disturb him and, smoking languidly, he looked about the room.

A bunk like a shelf ran along one wall; his slickers and working clothes hung at its end, and his muddy long boots occupied a corner. The floor was rough and cracked, and a pile of cordwood stood behind the rusty stove. His lodging was rude, but on the whole he liked its rudeness. The cordwood scented the room, and the resinous smell made one sleep soundly. Then he liked the control of the mine. He had improved its working, cut down expenses, and got out better

## CARSON RESUMES HIS OCCUPATION

ore. In fact, he was making good. Yet he felt his success was threatened, and he must think about this.

To begin with, Pelton's employers had given signs of a strange and hostile curiosity about the Rideau. The ore they raised was not worth much; the rock ought to have got better near the Rideau front, but did not. It almost looked as if the Forks people were willing to work without a profit in order to occupy the adjoining claim. One could not see their object.

Geoffrey resolved to let this go; he had thought about it before and seen no light. He wondered why Pelton had wanted the flood to reach the Rideau shaft. Revenge for his rebuff when he offered a bribe hardly accounted for his meddling, but he would, apparently, have got nothing else had he forced the Rideau's owners to undertake the expensive pumping that would have been needed to clear the mine.

It was plain that Geoffrey must tell Hilliard what had happened, although he meant to make his statement very matter-of-fact. Business men did not like romantic tales. Moreover, if one looked at it carelessly, the thing had not much significance. There was bad feeling between the two gangs and miners working adjoining claims sometimes indulged in savage disputes. Then, in a sense, Pelton's excuse for meddling was plausible; he did not mean his neighbors to fire blasting shots on the Forks property. Geoffrey saw he must not exaggerate the importance of the incident, although he felt it was important. However, since there was no clue to the puzzle, he must wait and watch.

His reflections were broken by a tramp of feet and a knocking at the bunk house door, and a few minutes afterwards Ross came in. Two men, sent down to the settlement to order supplies, had returned and brought Geoffrey's mail. Geoffrey opened a letter from Hilliard.

"They're satisfied at the office with our progress," he said to Ross. "Tell Carson I want him."

When Carson came Geoffrey indicated a chair. "I've got the assayer's report on the specimens I took from the Forks and some ore from our workings at the bottom of the vein. They tell me nothing fresh, but you can look at them and let me know what you think."

Carson studied the reports and when he put down the papers his face was thoughtful.

"Practical chemistry is not as exact a science as some people think, and an analysis is made with one of two objects," he remarked. "The first is utilitarian; you want to learn the proportions of useful metal, and dross that must be got rid of by refining. The other is different; you mean to investigate, as far as your knowledge will allow, the complicated actions of the metal and its alloys."

"You mean the assayer is generally satisfied to look for what he thinks it's useful for a miner to know?"

Carson agreed and picked up the reports. "These are pretty good examples of the commercial assay. You generally note there's a small *residue;* earthy matter, insoluble ash, and so forth. To the miner it's not important, but the scientist finds some interesting problems there."

"The residue is larger in the Forks specimens I got from the top of the lode."

"It's significant. In fact, there's something curious

# CARSON RESUMES HIS OCCUPATION

about the analysis. If I could work out the combinations that account for the residue, we might get a useful hint."

"You'll get a chance," said Geoffrey, smiling. "Our people at Montreal promise to send the apparatus you talked about."

Carson's eyes glistened. "I owe you much already, Mr. Lisle, and now perhaps you have done more than you know. The strange thing is, when I had time for research I got tired and slack, and in South Africa I threw up a good post because limited experiments with commercial objects soon get monotonous. In this country, I've lived by cooking at mining and lumber camps, but now, when much of the skill I had is gone, the fascination of research comes back. I'm getting old and the rude life will soon knock me out. It's some satisfaction to know that for a time I've got a scientific job again."

He spoke with feeling and Geoffrey understood and sympathized. It was much to be allowed to use one's best abilities and do the work one knew.

"All the same," he said, "we don't need an analyst and we do need a cook."

Carson smiled and got up. "I'll make time for cooking and some study. If the boys grumble about the food, you can stop my experiments and fire me out. Well, I'll fix your stove before I go."

He threw on fresh wood and regulated the draught. "She'll burn until morning," he resumed. "I'll go along and get things ready for breakfast. Good-night, boss!"

When he had gone Geoffrey laughed. Carson had meant to indicate that he knew his job and did not expect promotion. He was going to make the experiments because he was a chemist and not for a reward. Yet Geoffrey resolved that if his researches had useful consequences, some reward should be his.

A month afterwards, Hilliard called him to Montreal, and although Geoffrey might have traveled smoothly by canoe, he left the mine on foot, with food and a blanket strapped upon his back. Summer comes swiftly in the North and he wanted to be alone in the woods. Since he reached the mine he had hardly stopped work except to sleep. Now he could relax, and he went leisurely, enjoying the march.

The country had lost its forbidding sternness, and a soft west wind blew. Sunshine warmed the rocks and small red trunks; here and there hardy maples and groves of willows broke into shining green; fresh bright-colored shoots relieved the somber monotony of the pines. The woods were musical with the noise of running water and fragrant with sweet smells. Geoffrey skirted lonely lakes where the ice-worn bowlders gleamed among the reflections of the trees, and followed the banks of swollen creeks that sparkled in the sun and plunged into soft blue shade. He felt romantic and light-hearted and sometimes sang. Winter had gone. Mind and body reacted after the long strain, but Geoffrey was half conscious that in part his satisfaction sprang from knowing the strain had been borne. He had done all he had engaged to do and was making good.

When he reached Montreal by the afternoon train from Ottawa, Hilliard met him at the station and took him to his house at the foot of the Mountain. Florence Hilliard joined them at dinner, and Geoffrey, who had met her on his last visit, wondered why he had forgotten the attractive, animated girl. Florence was frankly modern, her clothes were in the latest fashion, and she talked much about sports, but she had grace and gave hints of a shrewdness Geoffrey approved. It was plain she knew something about business and a remark of hers indicated that she had not forgotten him. Geoffrey imagined Hilliard had talked to her about the mine; and then felt embarrassed because he saw she was studying him with a smile.

When Florence left them Hilliard took Geoffrey to his smoking-room and they weighed plans for economies at the mine and enlarging the output of ore. Geoffrey liked his post. Hilliard was just, and Geoffrey got a hint of a kindness he thought was perhaps accounted for by the other's friendship for Stayward. Stayward's friends were not numerous, but it looked as if they stuck to him.

"Well," said Hilliard after a time, "in Canada, we're generally blunt, and I must state that I and the others are satisfied with you. Since I want you to see them, you must stop with us for a week. Ross can keep things going and you have earned a holiday."

Geoffrey was flattered, but when he began a deprecatory reply Hilliard smiled.

"Your uncle declared you were the man for the post, and for people who know John Stayward his statements carry weight. Anyhow, you don't owe us much. The post is not well paid. Are you willing to keep it?"

"I'd like to hold on until we see if it's possible to make the Rideau pay."

Hilliard nodded. "On the whole, I think you're

prudent, and since you came we have gone some distance." He paused and added thoughtfully: "I'd like to know if the Forks gang made much progress and where they aim. So far as one can see, their claim is not a business proposition; but it's obvious they have money to spend. The strange thing is, they spend it on a mine that gives them nothing back."

"I see no light yet," said Geoffrey. "All the same, you have not got much money back from the Rideau."

"We have paid expenses, and mining's a gamble. You may squander all your money by holding on, and you may let go a day before the luck turns. Anyhow, Stayward has refused to sell and the Rideau's, so to speak, a side venture for the rest of us. So long as we don't lose money we'll keep things going."

"I rather imagine my uncle kept his shares in order to give me a job."

"He could have given you a job at the coke ovens."

"He said I was not a chemist," Geoffrey replied with a smile. "I agreed and hinted that anyhow I didn't think I'd take the post. We were generally pretty frank. But you know my uncle!"

"I have known two or three Staywards; you're an obstinate lot," Hilliard rejoined with some dryness. "Has John written to you recently?"

"Not for some time and he did not tell me much. We don't write often. I really think we are good friends, but somehow we keep our own confidence. Until he sent me to Canada, he didn't talk about my plans; I never asked his."

Hilliard's eyes twinkled. "I reckon I understand. After all, I'm a North-country man. Well, perhaps you know John has got over the trouble into which his partner dragged him, and it looks as if he might get rich. He's now making a dye-stuff that commands the highest price on the market."

"I'm very glad; he has had a stubborn fight," said Geoffrey, with some feeling. "Still, it's rather strange to imagine my uncle's getting rich. He's as frugal as a hermit. I don't know how he'll spend his money, unless he builds larger works."

"The subject ought to interest you. You are his nearest relation," Hilliard remarked.

Geoffrey laughed. "It doesn't really. Of course, I'm his nephew, but I haven't thought myself his heir. In fact, I don't want to think about the thing. The money's his, he earned it hard, and I hope he'll enjoy it long. Besides, I rather imagine we got on because he knew I meant to take the line I thought best."

"You mean, he knew you expected nothing from him?"

"Yes," said Geoffrey, "I think I did mean something like this."

Hilliard gave him a thoughtful glance. He saw Geoffrey's carelessness was sincere, and because he knew John Stayward thought he knew his nephew. Geoffrey was not as shrewd as the other, and did not calculate so far, but he had a number of John's qualities. Hilliard approved the young man.

"Did you know your uncle's partner?" he asked.

"I did not, although I met the fellow. A spirit tank exploded, and when I went to the office, after helping to put out the fire, my uncle and Creighton were talking. I believe he told Creighton I was his nephew, but I didn't see the latter. He was sitting by the door and my eyes were dazzled by the blaze. Then I'd burned my arm and went behind the partition to wash. I said something across the top and Creighton answered before I went out another way to get some oil. I didn't meet him again, but after he went stories got about that my uncle had not been just. Of course, I knew this wasn't so, and I wondered why he didn't deny the tales."

Hilliard smiled. "I don't think John often bothered about what people thought of him. Besides, it would perhaps have hurt to admit he had been robbed."

He stopped, for Florence came in. She declared they had talked enough and she felt neglected, and they went with her to the drawing-room.

## CHAPTER IX

### GEOFFREY'S HOLIDAY

IN the morning Geoffrey was occupied in the city with Hilliard, who said Florence would amuse him after lunch, and in the afternoon they set out together.

"We'll go to St. Peter's and then to the Mountain," Florence announced. "Montreal has some fine buildings, but, as a rule, you can't see them for scaffold poles. Soon after we finish a handsome block we begin to pull it down, and when we have got the last thing in pavements fixed somebody lays a new electric main, and we move the street-car lines about. I suppose one can't have progress without some mess."

Geoffrey laughed. He imagined Miss Hilliard was talking discursively in order to give him a start, and he wondered whether she found him dull. She was very pretty, her summer clothes were fashionable, and she wore, without its being too marked, a stamp of confidence. One felt Miss Hilliard knew her value. Yet Geoffrey liked her and thought she meant to be kind.

"You are progressive," he replied. "It's strange, but your temperament's not ours. America's your model."

"It looks like that. I expect we do copy our neighbors; the long, open frontier unites us. There's not a fort or strong camp all the way across. But we're not American; when you get to know us, our type's different. So far as we are British, I think we get our characteristics from the Scots. We weigh a bargain long; while we seem to hustle, we're really not quick to move, but when we do get started we don't stop. Perhaps you ought to understand us. Don't you come from the Scottish border?"

"In Cumberland, we are rather hard to move. All the same, we certainly don't pull things down until we are forced. Our object is to make things last; we're a frugal lot."

"Yet I imagine you, yourself, can move," Florence remarked. "For example, didn't you get about pretty fast, the night the Forks gang tried to put you off the claim?"

"Then you knew about that?" Geoffrey said, with surprise.

Florence gave him an amused glance. "Of course! I'm a girl and curious. You're a man—I really think you forgot you met me. They don't all."

"I'm afraid I'm sometimes dull, but I only talked to you for three or four minutes. Then I was kept occupied at the mine——"

"Yes," said Florence, "one's occupation comes first! Although the thing's not flattering, I suppose it ought. However, we'll cross the street. St. Peter's isn't old yet, but I like it. It's calm."

When she took him into the cathedral, Geoffrey agreed. The domed building had dignity. It was not like the ornate, Gothic, Notre Dame; one got a sense of austere quietness and strength. They went about in silence, trying instinctively to soften their

# GEOFFREY'S HOLIDAY

echoing steps, and when at length they reached the square outside Florence gave Geoffrey an approving glance.

"St. Peter's takes one back to the great beginning," she said. "The note it strikes drowns the little noisy quarrels of our Orangemen and the Catholic *habitants*. Our Cathedral stands for Canada, the land of wide plains and limitless quiet pines. A big clean, new country! One wonders what we'll make of it!"

They crossed the square and Geoffrey indicated the steep, wooded slopes in front.

"How does one get up the Mountain?" he asked.

"It depends on your age and temperament. There's an elevator and there are cabs, but sensible people walk. The automobile habit's insidious. I walk when I can."

Geoffrey noted her light step and the way she carried herself. It was a new and pleasing experience to move in harmony with a companion like this, and he wondered when he had walked beside an attractive girl before. Perhaps it was strange, but he could not remember. He began to think he had missed much. Then he looked about as they skirted the bottom of the hill; at the fine stone houses with pillared stoops and unfenced lawns where nickeled sprinklers threw glistening showers across the grass; at the trees that shaded the sidewalks, and the fresh green of climbing woods in the background.

Florence stopped in front of the shining walls of McGill, and he admitted that the famous college stood grandly on the slope above the town. Then they went up by roads that wound through the murmuring wood while the warm wind shook the branches and sunshine and shadow checkered their path. After his concentrated labor in the snowy wilds, Geoffrey responded to the call of Spring. His blood stirred and he felt a new exhilaration. For a time, he had done with work, and he meant to get all the satisfaction his rare holiday could give. Afterwards, he wondered how far Florence's society accounted for his buoyant mood. He liked her gay laugh; her voice broke charmingly through the rustle of the leaves. The wood had not much beauty, since the trees were small. There were no flowers, and in places the ground was trodden bare.

At the top they reached a platform bordering the steep edge of the hill. Benches ran along the parapet; behind were stalls for the sale of photographs, Indian curiosities, and enameled silver. Geoffrey bought one or two articles blazoned with the arms of the provinces; the Maple leaf, the Ship, the Wheat-sheaves. When he brought them rather diffidently to Florence, she gave him a curious, smiling glance.

"They're pretty and I like your choice. Perhaps you know this enameled ware is rather good."

"I didn't know. The warm color on the white metal took my eye. Still I'm glad you're pleased—you see, I hesitated."

Florence laughed. "Because you know the woods, but not our cities? Well, perhaps your hesitation was rather nice. I wonder whether you have often brought pretty things for a girl."

"I have not," said Geoffrey. "Now I come to think of it, I sometimes envied men from whom girls took gifts. All the same, I really think you didn't wonder much."

# GEOFFREY'S HOLIDAY. 185

"Do you mean your temperament's obvious? Had you not friends in England?"

"A few men," said Geoffrey, with thoughtful frankness. "They were, for the most part, men with whom I worked. You see, I was poor and ambitious. There was nobody who could help; I must concentrate on making my career. But you'll soon get bored——"

He stopped and turned his head to look across the spacious landscape. The city, dotted by green squares and rows of trees, crept up to the Mountain's foot. It was not dingy, like English cities, for there was no smoke, and the blocks of tall buildings, dwarfed by distance, stood out sharply, silver-gray and red. One noted the C.P.R. station, the dome of the cathedral, and the towers of Notre Dame. The great river, shining like a silver belt, formed the city's boundary. On the other side, the plain rolled back, in shades of fading color, until the hills of Vermont, ethereally blue, cut the dim horizon. In the foreground, a big liner moved up stream and the smoke of locomotives drifted about the water-front.

"It's a noble view," he remarked. "Perhaps our misty hills, where the colors change as every cloud sails past, are more beautiful; but there's something about the Canadian landscape that ours has not got. Something that braces you and gives you confidence. I expect your clear skies account for this."

Florence smiled. "We were not talking about the Canadian landscape. I'm curious. Tell me about your life in the Old Country."

Geoffrey told her; drawing with unconscious skill the ugliness of the mining towns and the sternness of Nethercleugh. Florence thought the tale dreary, although it seized her interest. The man had lived to work. She was vaguely sorry for him.

"Well," she said, "it's plain you saw where you meant to go, and did not look back. I don't think you often looked about. One gets forward when one marches light, with eyes fixed ahead, but to travel like that has drawbacks. Did you not feel the trail was lonely?" She paused and gave him a direct glance. "I'm not bored at all. You're rather a new type. I want you to talk."

"The strange thing is, I see now I was lonely; I didn't feel it then."

"But did you never meet somebody who needed companionship, or perhaps needed help? I mean a woman——"

Geoffrey hesitated and as he looked out across the wide Laurentian plain the shining river faded and the Vermont hills got dim. He knew what he was going to see, and the picture came; the red heath above Nethercleugh and a girl with a violin case toiling along the dusty road. He wondered whether he could draw the picture for Florence, and he tried.

"She looked lonely and somehow pathetic, and I stopped," he said. "We talked while I mended the bicycle. It was plain that she had pluck, but I think she found the road was long, and was getting tired." He paused and added naively: "I don't mean she was bodily tired, though this was obvious."

"So you stopped and helped her on?" Florence remarked in a sympathetic voice. "Well, I suppose it was something; perhaps it was much. But was that chance meeting all the romance you know?"

"In a way, it was not romantic. The side-car was

empty; her boot hurt. I don't know who she was and never saw her afterwards."

"But you have not forgotten? I wonder if she has——"

"Perhaps it doesn't matter much," said Geoffrey. "I don't expect we'll meet again."

Florence smiled, a friendly smile. "You're not a sentimentalist, but a touch of sentiment sometimes takes one far. After all, an engineer needs imagination."

"To-day, I'm not an engineer. I left my occupation when I left the mine. The winter's gone, the sun shines, and I feel like a boy who has got out of school. I want to do something——"

"I think I know," Florence remarked. "Have you any particular plan?"

"None at all. It ought to be something fresh and not too sober. Something frivolous and up-to-date, if you understand!"

"There's Dominion Park," said Florence thoughtfully. "In the evening, it's quite up-to-date, and not remarkably sober."

"What's the Dominion Park?"

"A friend of mine calls it a pandemonium. Colored lights, side-shows, music and noise; something like Coney Island with a subdued touch of the *Moulin Rouge!* Anyway, it's one of our popular shows. If you like, I'll take you. We'll go by street-car and not in the automobile. You see, although father doesn't meddle much, he's English, and I doubt if he'd approve."

Geoffrey pondered and Florence laughed. "Oh," she said, "I'm modern and like adventure. You declared you had got out of school, and to-night we'll both be truants for an hour."

Soon afterwards they left the platfrom and went down through the wood. When dinner was over and the big lamps began to burn among the trees in the avenue, they stole from the house and got a street-car at the Grand Trunk station.

Geoffrey found Dominion Park all that Florence had said, but his sharpest memories dwelt upon her frank enjoyment and his buoyant spirits. He noted her gay confidence, her keen curiosity, and her rather startling knowledge of human nature. In fact, he got illumination, without a jar. He had not thought girls of Miss Hilliard's stamp were like that, but his study of her persuaded him the freedom was good.

For the rest, he was somehow moved by the glaring lights, the women's summer dress, the music, and the noise. The shadows between the big lamps gave a hint of mystery to the scene, and just outside the glitter, the great river, touched by confused reflections, rolled into the gloom. When for a few moments the noise got less, one heard the current wash among the reeds.

Florence took him into side-shows and they shot with rifles for tinsel prizes. In an interval, they went to the water's edge and watched a liner forge up stream. Her long hull was pierced by innumerable lights, set in rows that marked her flowing lines and tiers of passenger decks. She looked like a fairy palace, not a ship. The great funnels and boat-deck loomed, vague and mysterious, high up in the dark. When she steamed past the deep throb of engines and measured beat of propellers drowned the noise of the

# GEOFFREY'S HOLIDAY

bands. Her long lines fore-shortened, the displaced water broke in angry waves against the bank, and Florence and Geoffrey went back to the crowd. The girl stopped and watched the moving figures.

"They swarm like ants, but they are playing, and the ants work," she said. "Men with brains and men with muscle built that splendid ship. Isn't it rather fine to be an engineer?"

"Sometimes it's a strenuous, and sometimes a dreary, job," Geoffrey replied. "Now, however, I'm out for a holiday."

They entered a noisy show and by and by left the park. The street-car was crowded, but the journey across the town had a thrill for Geoffrey. It was strange, he thought, but he had not before enjoyed an evening's gay amusement with an attractive girl. Still, he must be satisfied with his first experiment. Girls like Florence Hilliard were not numerous, and in a few days he must resume his work in the lonely North.

When they reached the house Florence left him outside Hilliard's smoking-room. She said nothing, but she smiled and made a sign, and Geoffrey, understanding, felt their stolen adventure was a tie. All the same, it was done with, and he went in to talk to Hilliard about silver ore.

Florence and Hilliard went with him to the station when he returned to the mine, and the girl gave him her hand and wished him good luck. Looking back from a lurching platform as the cars rolled out, he saw her wave to him, and lifted his cap. Then he went to the smoking-compartment and lighted up his pipe. He had enjoyed his holiday, but it was over. Florence was kind; he had owned his path was lonely, and she had cheered and sent him on his way with a lighter heart. This was all. She was a rich man's daughter, and he was the manager of an unprofitable mine.

## CHAPTER X

### CARSON'S ADVICE

SUMMER was going, and the sun was low, but the evening was very hot. The Whitefish had shrunk and a few threads of water marked the front of the Rideau fall. Its roar had dropped to a faint splash that hardly broke the silence of the bush. Not a breath of air touched the clearing and the pine-tops were motionless, but Geoffrey, standing by the pool, thought he heard angry voices and put down his rod. When the shadow crept across the eddies he had gone fishing.

He looked at his watch and saw he had been longer than he thought. It was a few minutes after supper time and the men had stopped work. Some had labored on the ore dump in the scorching sun, and Geoffrey imagined he knew the grounds for their discontent. They were tired and hungry, and supper was not served. This had happened before and Geoffrey, feeling himself accountable, climbed the steep bank. At the top he met Ross.

"The boys are getting riled," the foreman remarked. "They like old Tom, but they won't stand for waiting for their hash. I've put him wise, but maybe you'd better——"

"I'll see him about it," Geoffrey replied.

Somebody hammered an iron sheet, and while the noise rang across the woods groups of men hurried towards the bunk house. Geoffrey joined them at their meal; the rough tables had been carried outside, for it was cooler in the open than in the low shack. The food was good and plentiful, and when they had drained the last can of strong green tea the men's annoyance had vanished. For all that, Geoffrey presently crossed the clearing to the edge of the bush, where Carson was occupied.

The pines threw long shadows across the rows of stumps, among which fern and wild berries grew. Here and there a sunbeam, piercing an opening, touched with glowing color a straight trunk, and a trail of blue vapor, very faint and diaphanous, floated across the light. The vapor came from a small clay furnace, in front of which Carson fanned his charcoal fire with rude bellows. He wore an old slate-colored shirt, such as railroad hands use, greasy overall trousers, and broken long boots. His look was intent and he did not move when Geoffrey sat down.

"Supper was late again, Tom, and the boys were grumbling. You mustn't make them wait," Geoffrey remarked.

"Sorry," said Carson. "Don't talk for a few minutes, please!"

Geoffrey lighted his pipe. He meant to see that meals were punctual, but he rather sympathized with Carson. The fellow was very keen about his experiments. After a time, Carson took a small crucible from the furnace and putting it aside to cool, turned to Geoffrey.

"I forgot the time. I'd got the heat I wanted, and if I hadn't used it, might have been forced to blow for an hour after the fire got down. Besides, if I'd kept the crucible white-hot, the stuff would have oxidized."

"All the same, you mustn't neglect the boys' supper."

"Very well! I'm cook, not chemist. I meant to remember this, but when you get on the track of a new combination it's strangely hard to stop."

Geoffrey nodded, for he knew the lure of absorbing work. He thought he was fortunate, because he could concentrate on his proper business, but Carson could not. It was three months since his short visit to Montreal, and sometimes he could hardly persuade himself that he had gone. His strange, buoyant mood had vanished when he returned to the mine, and when he looked back to the few joyous days he felt as if somebody else had gone with Florence to Dominion Park.

"I'd have liked to give you proper time for your experiments and better pay," he said. "In fact, I talked about it to Hilliard, but he declared the mine was small, and when they wanted an analysis they went to an assayer. Then he hinted that my business was to cut down expenses."

"When you open a mine you must trust your luck and spend," Carson rejoined. "If the Rideau does not pay, why do the directors hold on?"

"They'll hold on so long as they don't lose money."

"You mean they'll try to be satisfied with the very small profit you earn?"

"I imagine so," Geoffrey agreed. "Hilliard said something about the Forks people's wanting to buy our block, but at a price that would not give the investors their money back."

Carson looked at him thoughtfully. "Your employers are a cautious lot! They haven't the miner's pluck. Well, I expect you see the Forks gang's inducement to keep things going is smaller than yours. Yet they don't stop."

"Their obstinacy's puzzling," Geoffrey admitted.

"Doesn't it look as if they imagined there was some useful metal in the vein that you don't know about?"

"The thing's obvious. You could go farther; they think there's more of the stuff in the Rideau property than in theirs. All the same, I can't imagine what the metal is. Can you?"

Carson was silent for a few moments and Geoffrey saw he was thinking hard. His lined face was rather grim, and his look indicated that his thoughts were disturbing.

"Had it been twenty years since, I believe I'd have solved the puzzle," he said. "I've lost and squandered much. Indulgence and hardship are blunting, and when you get old it's too late to pick up threads you broke. Well, I don't know what the metal is; I'm trying to find out."

Geoffrey filled his pipe again. It was getting dark and the mosquitoes bothered him, but his work for the day was done, and the faint wind that began to move the pine-tops was cool. He liked the smells that drifted out of the gloom and the languid splash of the fall was soothing. The charcoal fire glowed brighter in the shadow, and its reflection touched Carson's face.

Something in his look roused Geoffrey's sympathy. The fellow was, no doubt, paying for past slackness, but to pay was hard. Now he was old he needed the talents he had carelessly squandered. Yet, although his eyes and brain were dull and his hands had lost their delicate touch, his occupation called. The man who had commanded the resources of modern laboratories was working with rude and broken tools because he felt he must.

"How far have your experiments carried you?" Geoffrey asked after a time.

"Some distance," said Carson quietly. "I've found your assayer's analysis roughly accurate; that is, the percentage of silver and non-metallic elements. The problem's in the residue your man neglects."

"Then, if the Forks people expect to find a metal there, it must be valuable. Allowing for alloys, there's not much stuff in four or five per cent. to pay for refining."

"That's plain," said Carson, with some dryness. "I may find a clue, and I may not. Sometimes I feel I'm near it. The trouble is, I'm forced to cook."

"I'm afraid you must. The directors turned down my suggestion that you might take your proper job on business lines."

Carson smiled. "Research with a commercial object palled before."

"After all, running a mine is a business proposition," Geoffrey rejoined. "Well, I don't know if you want a reward or not, but I think I can promise that if you find out something useful, you will gain. Now we'll let the thing go. You mustn't keep the boys waiting for meals."

He knocked out his pipe and went off, but at the door of his room he turned and saw Carson sitting motionless by his furnace. His bent figure was outlined against the dull glow; he looked absorbed. Geoffrey hoped he would get things ready for breakfast and went to bed.

Breakfast was served at the proper time, and afterwards meals were punctual. Carson was generally occupied by cooking, and Geoffrey imagined he had lost his keenness for research. Indeed, he began to wonder whether the fellow was not finding out that he had been the victim of an illusion. He, however, reflected that if one took this for granted, there was nothing to explain the Forks manager's curiosity about the Rideau mine.

The weather soon got cold. For a week or two, great flocks of ducks and Brant geese crossed the Whitefish, flying south, and then in the mornings the pines glittered with frost. A little dry snow fell, ice began to gather in the slack below the fall, and it was obvious that Carson could not carry on his open air laboratory. Geoffrey told him he might use his room when he went down the shaft, and Carson thanked him but said nothing about his experiments.

Then, one day when the frost was Arctic and all the pines were white, Geoffrey got a letter from Hilliard. In the evening, he sat by the stove and pondered the letter.

"The Forks Company offer to buy the Rideau at a price that would give a small profit on our investment," Hilliard stated. "We can't raise them, and they hint we had better sell; our boundary survey and frontage, as given in the patent, is open to dispute, and so forth. It looks as if they want the mine, and if they have money to burn, they might make us spend a good sum in law expenses. My partners don't like to be bluffed, but since they see a chance of get-

## CARSON'S ADVICE

ting out with a profit, we resolved to let you know and will weigh your views."

Geoffrey folded the letter and knitted his brows. To begin with, he admitted that his views were not worth much. He did not want to give up his post, but if he advised the directors to hold on and the ore did not get much better, the responsibility for losing a favorable chance of selling the mine would be his. It was plain that much depended on the quality of the ore he raised in the next few months, but he frankly owned he did not know if the rock he had not yet bored was better than the rest. In fact, he had nothing to go upon but his cook's rather strange persuasion that there was valuable metal in the lode. By and by he sent for Carson and read the letter to him.

"I can't see my way," he said. "If I urge it, I think the directors will refuse. However, the prudent line is to sell."

"You are not rash," Carson remarked. "For all that, caution's a handicap. One can't get far unless one runs some risk."

"In this case, somebody else will run the risk. I'd gamble with my employer's money."

"That is so. All mining's a gamble. Your uncle's a shareholder. What line do you think he would take?"

Geoffrey looked up with surprise. So far as he could remember, he had not told Carson about Stayward. He, however, let this go.

"My uncle certainly does not like to be bluffed. I don't imagine he'd sell his property because the buyers threatened him. He's not that kind of man."

Carson smiled. "Very well. My advice is, stick to the mine."

"Let's be frank. Have you found out something fresh?"

"In a sense, I have not, but I've got a very curious reaction the tests I made before did not give, and feel I'm on the right track. Wait another two or three weeks, and I'll engage to tell you something that will justify your holding on."

"You'll *engage* to tell me?"

"Yes. It's a firm promise. I don't think you'll regret you refused the Forks Company's offer."

Geoffrey said nothing and after a few moments Carson resumed: "To make a plunge costs something, and one understands why you hesitate. The safe plan is to sell, and you know nothing about me except that I claim to be a chemist. I haven't supported my claim yet, and my idea that the vein carries a valuable metal may be an illusion. I'm a broken man, a knockabout camp cook. To trust me enough to urge your employers to keep the mine, because I recommend it, would be ridiculous."

"Well," said Geoffrey, "I must admit I did argue like this."

Carson gave him a strange smile. "All the same, if you tell the directors to hold, it will pay you. I *am* a chemist, and although I was a better chemist once, all my skill has not gone. Besides, I owe you something; perhaps more than you know."

Geoffrey looked at him hard, and getting up threw fresh wood in the stove. For a moment or two he stood motionless, knitting his brows. Then he said,

"In a sense, it is ridiculous, but I'll tell Hilliard to keep the mine."

He let Carson go, and sitting down wrote a telegram to Montreal:—

"Hold. Wait my letter."

To take the plunge was something of a relief. It was too late to doubt; he must go forward resolutely. For all that, Geoffrey felt he had put off an awkward job. He had promised to write to Hilliard and since the settlement was some distance off, his letter must go with the telegram. In the morning he must justify the bold line he had taken, and he did not know what arguments he could use.

## CHAPTER XI

### GEOFFREY'S TRIUMPH

THERE was no wind, the men in the bunk house were asleep, and all was very quiet in Geoffrey's room. The stove shone dull-red and the smell of hot iron drowned the resinous scent of the logs, but Geoffrey wore his skin coat and shivered now and then. The table was covered with bits of roasted ore, bottles of acid, and glass retorts, and Carson crouched beside the open front of the stove. He said nothing, but his look was intent as he watched a small crucible.

Geoffrey was tired and dull. It was nearly midnight, but curiosity conquered his drowsiness. Carson had told him the experiment he was now making would give him a clue to the puzzle that had bothered them long. Geoffrey doubted. Carson had said something like this before. Besides, he had not kept his promise; the stipulated time was gone, and if he was, as he declared, on the right track, it had led him nowhere yet. Indeed, Geoffrey wondered whether Hilliard was annoyed he had been persuaded not to sell the mine.

All the same, it was perhaps important that Pelton had recently driven his tunnel into the Rideau block. Geoffrey knew this by the muffled noise that pierced the stone. The Forks gang, with strange obstinacy, were again working the top of the lode. Geoffrey did not expostulate about their trespassing. The ore was poor, and he waited one night until he knew the Forks men had gone; and then, when all was quiet, fired a heavy shot. The explosion blocked his tunnel, but this did not matter, since he had begun to build another, and he imagined the shot had destroyed his antagonist's.

Presently Carson took out the crucible, and skimming off some dross, shook the rest of the material into a retort. He looked excited, and when by and by he poured some acid on the small gray lumps his face was strangely intent. Geoffrey, however, said nothing and tried to be calm. He was not going to let Carson's optimism cheat him again. Yet calmness was hard. Carson looked confident; although his hands shook when he began the experiment, his touch was now firm. One felt the fellow was satisfied.

For half an hour he occupied himself with his apparatus, and then quietly put down a glass tube he had heated.

*"I have got it,"* he said.

Geoffrey looked at him sharply and saw his eyes shone.

"What have you got?"

"The metal that eluded me. I knew it was there a month since, but couldn't break up the combination. Now I've reduced it to a simple oxide. I've made different tests and all agree."

"Ah!" said Geoffrey. "What is the metal? Will it pay to smelt? The quantity must be small."

"It's called Millinicum. Mills, the analyst, first discovered it. The stuff has not been found combined with silver. The price is very high; any quantity will pay to smelt."

Geoffrey thrilled. He had heard about Millinicum and knew its importance.

"It looks as if the Forks people knew," he said. "Now one sees why they wanted the Rideau!"

"They did know. I think their working the top of the vein gave me the first hint. The new metal's specific gravity and melting point are low; one would expect to find it above heavier ore. There's another thing; you'll get the richest stuff by abandoning the headings you've cut, and boring the other way, where the lode is highest. In fact, an open cut from the surface might give the best results. But this is your business; I'm not an engineer."

"I'm not a chemist, but I think I understand," Geoffrey remarked. "A light metal, that melts and vaporizes soon, would occupy the top of the vein when the mass consolidated after the subterranean fire that forced it up had cooled."

He stopped and pondered for a few moments. "The thing means a remodeling of our working plans," he resumed. "Perhaps we'll need fresh capital. I must see Hilliard and persuade him the venture's warranted. Are you satisfied about your analysis?"

Carson smiled. "One is sometimes cheated, but I've recorded my experiments and you can take my notes to somebody your directors trust. Pay a big fee and go to the best man in Canada. If you like, I'll give you his name. I think he'll tell you I am right."

"I'll get off in the morning," said Geoffrey quietly. He was excited, but meant to use stern control. "I'll stop at Ottawa," he added. "Our patent gives us the silver and any lead and copper in the alloy, but

## GEOFFREY'S TRIUMPH

it may be needful to file a fresh discovery claim for the new metal, and I'll see the head of the Crown minerals office. But you're the real discoverer."

"Oh, well," said Carson, giving him a curious glance, "I owe you something, and didn't work for a reward. It was, so to speak, my last opportunity to justify myself. However, if the directors offer me shares of money, I won't refuse. I would like to send a sum to somebody in England who loved me well."

For a moment or two he was quiet and his look got strangely gentle. The stamp of hardship and indulgence vanished and his eyes were soft. Then he got up and methodically put away his bottles and retorts.

"In the morning I'll give you my notes and all I think you'll need," he said and went out.

At daybreak Geoffrey and two miners took the trail. When his companions were ready to start he gave Carson his hand, and the other touched his old fur cap as the little party moved off. Geoffrey imagined the salute was a formal recognition of his authority and was somewhat moved. After all, his cook was an Old Country gentleman. At the edge of the bush, Geoffrey looked back. Carson stood in the snow, watching him. His figure was bent, his skin coat was ragged, but somehow he had a touch of dignity. Geoffrey remembered this afterwards.

The frost was bitter and light snow fell, but the party reached the railroad settlement and Geoffrey stopped next day at Ottawa. Then he went on to Montreal, and in the evening he and Hilliard talked in the latter's smoking-room.

"You have done well," Hilliard remarked at length.

"If your cook's analysis proves accurate, we won't have much trouble to get the money we need to remodel our mining plans and build a smelter. Stayward will help us. When he sent you out he said we could trust you and now I think he'll be satisfied."

Geoffrey colored. He was young and to think he had won the stern old man's approval was something.

"Can he help?" he asked.

"I imagine so," Hilliard answered with a smile. "It looks as if John were rich. You know about the dye he was the first to produce cheaply. Well, the stuff is getting famous, and a big combine is negotiating to take over his works. I understand Stayward is willing. He knows when to buy and when to sell. However, I think Florence is waiting for us. We'll talk about your uncle again."

They went to the drawing-room and when Hilliard was called to the telephone Florence said to Geoffrey:

"You have made good. How does it feel to come back in triumph?"

"The triumph is not altogether won, though I think we'll put it over," Geoffrey replied. "On the whole, I'm half surprised we pulled it off. Anyhow, it's the first really big thing in which I've helped, and when one's friends are kind——"

"I think you're rather nice, and you haven't disappointed us, although after your uncle's remarks about you, we expected much."

"It's strange. John Stayward never said much to me about his belief in my talents."

"He is your uncle; perhaps this accounts for something. One's relations often use a cautious reserve. They feel their approval might lose its value if it was

# GEOFFREY'S TRIUMPH

given frankly, and only indulge their family pride when they talk to strangers. All the same, I expect he's glad to own you have made good."

"I was lucky and ran some risks. For one thing, I trusted my camp cook. He found the metal."

"One must run risks," Florence remarked. "People who hesitate don't go far. Then to know whom you can trust is something of a gift. However, I mustn't philosophize. You have got sober in the woods and need a holiday."

"My last holiday was glorious," Geoffrey declared. "Can't we go to Dominion Park again?"

Florence smiled, rather curiously. "Dominion Park's a summer festival, and summer is gone. Besides, you can't recapture a mood."

"I wonder—. Well, perhaps the thing's impossible, but that evening's adventure was exhilarating. It made work lighter and helped me forward."

"For a time!" said Florence, giving him a level glance. "Then the work did not need lightening and resumed its claim. You forgot you had neglected your occupation for a frivolous week?"

Geoffrey was honest. Moreover, he saw Florence knew him, although her doing so was strange.

"After all, one doesn't control a mine for nothing, and one must pay for making good," he said. "I expect it generally implies concentrated effort."

"You were willing to concentrate and you have made good. You ought to be satisfied," Florence rejoined. "Well, we can't go to Dominion Park, and if we could, we'd probably find it vulgar and noisy; but I'll take you to the toboggan slide. The amusement you'll get there is of another kind."

Then Hilliard came back, and when Geoffrey went to his room he sat for a time by the radiator, thinking rather hard, but not about the mine. He liked Florence Hilliard. She was clever, bright, and kind, and he could not forget altogether the holiday she had helped him to enjoy, although he had forgotten for a time. Indeed, when he started for Montreal he had looked forward with keen satisfaction to meeting her again. All the same, it was perhaps important that he had not thought about her much until he left the mine. The strange thing was, she seemed to know this.

She had generously welcomed his success, and he thought her sympathy sincere. She was friendly, but he felt an elusive difference in her attitude. On his other visit she had been his frank, inspiring comrade; for example, without her he would have been bored by the noise and glitter at Dominion Park. Yet she had declared that one could not recapture a mood and summer had gone. He wondered what she meant, but thought he half understood.

Well, suppose their comradeship had gone as far as it could go? There was another, closer relation. Florence was all that he approved, and he had now begun to make his mark, and imagined he was a rich man's heir. His drawbacks were vanishing and, from one point of view, the advantages of his marrying Florence were plain. He began to weigh them coolly, and then pulled himself up and smiled, for he felt his coolness was significant. Then he looked at his watch and went to bed.

Next afternoon Florence took him to the toboggan slide on a slope of the Mountain, and at the top brought a small sledge to the edge of the run. The straight

# GEOFFREY'S TRIUMPH

track, beaten in the snow, looked remarkably steep, and near the bottom, vanished at the brow of a sharper pitch. Geoffrey wondered how far the toboggan would plunge when it leaped the bank.

A young man and a girl, lying flat, went down on another sledge, and Geoffrey watched their swift descent. He heard the steel runners scream and saw fine snow curl up like foam. One got a sense of furious speed, and then the toboggan jumped the edge below and vanished. Geoffrey turned and saw Florence looking at him with a smile.

"The slide's pretty fast to-day," she said. "If you're ready, get on first and give me room."

"I suppose I'm a passenger?" Geoffrey remarked.

"That's all," said Florence, with a twinkle. "I imagine you don't like to leave control to a girl, but tobogganing's like mining. One must learn the rules."

"I expect that's so," Geoffrey agreed. "Well, I got a thrill at Dominion Park and expect another now. It looks as if you had some talent for thrilling people."

"Get on board and hold fast," Florence commanded. "This thrill is going to be different; you ought to like it better."

Lying on the tail boards, with feet in the snow, she pushed off the sledge, and when it gathered speed Geoffrey gasped for breath. An icy wind swept up the slide; dusty snow that stung the skin whipped his face. He felt the sledge rock, and now and then heard the runners, but it was difficult to imagine they traveled on the ground. One seemed to be flying; the speed was tremendous. Yet the sledge was narrow and would easily capsize. Geoffrey was an engineer and had half consciously measured its width. He knew a long, narrow object going very fast must turn over if it did not go straight.

The sledge went straight. Geoffrey could not see his companion, but he felt her firm control. A moment's hesitation or unsteadiness and they would be hurled off, but the light frame to which they clung sped on without swerving. Geoffrey was confident; Florence was a girl to trust when nerve was required. He laughed with strange excitement when they reached the edge of the dip. A shower of snow beat his lowered head; he heard the wind scream and the runners hiss as they hit the ice. The snow had been ground down and beaten until it turned to ice. Then the sledge leaped out. There was nothing beneath the runners; the thing was flying. The cold pierced his furs, the speed cut his breath, and then he felt they were on the ground. He could not see; it was impossible to look ahead. All he could do was to hold fast.

The strange excitement lasted for a few moments, and then the sledge tilted up and slowed. Geoffrey moved and tried to look about. Florence shouted, there was a jerk, and Geoffrey, thrown forward, rolled in the snow. He did not stop for a moment or two, and when he got on his feet and picked up his cap Florence stood smiling at him a short distance off.

"You should have conquered your curiosity," she remarked. "One must trust the person who runs the machine."

"It's obvious," Geoffrey agreed. "I oughtn't to have moved, but it wasn't from want of confidence. You see, I've got the habit of controlling things, myself. I've generally been forced."

Florence laughed. "Then perhaps it's strange we

# GEOFFREY'S TRIUMPH 209

haven't jarred, but our business is to get back to the top. I expect you'll find coming down was easier."

"That's often so," said Geoffrey. "Anyhow, I'll own you boss and I can obey orders now and then. Shall I take the trace and pull?"

She nodded, and he began to haul the toboggan up the incline. There was a track, where the snow was loose, near the slide, and he went up with the light step and easy balance of a mountaineer. Florence walked close by. She wore a thick blanket-dress, and the swift descent had brought the color to her skin and a sparkle to her eyes. She looked strangely alert and virile, and Geoffrey felt her charm. For all that, he half-consciously resisted. The thing was puzzling, and with an effort to banish his thoughts he looked up the hill.

The sun was setting, and in places faint rose-pink reflections touched the snow. Outside the light, it glimmered with soft shades of blue. The trees, bending under their white load, sparkled where a branch caught a slanting beam, and here and there one saw the saffron sky between their trunks. The slide was in the shadow. It ran straight up hill, and, vanishing over the edge of an easier incline, gave one the illusion of its being very long. Marked by the blue line of the toboggan track, it looked like a road that led up to the sky. While Geoffrey plodded up the illusion got stronger and his imagination began to work. The glittering white and cold blue faded and the slope of the Laurentian hill got dim. He knew he was going to picture another road that ran into the sky. In another moment he would see a lonely figure on the crest of the rise in front. He pulled himself up and turned to Florence.

"Canada's a hard country and our winter's long," she said. "You're thinking about England."

"I really was," he owned. "I don't know how you know."

She laughed. "Oh, well, you're rather obvious, Mr. Lisle. However, when the Rideau mine is famous, you can, of course, go back to the English hills and Nethercleugh."

"I wonder—I don't know yet. After all, I was sometimes lonely in England; in Canada, I have friends."

"One meets people one likes," Florence remarked. "For a time, perhaps, one travels in company; then the others stop or take another trail. Sometimes one gives them a friendly greeting and that's all."

"It's much," said Geoffrey. "A friendly greeting helps the traveler. But it's strange you knew I was thinking about a road."

"The road was in the Old Country," Florence replied. "You'll go back and take that way again. Perhaps it won't be lonely. When you start, your Canadian friends will wish you good-luck." She paused and, for they had crossed the ledge, looked up to the stages where the toboggans went off. "Now push along," she resumed. "It will soon be dark and we're some distance from the top."

Geoffrey tugged at the sledge-trace and said nothing. Florence was clever and he thought she had an object for her humorous philosophy. In a sense, perhaps, she liked him, and her friendly greeting had helped him on his way, but he imagined she meant to intimate that his way was not hers. Well, if she left him where the trail forked, he would remember her long.

## CHAPTER XII

### CARSON'S LAST JOURNEY

DARKNESS was creeping across the woods, the sledge ran heavily, and the team labored over the beaten snow. The trail, however, was clearly marked, since the traffic between the Forks and the settlement had kept it open, and the freighter was bringing up a load of machines and tools Geoffrey had bought at Montreal. Another lot was on board the cars, for Hilliard had approved the spending of the rather large sum Geoffrey thought necessary to develop the mine.

He walked beside the half-breed freighter, who urged on his tired horses in uncouth French. Frost glittered on the men's furs and their breath floated in a white cloud about their heads. Their hands and feet were numb, but they expected to reach the Forks soon after dark. Plodding forward doggedly, Geoffrey looked about and mused. The bush was thin and a bright new moon hung in the clear sky. The snow sparkled faintly and the pines stood out like small dark spires. One could see far back into the shadow between the trunks.

Geoffrey dwelt upon his stop at Montreal, which he had frankly enjoyed. After working long for small pay, it was soothing to feel that he had made good and forced his employers to own his talent. Then Florence's generous satisfaction had made his sense of triumph keener. She was very kind, but he had felt she was not the girl he had met on his first visit. Geoffrey pondered this.

Her charm was strong, but he had somehow braced himself against her and he began to think she knew he had done so. All the same, she liked him and perhaps, at the beginning, had he pursued her resolutely she might have given way. But he had not pursued, and now he felt she had, so to speak, let him go. Yet they were friends and he knew their friendship would last. Geoffrey owned himself romantic and perhaps ridiculous. Florence had beauty and qualities he admired, but between him and her stood the memory of a tired girl whom he might not see again. After all, he imagined Florence knew this. She was clever and had declared he was rather obvious. Well, he had been honest, and if he had been rash, the thing was done with. Florence Hilliard was not for him.

Geoffrey began to think about Carson. In a sense, his triumph was really Carson's. The fellow had found the metal that would make the Rideau mine famous and was entitled to his reward. He had not stipulated for a reward, but Geoffrey had talked about it to Hilliard, who agreed that if much profit was earned when they refined the metal, a part must go to its discoverer. In the meantime, one could not fix a sum.

For all that the sum would not be small and Geoffrey wondered how Carson would spend the money. The old fellow had long been poor; he had lost his friends, and wore the stamp of hardship. If he went back to the Old Country, he would be a stranger in the circle to which he had belonged. There was something

# CARSON'S LAST JOURNEY 213

pathetic about it. One felt that Carson had mended his broken fortune too late.

Then a pale gleam among the trunks caught Geoffrey's eye and he touched the freighter who urged his team. The tired horses strained at the traces and the sledge lurched forward. The gleam got brighter and broke into separate lights, and presently the low shape of the bunk house loomed ahead. Geoffrey left the freighter and went to his room.

The lamp was lighted, the red stove snapped, and Geoffrey, throwing off his coat, dropped limply into a chair. The dry warmth made his head swim and the smell of wood and hot iron was nauseating. When one was numbed and exhausted by a long march across the snow, the reaction was sharp. After a minute or two, a man whom Geoffrey had not seen before came in.

"Are you fixed all right, Boss?" he asked, and went on: "Your supper's pretty near ready. I'll bring it along."

"Who are you?"

"The new cook. Mr. Ross hired me at the settlement."

"Then where's Carson?"

"He's in the store, waiting till the freighter goes back. Ross allowed you'd like to have him sent to the settlement. The Episcopalians have opened a cemetery lot."

Geoffrey started. "Do you mean he's dead?"

"Sure," said the other. "Looks as if you hadn't heard about the accident! Well, it happened before I took the job. I'll send Mr. Ross along."

He went off and soon afterwards the foreman entered.

"I guess the cook has told you old Tom has pulled out," he said. "The boys surely liked him and he's going to be missed, but I reckon I'd better put you wise. Well, we wanted to fire a shot in the new heading at the top of the lode, and the giant powder was frozen bad. Carson allowed he'd thaw some out at the cook-stove; he was mighty keen about the shot. I let him. He'd fixed the stuff before and knew his job."

Geoffrey nodded. Giant-powder freezes and must be gently warmed to restore it to its semi-plastic state. As a rule, this can be done without much danger, but the material is unstable and now and then accidents happen.

"I left Tom with it and went to the bunk house," Ross resumed. "While I was looking for something there was a crash, and when I ran out the cook shack had gone. The hot stove was sizzling in the snow, smashed posts and shiplap lay around. We found old Tom under the wreck and knew he'd hit the trail before we got him out."

"Ah!" said Geoffrey. "Was he——?"

"No," said the foreman. "It was some relief to all of us. We liked old Tom. Giant-powder's curious, the way she gets one thing and leaves another. There was a bruise where a roof-tie had pinned him down; not much else to talk about. I allow it was concussion or mebbe his heart was bad. Well, we reckoned we'd send him to the settlement, and the boys have fixed him for the trail. When you're ready I'll go along to the store with you."

## CARSON'S LAST JOURNEY

An hour afterwards, Geoffrey took a lantern and went with Ross. Carson, wrapped in his skin-coat, lay on some dark fir branches that neatly covered two boards. The old coat had been recently mended and somebody had put in his hand the string of a little bag that held bits of ore.

"He was sure keen on those specimens. We allowed we'd let him take them along," remarked the foreman.

Geoffrey said nothing, for he was moved. It was plain the boys had liked old Tom. They could not do much, but all that was possible for rude kindness had been done. Geoffrey lifted the light, and for a moment or two studied Carson's face. There was no mark; Carson looked younger. The capricious explosive that sometimes mashes a hard rock to fragments and leaves the soil a few yards off undisturbed, had not disfigured him. The lines that had seamed his forehead were gone; Carson was strangely dignified in his frozen calm.

Then Geoffrey began to puzzle. There was something about the quiet face he felt he ought to know but did not. It was curious, since he had felt he ought to know Carson's voice. He got no clue, however, and lowering the light, signed to Ross.

"Was there anything in his pockets? Letters, for example?" he asked when they went out.

"Nothing. We looked," said Ross. "We put his truck together and left it for you. I'll send the things to your room."

Geoffrey carefully examined Carson's belongings; a Hudson Bay blanket, a deerskin bag of odds and ends, and a few old clothes. There were no letters. His pipes, metal tobacco box, and watch were not engraved. The cheap watch was made at a Connecticut factory whose goods were sold all over the United States and Canada. It gave no clue.

After a time Geoffrey put the things away and, lighting his pipe, sat by the stove and mused. He remembered Carson had smiled when he gave his name, but had not thought this curious. In Canada, one met men who had broken ties that galled, and some who sought forgetfulness of follies and sorrows in the past. He did not know Carson's story and perhaps would only know its tragic end. The end was tragic, for the man had labored long with broken tools, fronting many obstacles until by dogged patience they were removed. He had won, but he had not tasted his triumph and his reward would go to strangers. For all that, he had found the new metal, and Geoffrey resolved he would go with him to the settlement, and leave him to be buried in the Episcopal cemetery with such honors as one could give. Then he knocked out his pipe and went to bed.

Two or three days afterwards, Geoffrey and the freighter set out, and the miners, with pitlamps lighted, stood in the biting cold to see them start. Carson occupied the sledge, and day was breaking when the horses plodded off into the gloom of the pines. Geoffrey long remembered the march. The freighter was a taciturn half-breed who spoke uncouth French. For the most part, both were quiet. At night they made a fire behind a bank of snow where the pines were thick enough to keep off the wind, but Geoffrey would not have the sledge left outside the flickering light. He owed Carson something and was not disturbed when the trembling reflections touched the motionless object under the Hudson Bay blanket.

Carson had cooked for him and cleaned his room. They had talked long, about mining chemistry and their experiments, on bitter evenings. The man who found the metal was his friend. Geoffrey, smoking his pipe behind the snow-bank while the shadows wavered round the sledge, thought about him with gentle melancholy.

On the last day, a blizzard raged and they struggled, with lowered heads and freezing bodies, beside the horses, using all the strength they had to finish the march. Dark came before they made the settlement and when they plodded into the beam from the hotel windows horses and men were white and moved without noise like ghosts.

Afterwards Geoffrey went back to the mine, where there was much to be done, and until the frost broke he was keenly occupied. A new tunnel must be driven into the top of the vein, and as he bored back from the old workings the ore got richer. The new metal had sought the surface and sometimes he got excited when the assay reports arrived. The Rideau was going to pay its owners well.

Some time after his return Geoffrey got a letter from Stayward, who stated that he had sold his coke ovens for a "canny price." He added, as if in excuse, that he was beginning to feel his age, and concluded: "You have done well. Gan forrad and finish the job. but come home then. You're all the kin I've got and I may need you, lad."

Geoffrey was moved. He was not a sentimentalist and his relations with Stayward had rather been marked by a half-humorous forbearance than affection. It was, he thought, the first time his uncle had shown much warmth of feeling, but Geoffrey owned he had long felt a keen respect for the hard old man. With all his dry reserve, Stayward had been kind, and it now looked as if his kindness was deeper than Geoffrey had thought.

He had, however, much to think about, and the development of the mine absorbed him, until, when the frost was breaking, the freighter brought him a telegram from Hilliard.

"John is ill and wants you. Fix things with Ross and start. We must let you go."

For a few minutes, Geoffrey hesitated. Spring was coming and the ore he had raised must soon be sent off to the smelter. The prosperity of the mine meant much to him and he had not finished his job, but Stayward had called and Geoffrey knew he would not have done so had his need not been strong.

He sent for Ross and at dawn next day started for the settlement across the melting snow. He did not see Florence at Montreal; she was with friends at Toronto, but had left him a kind note. Geoffrey talked for long with Hilliard and next day set off to join the Liverpool boat at Quebec.

# PART III

THE STRUGGLE

# CHAPTER I

### GEOFFREY'S RETURN

SPRING had come in England, but the evening was cold and bitter wind wailed about Nethercleugh. The narrow windows rattled, the bare branches of the ash trees clashed in the savage gusts. At the bottom of the long hill, the smoke of collieries and furnaces blew along the shore; and torn clouds sped inland before the gale.

It was getting dark and two candles flickered in the draughts that swept an upper room. Although a small fire burned, the room was cold and Geoffrey, sitting by a window, shivered now and then. He had arrived from Liverpool a few hours since, and knew he had not come too soon.

Stayward, supported by pillows, occupied the old tester bed, from which it was characteristic the hangings had been stripped. A worn-out rug his mother had made covered part of the dark, worm-eaten floor; there was no unnecessary furniture. Stayward was very gaunt and his face was pinched, but his eyes were keen. His voice was hoarse, and when he stopped for breath and the doctor expostulated, he frowned angrily.

"I'll be quiet long enough, and I'll talk while I can," he said. "Let me be and git oot. You'll ken when to come back and finish your job."

The doctor shrugged and went out. He was young and had not yet contended with a patient like this. Stayward had some time since banished his nurse, but the doctor admitted that the old housekeeper had tended her master with a skill and patience that did not mark all the nurses he knew. When the door shut, Stayward beckoned Geoffrey to his bed and began to pick up the documents scattered about.

"Put them in box," he said, indicating a padlocked deed-case. "Nethercleugh and aw that's mine is yours; Faulder has the will. If you want advice, you can trust him. For a lawyer, he's an honest man, and not such a fool as some. But I would like you to live at Nethercleugh. Margaret was aw a Stayward, the last but me, and you're her son. Noo give me a drink."

Geoffrey went for a draught old Belle had left, and when Stayward drained the glass and was quiet began to muse. He understood his uncle had mended his fortune, but nothing at Nethercleugh indicated this. All was the same and Belle used the stern economy that had long marked her rule. Although John Stayward was sometimes hard to others, he did not indulge himself. But Geoffrey knew his self-denial did not spring from greed. He was something of an ascetic and his austere pride scorned to yield much to his body's claims. A grim man, but all the same, somehow fine.

"Did you iver hear aught o' music teacher you met long sin'?" he asked.

"I did not," said Geoffrey, wondering where the remark led.

"Weel," resumed Stayward, "mayhappen you will marry by and by, and a bit money cannily spent would modernize the hoose. I would not have you alter much, but you could make it comfortable. T'oad fellside breed is dying oot and womenfolk are soft. You'll mind I saved and sweated to buy the land that was Nethercleugh's."

Geoffrey signed agreement. The estate was small and the soil was barren, but his ancestors had owned it and there were minerals that might be mined by up-to-date methods.

"I suppose this was your object when you started the coke ovens?" he said. "You had a struggle then."

"Up hill aw the way and Creighton kept me back. He robbed me and I broke him; the man who robs me pays. For aw that, he kenned I was just, and I think he bore me no grudge. If Tom and me had met again, we'd have met like friends. But you'll find aw aboot it in box; our agreement, some letters, and a receipt in his hand. You can read them when I'm gone."

Geoffrey had known his uncle's pride and stern reserve. He had let Mrs. Creighton's stories go, and now he felt his statement was enough. He did not bother his nephew to study the proofs he had kept.

"Does Mrs. Creighton live in the neighborhood yet?" Geoffrey asked.

Stayward gave him a curious glance. "Then, you did not ken? She lives at Beckfoot—in my hoose. I bought mortgage from her cousin's creditors when I sold coke ovens. With the garth, a canny bit property that rounded off mine."

He paused and smiled, rather dryly, when he saw Geoffrey's surprise. "You'll let her stay," he resumed.

"We do not fratch with women, and if the rent's no paid varra regular, it will not cost you much."

"Does she know the house is yours?"

"She does not. For my sake, she'll hate you, lad. Weel, in t' meantime, you can let her talk, though she has a bitter tongue; your neighbors ken the Hassals. But, if you feel she's power to hurt you, let her see t' papers you'll find in box."

"I don't expect Mrs. Creighton can hurt me," Geoffrey remarked.

"Mayhappen not," Stayward agreed, with a curious faint smile. "Janet's a proud, foolish woman and drove her husband on. Tom was soft and a fool at aw but chemistry. It's possible she's borne her grudge so long she's forgot the truth and persuaded herself I robbed her man. There's a daughter, Ruth, a canny lass. I met her noo and then and thought her heart was good. Tom paid and the score's wiped out. I would not have t' lass suffer for his sake."

"I won't disturb her or Mrs. Creighton," Geoffrey promised.

Stayward's eyes began to shut. "Let them bide," he said in a sleepy voice. "T' lass works hard and her heart is good. Tom's daughter, and Tom was not a cheat, but weak! His foolish wife——"

He turned his head from the light and presently Geoffrey, seeing he was asleep, took the deed-box and stole from the room. Going to the kitchen, he sent up the housekeeper, and sat by the hearth where a peat fire burned. Nethercleugh was big and cold, but Belle was frugal and had not lighted another fire. Geoffrey put the lamp on the table, and taking the

# GEOFFREY'S RETURN

papers from the box, found those he wanted neatly tied up and docketed.

He was keenly interested by the story the letters, bank-book, and receipt told. Stayward was methodical, and had left out nothing that related to his breaking the partnership, and Geoffrey was soon convinced that his uncle was justified; Creighton had come near to ruining the house. Stayward's using his partner's invention was, however, another thing, and Geoffrey carefully studied the specification of the patent and the plans of the retorts and machine Stayward had made.

To begin with, he thought Stayward would not have been able to manufacture the dye that had made him rich had not Creighton put him on the right track. For all that, Creighton had not done more than indicate the way. Stayward had taken it and pushed on with characteristic stubbornness. He had gone farther than Creighton saw, and on the whole Geoffrey did not think he had infringed the other's patent. Moreover, this was really not important, since Creighton admitted he had no legal claim and his receipt for the sum Stayward gave him was with the other documents. The sum, of course, was ridiculously small; but if one reflected that Creighton had squandered his partner's capital, it looked as if the latter's not paying him more was ethically justified. Anyhow, the receipt would satisfy a lawyer.

Geoffrey put back the documents. The house was very quiet but for the wind. One got a sense of loneliness and bleakness. Geoffrey, however, had heard wilder winds break the roaring pines when the thermometer was below zero, and had known the loneliness of the frozen North. He began to think about Stayward with a curious tenderness; he liked his scornful silence when the woman who hated him declared him a thief. John Stayward could have stopped her, but he did not quarrel with women. Then he had talked about his partner gently, as if their dispute were done with, and had said Creighton's daughter had a good heart.

Geoffrey felt some curiosity about Ruth Creighton. Stayward had said she worked hard, and this seemed to indicate she was paying for her father's fault, since had Creighton not used his partner's money, part of Geoffrey's inheritance would have been hers. Geoffrey resolved that if he thought he could make things easier for Miss Creighton, he would try.

He began to get drowsy. The wind was louder and the red peats glowed in their bed of feathery ash. The lamp burned low and wavering reflections from the grate touched Belle's old copper pans and twinkled on dark oak. The other end of the big kitchen was dim and the draughts were cold, but Geoffrey was not luxurious, and half-consciously rejoiced because he was at home. Now Nethercleugh was going to be his, he knew he loved the house.

For some hours he slept in his chair, and then, when Belle came down for something, sent her to bed and went back to Stayward's room. Stayward did not talk, and slept quietly when at daybreak Belle resumed her watch. In the evening Geoffrey sat by the window reading, but got up when Stayward beckoned.

"It's aw yours," he said, very feebly. "You're Mar-

## GEOFFREY'S RETURN

garet's son; I won it back for you. You'll guard it weel, like a canny lad."

Geoffrey promised and Stayward said no more. At midnight the doctor came in and stopped for a time. The wind had dropped and the night was cold and calm. The window was open and now and then Geoffrey thought he heard the distant rattle of colliery winding-gear. At daybreak the dry bent-grass began to rustle and the dark ash-branches moved. The candles flickered and the doctor went to Stayward's bed. He signed to Geoffrey, who picked up a candle and crossed the floor.

Stayward's eyes were open and Geoffrey thought he knew him, but in a few moments the wrinkled lids shut. The doctor stooped and soon afterwards touched Geoffrey's arm. Geoffrey shivered and went out with head bent. He felt desolate, although he knew Nethercleugh was his.

While he sat by the kitchen fire Belle came in. Her eyes were dry, for the dalesfolk are not emotional, but she looked very old and sat down slackly.

"I kenned he would go by morning; he waited for you," she said. "It will be lang or you meet anodder like him; but noo you're master you'll do weel to tak' his road."

Geoffrey agreed that his uncle's road was straight. There was something fine about his bluntness; Stayward feared nobody and never used a shabby trick. Geoffrey had long known him just, but it soon began to look as if many had found him generous.

He was buried with his ancestors at a ruined church on the fellside, and Geoffrey wondered when he saw the crowd that came to his funeral. Old servants who now worked for another master had lost a day's pay to join the procession; men with whom Stayward had grimly disputed left furnaces and pits; and rugged sheep-farmers drove from the lonely dales. Geoffrey stood at the gate and gave his hand to all who entered, although there were many he had not seen before. He was moved and conscious of a touch of pride. After all, he was half a Stayward, and it was something to feel the respect the men from mines and dales bore the head of his house.

When the funeral started it began to rain, but nobody left the long procession that moved up the hill. Mist rolled about the fell-tops above the hollow in the moor where the crowd gathered round the broken walls of the lonely church. A beck brawled in a wooded ghyll, and now and then drowned the voice of the clergyman. Geoffrey, standing by a clump of ragged firs, saw rows of quiet faces against a background of mist and rain.

Afterwards he went back to Nethercleugh, and for a time talked with his lawyer. He knew one phase of his life was finished and another had begun. He had long known poverty and now he was richer than he had thought. But his wealth brought responsibility; he must use it as Stayward had meant it to be used, and to begin with, he had promised to live at Nethercleugh. When the lawyer drove off he pondered long.

## CHAPTER II

#### GEOFFREY MEETS MISS CREIGHTON

A MONTH after his return, Geoffrey stood one morning in the garden of a white hotel by a river of the North. The river was swollen, for it had rained at night, and the tops of the hills across the slopes were deep blue, and when the faint gleams of sunshine that picked out wet rocks and wooded hollows passed, looked forbiddingly dark. Geoffrey thought the rain would return, but this did not bother him much, although he meant to cross the mountains to Nethercleugh. He knew the rocks and, because he knew the weather, wore old clothes he had used at the Rideau mine.

For a month after the reading of Stayward's will, he had been rather closely occupied informing himself about his inheritance. It was larger than he had thought, for Stayward had got a high price for his works and had made a number of lucky speculations, besides buying back land that had belonged to the family. On the latter were limestone quarries, beds of sand steelworkers used, and a thin vein of lead that might perhaps be mined. When he had examined all, Geoffrey took a few days' holiday and went across the fells.

Stopping in the evening for dinner at the hotel by the waterside, he opened the visitors' book. If the house were full, he meant to go on to a village up the valley. There were not many guests, but an entry recorded the arrival of a party the day before and he noted with keen curiosity the name Ruth Creighton. Geoffrey did not sign the book, although he asked for a room, and when he made cautious inquiries a waitress told him that Miss Creighton and Miss Chisholm had gone to a friend's house and would not return for dinner.

Geoffrey ordered an early breakfast, and since the waitress said the party was going across the hills, waited to see it start. He was curious about Miss Creighton and sorry for her. Had her father been honest, she would have enjoyed a share of the prosperity that had rewarded Stayward's efforts, but she and her mother were poor. Then Mrs. Creighton declared that Stayward had robbed her husband, and the girl, no doubt, imagined Geoffrey had inherited money that ought to be theirs. If he met her, he must be cautious.

By and by a young clergyman and another young man came out of the hotel. They carried sticks and rucksacks, and, lighting pipes, leaned against a mossy wall and looked up at the hills.

"If we are going, we ought to get off," the clergyman remarked. "Where are the girls?"

"They're waiting for our lunch. Of course we're going," the other replied.

"The landlord tells me we'll have a rough climb, and the mist is often baffling," said the clergyman. "Miss Chisholm's keen, but not very strong. I suppose you're confident you can find the way, Jim?"

"I went over the ground some years since. Nothing

to bother a healthy person, and Maud will keep up all right. People who want a guide for a summer walk across the hills are ridiculous."

The men were obviously from the cities, but Geoffrey knew a number of good cragsmen were lawyers and professors. He kept in the background and presently three girls came out.

"Are you ready, Maud? Where's Ruth?" the man called Jim asked.

"She's getting some sandwiches," the girl replied, and Geoffrey imagined she was Miss Chisholm. He agreed with the clergyman: she hardly looked strong enough for a laborious walk in bad weather.

"Here's Ruth!" she exclaimed next moment, and Geoffrey's heart beat.

Another girl came out of the porch. She was tall and wore a rather short and shabby gray cloth dress. A rucksack and a mackintosh were strapped on her shoulders and Geoffrey noted her firm step and thick boots. This girl was a mountaineer. She did not see him, but he knew her calm look and graceful pose. Her face had haunted him when he mused by the stove at the Rideau mine. Ruth Creighton was the girl he had long since driven across the moor.

"The padre's doubtful about starting," Jim remarked. "You know the fells, don't you? You'd better persuade him."

"I know the other side best," said Ruth. "There's some very rough ground before you get to the top ridge and drop down to Netherdale, and I think it's going to rain. However, we ought to get across."

"Summer rain!" scoffed Jim. "We have a good

map, a compass, and lots of food. Let's chance it and start!"

Geoffrey thought the clergyman and Miss Chisholm hesitated, and lifting his cap, he advanced.

"I am going to Netherdale and know the way," he said. "If it's some help, I could see you across the one or two awkward spots."

He imagined the clergyman was relieved. His clothes were rough and shabby, and his skin was very brown; no doubt he looked like a small sheep-farmer. Then Miss Creighton turned and Geoffrey thrilled, for he saw she had not forgotten him. Her glance was frank and gracious, but he thought a faint touch of color came to her skin.

"Of course it would help," she said. "If we will not bother you and keep you back!"

Geoffrey replied politely and they started. The road was wet, and when they crossed a rough pasture the boggy soil was soft. Then they followed a beck up a stony valley, and Geoffrey noted with amusement that Jim went in front and picked out the landmarks he had obviously noted in a guidebook. Once when the fellow gave the others some directions Geoffrey looked at Ruth, who smiled.

As they climbed out of the valley thick mist gathered about the heights, and by and by Geoffrey, firmly passing Jim, led the party along a narrow ridge. One could not see much. On one side, across a belt of vapor, dark rocks loomed faintly against driving cloud. On the other side, one looked down on rough wet screes and the mist that hid the bottom of a forbidding gulf. The stones the party disturbed rolled away with a harsh tinkle, and now and then a bank slipped

# GEOFFREY MEETS MISS CREIGHTON

down and one heard a roar below. Presently they came to a row of massive blocks, and Jim jumped into a gap.

"Some shelter here," he remarked. "We have come along pretty fast. What d' you say? Shall we stop for lunch?"

Geoffrey knew heavy rain was coming and wanted to get the party off the ridge. There was an awkward spot farther on.

"I think not," he said. "Anyhow, if you want to stop, you had better get off the high ground and drop down to the crossing by the tarn."

Jim gave him a rather supercilious look. "That's three or four miles farther and the book states there's a stiff climb out of the dale. Besides, the rule is never to lose height you must make up again. I won't take the girls round."

"Then you had better push on," said Geoffrey, and Ruth agreed.

They went on, and although it was perhaps not important, Geoffrey was strangely gratified by Ruth's support. For a time, she walked near him, and he studied her quietly. Her face was thin and her color faint; it was plain that she worked hard and her work was tiring. For all that, he noted her easy movements and her confidence on the slippery rocks. Her skin was smooth and delicate; she had wavy brown hair with an elusive touch of red, and he liked the sparkle in her eyes. The sparkle was somehow joyous; one saw she loved the hills and was not daunted by the dark and cold.

When the ground allowed them to walk together, she talked to him frankly about the rocks, and Geoffrey was relieved to note she did not yet know who he was. He thought Ruth Creighton had a high spirit and her will was firm. The strange thing was, something about her recalled somebody he had known, but he could not remember whom.

After they crossed the ridge and clambered, over large sharp stones, round the bottom of a crag, Geoffrey found a hollow in the rocks and they stopped and ate some sandwiches. It had begun to rain and the wind was getting strong, but they lingered over the meal, and afterwards nobody looked anxious to start. When they did get off Geoffrey remarked that Ruth's mackintosh was old and worn. He doubted if it would long keep out the rain, and this disturbed him. She was poor and, in a sense, he had gained much by her poverty.

For a time their path led across a wind-swept summit, and then, going down over a boggy heath, they stopped at a hollow between two crags, and Jim looked about. All were wet and the clergyman and Miss Chisholm looked tired. One saw indistinct wet rocks perhaps a hundred yards off, but this was all, except that on one side of the faint track a beck plunged into a ravine. The ravine was deep and its banks were gravel and wet soil. A shelf of peat and heather, about a foot wide, ran obliquely some way down and then broke off.

"Red Ghyll," said Jim. "We go down here."

Geoffrey looked at Ruth, who knitted her brows as if she were in doubt.

"I imagine we had better go up and cross by the Gap," he said.

"Why?" said Jim. "It's another five hundred feet

# GEOFFREY MEETS MISS CREIGHTON 235

and the girls have had enough. The Ghyll's nearer, and all you have to do is to follow the beck."

"To follow a mountain beck is not always as easy as it looks," Geoffrey rejoined and turned to Ruth. "What do you think, Miss Creighton?"

Ruth hesitated. "It's long since I went down, but I know the banks wash out. For all that, I don't want to take Maud farther than I must. The ghyll is shorter."

"Very well," said Geoffrey, and Jim went down the narrow shelf.

He dropped from its end and slid down the nearly precipitous bank below; then he held up his hands and steadied the girl who followed him. The clergyman went next, and Geoffrey gave Miss Chisholm some support. After a few moments he felt the boggy soil give way, and leaning against the bank, pushed her back. The shelf broke off and turf and stones plunged into the beck. Geoffrey, bracing his feet against a few inches of muddy earth, held the girl, who looked down and saw stones and angry water below. His face was tense and he breathed hard.

"Both hands on my shoulder; then get your foot on the rocky knob and creep back," he said.

Maud did so, but when he joined her at the end of the shelf she trembled and the others had vanished round a corner.

"You were very steady," she gasped. "If you had not held me fast——"

"It's not much of a fall," said Geoffrey, smiling. "You might have got your boots wet."

Maud looked down and shivered. "I don't think

that would have been all. But the others have gone. If they come back for us, they can't get up."

"It looks like that," said Geoffrey. "I don't think your friend Jim would try; he meant to go by the ghyll. Anyhow, it would be awkward for us to get down."

"I'm not going down," Maud declared.

Geoffrey turned to Ruth. "We'll start for the Gap. I don't expect the beck at the dale head will be flooded yet."

They resumed their journey, and presently followed up a little stream that splashed through a hollow and made pools among the stones and fern. The hollow narrowed and got steeper, until it ended at a bank of large rough stones. The top was hidden by tossing mist.

"Must we go up there?" Maud asked.

"I'm afraid you must," said Geoffrey. "It's the last stiff climb."

He went first, turning where the blocks were nearly perpendicular to help the tired girl. Her mackintosh was dark with rain, and he saw that Ruth's was torn, and did not keep out the water. The wind was cold and wailed angrily in the crags overhead. Miss Chisholm was obviously flagging, Ruth's look was rather strained, and Geoffrey began to get disturbed. It was raining very hard and he durst not let his companions stop on the bleak hillside.

Yet he was a little comforted by Ruth's firmness. Although she was tired, she encouraged the other and joked when they stumbled. He thought Miss Chisholm would remember the struggle to the top, but they were getting up, and at length he stopped among

# GEOFFREY MEETS MISS CREIGHTON 237

broken rocks. One could see nothing but the waves of mist that rolled up out of the dale in front, and the vast, dark pit seemed filled with the noise of elemental tumult. The wind roared, stones crashed down hidden screes, and the splash of water rose faintly from forbidding depths.

"Can you find the Green Tongue?" Ruth asked.

"I'll try," he said and took them across a slippery scree.

The stones stopped at the top of a grassy ridge, broken by strange round rocks, running down into the mist.

"I think our troubles are over," he remarked. "If it's necessary, we can stop and rest at the shieling near the dale head."

They went down through the vapor and at length reached the bottom of the dale, where banks of gravel were pierced by small ravines. There was no grass and one saw how the floods had tossed the stones about. The valley was wildly desolate and the rocks that walled its sides were torn by storms. Geoffrey went to the bank of the largest ravine. A savage torrent brawled across broken ledges and fifty yards off plunged over a fall. He could see no farther and for a few moments knitted his brows.

"The track's on the other side," he said. "We can't cross, but there's a better spot lower down. Might be awkward to find while the mist and rain are thick. I think we'll make for the shieling."

Ruth agreed and they set off across the stones.

# CHAPTER III

### THE SHIELING

AFTER a few minutes Geoffrey brought the others to a small hut, rudely built of stones from the beck. There was no window and the door had fallen, but the roof of rushes and heather looked good. The spot was wild and lonely. Steep gravel screes, and stony slopes where moss and bent-grass grew, ran up into the mist, and on the open side the dale was filled by leaden cloud. One heard the roar of water and wail of wind.

"We'll wait," said Geoffrey. "I don't think the rain will last."

They went in. The hut was cold, but a pile of dry fern and dead branches occupied a corner, there was a chimney, and in a few minutes Geoffrey lighted a fire. The girls took off their dripping mackintoshes and sat down near the blaze.

"It's a relief to get into shelter," Miss Chisholm remarked when her wet clothes began to steam. "But why did somebody build the hut in this desolate spot?"

"In spring the shepherds come up at night to see the rock foxes don't carry off the lambs," Geoffrey replied. "There is some orthodox hunting, although on the fells, we follow hounds on foot, but a number of the foxes are shot."

"You seem to know the dalesfolk's habits," said

# THE SHIELING

Ruth, who noted that he said *we*. "Didn't you tell me, another time, you were an engineer?"

"I am an engineer," Geoffrey answered, feeling strangely gratified that she had not forgotten. "All the same, I belong to the dales."

"But when one gets back from the coast, there are no mines and works to give you an occupation."

"That is so," Geoffrey agreed. "My last mining job was in Canada; developing a silver vein in the Ontario wilds."

"Did you find much silver?"

"We found another valuable metal, but I don't know if it was due to my efforts. My cook really found the stuff."

"Your cook?" Ruth remarked.

"Yes," said Geoffrey. "A strange old fellow! He was a good cook, but he knew more than I knew about mining chemistry."

Ruth thought about her father, and he wondered why her look got gentle. It was puzzling, but not important, and he resumed:

"We didn't finish all our lunch. I have some sandwiches left."

"So have I," said Miss Chisholm. "Ruth has got some cake. Suppose we pool?"

They divided the food and Geoffrey owned that it was long since he had so enjoyed a meal. The hut was getting warm and the reflections of the leaping flames played about the girls. Their society gave the rude shieling a strange homelike touch, they wore the stamp of high cultivation, and it was something to share his crushed sandwiches with Ruth. When the last was eaten he threw fresh branches on the fire and Ruth, leaning forward, held her hands to the blaze. Geoffrey noted they were thin and nervous but finely shaped.

"It's nice to get warm again," she said. "However, perhaps you oughtn't to be extravagant. Somebody has brought the fuel a long way on his plowsledge."

"We needn't bother about that," Geoffrey replied. "I don't expect the farmer would mind my burning his wood."

Ruth gave him a quick glance, and seeing she was puzzled, he resolved to be cautious. She would, of course, soon find out he was Stayward's nephew, but he did not want her to find out yet. He had grounds for imagining Mrs. Creighton had transferred to him the grudge she had borne his uncle.

"Anyhow, you and Miss Chisholm were cold," he resumed. "You looked tired and wet clothes are dangerous when one is fatigued."

"I am tired," Miss Chisholm declared. "It's my first adventure on the fells, and Ruth has not climbed for long. Still, I don't understand how you knew me."

"Your name was in the visitors' book," Geoffrey said and paused. "You see, when one thinks about stopping at a tourist hotel, one wants to know if the house is full."

"Exactly," Miss Chisholm agreed, with a twinkle that rather annoyed him. "But how do you think the rest of our party has got on?"

"If your friend Jim keeps the proper side of the beck, I expect he'll bring the others down all right,"

Geoffrey said and turned to Ruth. "It's some time since you were on the fells?"

"Yes. I found the climb to-day harder than I thought," Ruth replied. "You soon get slack in town, and I have only come home for a week or two because my mother is ill——" She paused and resumed with a smile: "Perhaps it's strange, but when I needed help another time you arrived. Do you go about helping people?"

"I can't claim the habit. In fact, I hesitated that other time, although I saw you some distance off, and imagined it hurt you to walk. The sky was full of yellow light and as you went up the hill your figure cut against the sunset. You were going resolutely, but you kept on the heather, and there was something about your pose; one knows when another's tired. Then the evening was very hot, the road was dusty, and when you were forced to stop I thought I might venture——"

Geoffrey imagined Miss Chisholm studied him and wondered whether he had said too much. Ruth was looking at the fire, but she turned.

"I was grateful. One is grateful for a kindness one feels is sincere," she said, and added with a laugh: "But your hesitation was obvious. You were very apologetic because the tire went down and took some time to mend. In fact, you were rather unnecessarily embarrassed. I didn't doubt that the tire leaked."

"After all, you hadn't much ground for your confidence."

"Oh, well! Perhaps one trusts by instinct. Then at the beginning, when the bicycle began to jolt, you frowned and I think you growled. It was plain you were annoyed!"

Geoffrey admitted this and wondered why Miss Chisholm was amused. He thrilled to note Ruth had remembered so much, and then it dawned on him that he had shown his memory was strangely good.

"How are we to get home?" Miss Chisholm asked.

Geoffrey went to the door. The mist was not so thick and one could see farther down the dale.

"I expect the rain will soon stop. If it does not, I must try to cross the beck and hire ponies at a farm I know. However, since this is your first climbing excursion, what do you think about our hills?"

"In the mist, they're forbidding, but I'm glad Ruth planned the trip. All I know of rural England is the smoky country round the towns where the tram-lines and tarred roads run; a tame country of dusty hedges and rows of telegraph poles, with groups of new, plastered houses where there is a pretty spot. Ruth has shown me an England I didn't know was mine; a stern wilderness that one feels is as rugged as it was at the beginning. All the same, I think its enjoyment needs cultivation."

"That is so," said Ruth. "The North is bleak and bracing. Let's hope the mountains will remain a wilderness where adventurous people can try nerve and muscle and front the rain and wind. England needs a playground like this."

Half an hour afterwards, Geoffrey went back to the door and beckoned the others. There was no rain, the wind had dropped, and the mist was rolling up the long rough slopes. Dim crags loomed in the thin

# THE SHIELING

vapour and wet rocks glistened with faint reflected light.

They crossed the stones to the ravine and when they had gone some distance stopped where the stream narrowed above a dark pool. Big smooth stones ran out into the flood, and on the other side a slender mountain-ash stretched its branches across the water that plunged, a few yards away, into a chasm between the rocks. The bank was precipitous, and the roar of the fall was daunting.

Geoffrey, going down cautiously, gave his hand to Miss Chisholm; he saw Ruth did not need his help. She had a mountaineer's steady balance and knew how to tread on stones that slipped and rolled. The big blocks at the bottom of the bank were level with the flood and he waited for a moment to get his breath before he leaped across. Then he turned and holding on by the mountain-ash beckoned Miss Chisholm.

"Not much of a jump and a pretty good path goes down this side. There's nothing to bother you after you get across."

The girl advanced to the edge of the stones and drew back with a shiver.

"I can't," she said, despairingly.

Geoffrey leaned forward as far as he could and held out his hand, but Ruth signed to him that he was not to help and sprang across. He saw she meant to encourage her companion, and admitted that the spot was daunting for a beginner. To jump short, or slip back, after alighting, meant that one would be swept down the fall. Then he frowned as he saw Miss Chisholm's doubts were not yet banished and Ruth was going back. It was plain that she had pluck, but her face was rather white and her look was strained. She jumped and reached the block.

"Brace up, Maud," she said. "It's only a rather long step, and one can't get down this side. You wouldn't like to scramble over rocks and awkward screes."

Miss Chisholm made an effort. Geoffrey saw her thin figure stiffen and her mouth set. She sprang across, and Geoffrey pushed her up a yard or two of the steep bank. Then he turned and saw Ruth balance herself on the other side. The ground was lower there, and he thought she had done too much.

"Wait a moment and get breath," he said. "I can nearly reach across and won't let you go."

She jumped and he seized her as she came down. Her foot touched the edge, but the stone was wet and rounded, and she slipped back. Geoffrey gasped, the mountain-ash bent and cracked, and he felt his fingers slide across the bark. The veins swelled on his forehead, he doubted if he could lift the girl to firm ground, but he would not let go. For a moment he saw Ruth's face, white and tense, but somehow confident; and then the strain slackened. He pulled forward and they fell against the bank.

"You ought not to have gone back," he said hoarsely.

Ruth looked slack and shaken, but she smiled. "If I hadn't gone, Maud would have stopped on the other side."

They followed Miss Chisholm, who was awkwardly climbing the slope in front, and soon afterwards found a green track that led down from the stony waste to rough pastures. The girls were quiet and

# THE SHIELING 245

Geoffrey did not talk. He thought the hour or two by the shieling fire and their adventure at the crossing had brought him nearer Ruth Creighton than he might have got had he known her long. When the strain had come she trusted him and he trusted her. Yet, in a sense, the strain had not been needed; she was all he had thought, and she had not forgotten their first meeting. When she came into the hotel garden they were not strangers.

He left the girls at a cross-road, and while he went on to Nethercleugh they took a field path to Beckfoot. Some time after they arrived Maud and Ruth sat by the fire in the small drawing-room. Maud lounged in an easy chair, with her feet on the hearth brasses.

"I hope I haven't scratched those things and burned your slippers," she presently remarked. "I'm not much used to drawing-rooms, and to-day's adventures have left me creepy and cold. Mountaineering's a strenuous hobby and I doubt if I'm up to it. But I wonder where Jim has taken the others. Jim was not his best after your engineering friend arrived; he likes to lead."

"They probably got down the ghyll and there's an inn not far from the bottom. The landlady's kind; I expect she would dry their clothes."

"We needn't bother about Jim and Gertie," Maud resumed. "Jim's pose is a Spartan athlete and Gertie's as hardy as a mule, but Peter's not like that. I don't imagine getting wet on your bleak mountains is the kind of change he needs. In fact, I tried to persuade him not to join our party."

Peter was the clergyman; a curate from the Rainsfield church, and Ruth said, "I thought you liked him much."

"If you like a man, you feel you ought to take care of him," Maud replied. "Anyhow, I feel I want to take care of Peter. A motherly instinct I can't lawfully indulge otherwise, perhaps! Besides, Peter's nearly all spirit, and what flesh he has is weak. I mean physically weak, because everybody knows Peter's morals are austere."

Ruth said nothing. She imagined Peter had asked Maud to marry him, and she had refused. Sometimes Maud was moody and sometimes it looked as if her rather ironical carelessness were forced.

"If your mother's not coming down, I'm going to smoke," Maud resumed, taking out a cigarette case. "She will, of course, smell the smoke, but the jolt will be less than finding me with the unwomanly abomination in my mouth. Anyhow, she has been spared one jar. In a sense, I'm probably enough, but suppose your climate had forced us all to take refuge at Beckfoot?"

"Oh, well," said Ruth, smiling, "for my sake she'd have tried to be kind. You must remember my mother is old-fashioned and has not enjoyed your advantages."

"I expect she'd call them drawbacks. However, she's lucky. Think of the strain she might have had to bear! Peter would pass; he's obviously your sort and a clergyman. When she'd found out something about him, she'd tell him your virtues. But Jim from the Co-op store, and tanyard Gertie——"

Ruth colored and stopped the other by a glance. As a rule, one made allowance for Maud, but sometimes she was remarkably perverse. This often happened after she had enjoyed Peter's society, and Ruth was sorry for her. She thought Maud felt the galling force of social conventions, and now and then rebelled. It looked as if she had resolved, at some cost to herself, that she would not spoil her lover's career.

"Suppose we talk about something else," Ruth said quietly.

"Very well. I liked your engineer. A well-balanced man. Brains enough, I think, but perhaps not too much, and a vigorous, disciplined body. Soft, indulgent men don't wear his clean, alert look. Then I noted that he saw we got the most part of his lunch. A small thing, but some small things count. Anyhow, I ate and was thankful. A man like that could walk all day without needing food; I can't. Why didn't you present him properly?"

"I don't know him. I met him once, some time since."

"On the road, when the sky was yellow and your figure cut against the light! One can see the picture. It's strange and perhaps significant he remembers so much. I imagined you remembered something, too."

Ruth colored, but forced a smile. "Oh, well, he was kind and I rather approved his honest awkwardness when he stopped his bicycle and asked if he could help. Then I was tired and moody after finding out that friends don't bother about you when you're poor. To feel somebody was willing to help was soothing. That's all, and it's not important. I doubt if I shall meet him again."

"I don't doubt. The young man's resolute, although his resolution's not aggressive, like Jim's," Maud rejoined. Then seeing Ruth's eyes sparkle she laughed and went on: "Yet, if you use a firm hand, Jim is a good sort."

"It's hard to see why Jim and Peter are friends," Ruth remarked.

Maud smiled gently. "Peter's romantic and believes in the real brotherhood of man. At the beginning, Jim jarred him, but Peter welcomes jars like that. He imagines they're healthy discipline and help him to conquer his prejudices. The poor fellow hates to feel he shrinks from honest rudeness, and when he does shrink he tries to find redeeming qualities in the offender. I think he does find them; people play up to him."

"He's a dear!" Ruth declared with frank enthusiasm.

Then the drawing-room door opened and Maud threw her cigarette into the grate as Mrs. Creighton entered. Her face was haggard and she looked ill.

"Dinner will not be long. I hope your fatigue is wearing off," she said to Maud, and crossing the floor slowly, opened the window.

## CHAPTER IV

### THE STACK

AT noon one day soon after his walk across the hills, Geoffrey packed up his fishing-rod by a tarn among the rocks, and sitting on the smooth gravel took out his lunch. A soft, south-west wind was blowing and the water sparkled in the sun, and faded as the shadows trailed across the hills. Two or three small trout lay behind a stone, and although the fish were not rising well, Geoffrey did not want to go. The air was balmy and the changing lights touched the landscape with melting color. Sometimes the rocks shone and sometimes got dim. The white bent-grass was flecked by delicate ochre when it rippled in the wind; the fresh ferns and mossy belts gleamed with gold and luminous green.

Geoffrey wanted to loaf and muse about Ruth Creighton, but knew he ought not. He had left his motor bicycle at a farm in the dale, and had meant to transact some business with a lawyer at a mining town some distance off. Then an architect, with whom he had planned the rebuilding of a farmstead, would probably arrive soon after he got home. Geoffrey did not put things off; although he now owned Nethercleugh and much besides, he was as punctual as when he worked for others at the Rideau mine.

For all that, he frowned when he rolled up his

sandwich papers and looked at his watch. In the North, summer is short and fine weather is not the rule. Then since he had met Ruth Creighton business had lost its charm. He wanted to think about her among the mountains, to which he felt she belonged. He pictured her going back, pale but confident, across the beck at the edge of the fall, and sitting by the fire while the rain beat upon the lonely shieling. She had pluck and her smile was bright, but she was often quiet and he liked her calm. Her charm was, so to speak, elusive; strong but somehow vague, like the elusive beauty of the fells when mist and sun came and went.

Geoffrey pulled himself up. He must not indulge his romantic imagination and neglect his business. There was time for a pipe and then he would start. Before the pipe was smoked out, however, he looked across the tarn and suddenly forgot the lawyer and the architect. A row of small figures came down the hill and he thought he knew the clergyman and Jim. Behind them were three girls, and Geoffrey would have known Ruth Creighton much farther off. She had grace and a mountaineer's balance; nobody walked like her.

When the party reached the tarn Geoffrey got up and for some minutes the others stopped and talked. They had finished their holiday and were making for a station; Ruth had led them across the hills but was going home. Miss Chisholm told Geoffrey this.

"Now we can see our line, we don't need a guide," she said. "We have brought Ruth some distance, and it's lucky she need not go back alone."

Geoffrey looked at Ruth, who smiled. "If one

# THE STACK

crosses the scree by the Stack, it is really not far," she said. Then she indicated the little shining trout. "Besides, one doesn't like to be disturbed when one is catching fish."

"I'm not catching fish; two hours have gone since the last rose," Geoffrey replied. "Then, if they were rising, the fish in this tarn are not worth bothering about."

"It sounds like a lawyer's argument," Miss Chisolm remarked. "Anyhow, Ruth has come far enough."

For a minute or two the girls talked and Geoffrey gave the men some directions about the path. Jim heard him without impatience and Geoffrey thought his trust in his map and compass was shaken.

"We were sorry afterwards we didn't stick to you," he said. "Landmarks that look plain in a guidebook are puzzling in the mist, and I imagine we went the wrong side of the Red Ghyll beck. Washed-down banks, little crags with mossy ledges, and patches of flooded bog are awkward to cross. When we got to the bottom we were tired out."

Geoffrey laughed and let him go, and when the party took the path below the tarn, Ruth and he went back up the hill. An hour afterwards, they stopped on a narrow sheep path that crossed a great bank of gravel. For some distance the stones ran down at so steep an angle that now and then the gusts of wind disturbed their equilibrium and they rolled away. Across the bog at the bottom of the bank, the shoulder of a mountain rose in a broken line and ended in a huge rock buttress that cut off the view. In places, where the water trickled down, the crag glimmered, but for the most part, the rocks looked dark and mysterious in the shadow. They were seamed by gullies, and the broken, tilted strata gave them a rude likeness to steps.

"The Stack looks very grand from here," Ruth remarked while her dress fluttered and her hair blew about the edge of her soft cap. "Not a first-class climb, of course, but there are awkward pitches! Have you gone up the Buttress?"

"I have not," said Geoffrey. "I'd rather like to go! Let's sit down for a few minutes and plan the line we'd take if we were going. There's a fascination about looking for your route up a fresh bit of rock. But perhaps you know the way?"

"I went up once. Four of us on a rope, and the first two were good cragsmen. That rather spoiled the thing, because they pulled me up like a bale of goods."

"You're an individualist, I expect, but to feel one must follow somebody else does spoil things," Geoffrey said with a laugh. "Well, I don't know the way and perhaps you don't remember much. This ought to give the climb a touch of adventure. Suppose we try?"

Ruth pondered. The rocks called, but she hesitated. For one thing, she ought to have returned sooner and Mrs. Creighton would be curious. Then she did not know Geoffrey, and although she had meant to find out who he was she had shrunk from talking about him to her mother. Beckfoot was lonely, Mrs. Creighton and Maud kept her occupied, and she had not been to the village. Besides, Maud had hinted something and Ruth, looking at Geoffrey sideways, felt vaguely disturbed. He attracted her and she had thought about him rather often since their journey across the hills. However, she had not lived with Maud at Rainsfield for nothing, and she was tempted to be rash.

"It's a glorious afternoon. The wind's not too strong and the rocks are dry," Geoffrey resumed.

"Very well," she said, and he thought the wind had brought the touch of color to her skin. Her eyes sparkled and when they went down the screes her step was light.

Geoffrey got a thrilling sense of adventure. He remembered his going with Florence to Dominion Park and his boyish enjoyment of the stolen excursion, but he was really not strongly moved then. To begin with, the stage, so to speak, was different. At Dominion Park, all was theatrical; colored lights, over-dressed crowds, noise, and popular music; here one had the serene grandeur of the mountains and the wild harmonies of the wind in the rocks. Then, although Florence was kind and clever, she was not the girl he had dreamed about on bitter evenings when the snow lay deep round the lonely mine.

Half an hour after they set off they stopped for breath at the bottom of a gully in the crag. The pitch was steep and big stones blocked the gully here and there. A few ferns grew in crannies and belts of rock were slippery with moss.

"Somebody else and a rope would be useful," Ruth remarked. "However, we ought to get up if the rest's not worse than this."

They went up for some distance without much effort, and then paused by a little pool where a block rested on the edge of a three or four foot fall. In order to get round the pool, one must step upon the block, and to slip might mean a plunge to the bottom of the gully.

"I think that stone will move," said Ruth.

"Try it," said Geoffrey, "I'll steady you. There's a good hold on the ledge when you get across."

The stone rocked when Ruth sprang across, but it did not fall, and Geoffrey cautiously prepared to follow. He was heavier and did not like the block. While he balanced himself it rolled under his foot and he stumbled. He must, if possible, fall into the pool, but he doubted if he could; if he struck the rock and fell back, he might not stop until he reached the bottom of the crag. Then Ruth, leaning out from the ledge, seized his arm, and next moment he stood, gasping, at her side. They heard the stone plunge down the gully and smash.

"Thanks!" he said. "One can trust you! If you hadn't helped, I'd hardly have got across."

"You'd have gone into the pool," Ruth declared with a laugh.

"I doubt——" he said and stopped, for Ruth had struck the right note. There must be no hint of strain, and when one climbed with a companion incidents like this were not unusual. One ran risks, counting on the help the other gave. Much help was not needed; a steadying touch was often enough. All the same, he was moved and turned his head, for fear Ruth saw and understood. She was a little breathless, her eyes sparkled, and the blood had come to her skin. Her head was lifted and her unconscious pose was beautiful.

They left the gully and made a traverse across the

## THE STACK

crag. The rock slanted and the hold was good. Perhaps it was not a traverse for a beginner, but there was not much risk and one could look about. White clouds sailed across, and sometimes touched, the broken summits; the great crag flashed like silver, and the hollow they had left looked profoundly deep and was colored a soft misty blue. Then they came to an awkward corner, where for a few yards the rock was nearly vertical. Ruth was in front and when she paused to feel for a hold her figure was outlined against the sky. Her shabby dress blew away from her, her hair streamed about her cap, and Geoffrey noted that her boots were old and torn by the stones. Yet as she clung to the gray slab, calmly confident, he thought her wonderful. With the sky behind her and the deep gulf below, she rather seemed a spirit of the mountains than flesh and blood. But Geoffrey pulled himself up; his business was to see she got round the corner safe.

"Try the knob to the left," he said. "Then if you can reach the crack——"

Ruth nodded and went round, but when she vanished Geoffrey thought the great rock looked desolate and the view had lost its charm. He followed, and for a time they climbed across broken slabs that ran up rather like a flight of stairs. There was no danger if one looked for a firm hold before one moved, but it was different when they came to the steep, rounded side of the summit. Shallow wet soil and heather covered the rock, and the small ledges that broke the surface were smooth. One's feet slipped in the bog and the heather gave way.

By and by Ruth seized a clump that came out with

its roots. She slipped back a few feet, until Geoffrey, bracing himself against the slope, stopped her. It was something of a shock, but his hold was good, and Ruth laughed when she clambered up. Then they found a precipitous channel from which the rain had washed away the soil. Here there was a better grip for foot and hand, and a few minutes' effort brought them to the top.

The top was a peaty dome, broken by little pools that reflected the sky and darkened when the white clouds rolled past. They sat down in the boisterous wind, and for a time looked about; across scarred peaks, sullen tarns among the rocks, and a sparkling lake in a deep dale, to the faint silver band that marked the sea. Now and then, however, Geoffrey looked at Ruth and his heart beat.

She was his equal in pluck and steadiness; indeed she was his equal in all except perhaps muscular strength, and when he was slow she was quick. He did not know if her face was beautiful by classical rules, but this did not matter; Ruth had a charm that was hers alone. Now and then, however, a look or a note in her voice puzzled him. He felt he ought to know the humorous smile and quick drop to a lower tone, but he did not. Although he had felt this before, he saw no light yet.

"It was a glorious scramble," she said, by and by. "Perhaps I enjoyed it better because we, ourselves, found the way. On the famous climbs, others have long since discovered how you can best get round the obstacles and you use their rules."

"To feel you're a pioneer is something," Geoffrey agreed.

# THE STACK

"Then, I suppose generosity made you let me choose our line?"

"It didn't cost much, anyhow. Perhaps it's human to grumble when you're forced to follow another's path, but when somebody else knows the job as well as I know it, I don't mind the second place."

"Really? You don't want to lead?"

"On the whole, I don't think so," Geoffrey replied. "At the mine in Ontario, two of us engaged to solve a puzzle. I was manager, the other fellow was my cook, but I was satisfied to let him take the lead. It was plain he knew more. However, this is not important; I mustn't bore you——"

He stopped. Somehow his talking about the mine seemed to give him a clue to the puzzling note in Ruth's voice, but when he tried to seize the clue it broke.

"Oh, well," said Ruth, "if you had not come, I could not have climbed the Stack, and in the North, days like this are not numerous. It will be something to remember when I am back in town."

"Then, you must go back soon?"

"I must," said Ruth rather drearily. "I wonder whether you know Rainsfield; it's a little dirtier and uglier than other manufacturing towns. Of course, to work is not a hardship, and if your work absorbs you, it doesn't matter where you live. But, when one meant to be a pioneer and is forced to struggle with the crowd along the beaten track——"

She stopped. To talk like this to a man she did not know was ridiculous.

"All the same," she resumed, "I must wait until my mother is better, and I may perhaps get on the hills again, although I doubt. I came to-day because Maud was going, but I ought to have turned back sooner. When we stopped on the scree the Stack looked tempting. You see, it's long since I got up among the big rocks."

Geoffrey sympathized. She loved the rocks, but was forced to labor in the town, and her tired look and shabby clothes indicated that her reward was small. Yet he could not help and must be cautious.

"I understand," he said. "A stolen holiday's better than a number you're entitled to enjoy! All the same, we're not going down the Buttress and the tourist path runs a long way round. I'm afraid you'll hardly get home for dinner."

Ruth glanced at her wrist-watch and got up. "We must start! It's later than I thought."

"I've a notion. My bicycle and side-car are at Ritson's in the dale. If you'll come with me again, you ought to reach home in half-an-hour after we leave the farm."

She hesitated for a moment, and then smiled. In a sense, she had been rash to climb the Stack with him, but rashness had a charm and she would keep it up. Besides, Mrs. Creighton needed her and might be alarmed if she did not return soon.

"Thank you," she said. "It's strange, but when I'm in a difficulty you and the bicycle arrive. However, I think some people are like that."

"A number of us have motor bicycles, if that is what you mean," Geoffrey remarked.

Ruth laughed. "You're very matter-of-fact. I think I meant it's something when people feel you're generally where you are wanted."

## CHAPTER V

RUTH'S PERSUASION

THE doctor was leaving Beckfoot, and stopping at the gate, looked thoughtfully at Ruth, who had gone with him across the garden.

"I'm bothered about your mother," he said. "Her heart, of course, is weak, but to some extent her illness is mental; nervous, if you like. She needs a change; fresh interests and associations as much as fresh surroundings. Can you take her away?"

"I'm afraid it's impossible," Ruth replied.

The doctor nodded. He knew something about Mrs. Creighton's affairs. "Then you must try to keep her cheerful and banish her rather morbid gloominess. She ought to go out, and although she must be amused and now and then indulged, you must use some firmness. Medicine won't do all that's needed; much depends on you."

He went off and Ruth felt disturbed. It looked as if she must stay at Beckfoot and this would be awkward, although she loved the dale and her work at Rainsfield often jarred. Maud and she were making progress, her help was useful, and Maud would be embarrassed if she left her. Besides, the small sums she earned were needed. Then Ruth had been at Beckfoot for some time, and had now and then found her mother's moods hard to bear. Yet her duty looked plain, and she went back to the house trying to be resigned.

Mrs. Creighton reclined in a long chair with tray and book rests, for which she had sent to London. Her face was thin and her eyes were dull, but weakness had not given her patience. She looked bitter and dissatisfied. The window was open and the afternoon was warm, but a fire burned in the small drawing-room. Mrs. Creighton liked a fire and Ruth agreed, although she knew the cost of bringing coal up the long, steep hill to the dale.

"Dr. Teasdale is strangely unsympathetic," Mrs. Creighton grumbled. "He said I ought to rouse myself, go out more, and undertake some light work in the garden. The thing is ridiculous! I might go out now and then if I could drive. Besides, old James would not allow me to touch his borders. Sometimes I'm tempted to send for the Mellerby doctor."

There was an obvious reason why Mrs. Creighton should not dismiss Teasdale, but Ruth said, "I don't see why James comes so often. The garden is small."

"You know I like flowers. Your father was generous and parsimony is not a fault of the Hassals. I don't know where you got yours."

Ruth smiled. She had been forced to study economy at Rainsfield, and since Maud's classes got larger had sent Mrs. Creighton the most part of the fees she earned.

"However, I imagine Miss Chisholm's example and society have had an unfortunate influence," Mrs. Creighton resumed. "It is a relief the girl has gone. She jarred me and I am glad you will not be able

## RUTH'S PERSUASION

to rejoin her for some time. No doubt Teasdale stated that I shall need you."

"Maud is my friend," Ruth replied, rather sharply, but stopped. Her mother was ill and must be indulged. "But let's be practical," she added. "Can I stay at Beckfoot? We owe a number of people money and the rent has not been paid."

"You are not kind. You know talking about these things brings on my headache. Then it does not matter about the rent. Beckfoot is my cousin's and Jack is not greedy. When I came here he promised——"

"I don't understand," she said. "Jack Hassal was in debt and his promise would not bind his creditors."

"You do not understand business," Mrs. Creighton rejoined. "But I wanted to talk about something else, and now I cannot. You argued and my headache is very bad——"

Ruth left her and when she returned by and by Mrs. Creighton said, "While you were out in the morning George came."

"Ah!" said Ruth and her heart beat, for George Hassal was a lawyer and had been making inquiries abroad about Creighton.

"He is persuaded your father died in Canada," Mrs. Creighton went on. "Although I had long given up hope, the shock was great." She paused and let her voice drop to a low note. "It was worse because George found out that when your father left Calgary he had been ill and was very poor."

Ruth was very quiet for a minute or two. She had for some time feared her father was dead, but it was harrowing to think he had died among strangers, perhaps neglected, and without the help and comforts sick people needed. In fact, she durst not think about it, and with an effort she roused herself to ask what grounds the lawyer had for his belief.

Mrs. Creighton told her and Ruth admitted there was not much room for doubt. Then Mrs. Creighton added: "It is long since your father wrote to us, but I knew he was not prospering. He was generous and meant to hide his poverty. One must try to be resigned, but the sense of loss is keen——"

She wept with an abandonment that disturbed Ruth. For all that, the girl was puzzled; she remembered that her parents had jarred and Mrs. Creighton had not been gentle to her husband. Indeed, Ruth had often pitied her father and tried to comfort him. It was not until he had gone her mother talked about him with tenderness and appreciation. Although Ruth was sympathetic, she felt her mother's grief was somehow artificial, but she tried to banish the uncharitable thought. Presently Mrs. Creighton got calm.

"In a sense, we were both prepared," she said. "Perhaps this has saved us some pain, but now we are left alone, we must try to draw closer and trust each other." She was quiet for a time and then, while Ruth indulged her grief, resumed: "Miss Chisholm talked about a man who went with you across the hills."

Ruth started. Maud had talked about Geoffrey, one morning in the garden, but Ruth had thought her mother was in the house.

"Well," she said, "we met a man at the hotel who knew the hills and were rather glad when he told us he was going our way. Soon after we started it began to rain and the mist was thick. If he had not helped, we might not have got down that night."

"One would not expect a stranger to be a useful guide. You imply you do not know him."

"I do not know him," Ruth declared, and Mrs. Creighton gave her a keen glance.

"What was the man like?" she asked.

Ruth told her and she smiled, rather cruelly. "I imagine the man knew you, although his object for joining your party is not very plain. He is Stayward's nephew, Geoffrey Lisle."

The blood came to Ruth's skin and her pose stiffened, for she felt she must brace herself. She had thought much about Geoffrey since she met him on the moor, and he had come to stand for all the romance she knew. When she met him again, in the garden at the hotel, it was rather like a reunion with a trusted friend. He was strong and frank and honest, and she owned that she had tempted him to suggest that they should climb the Stack, for the pleasure of adventuring in his society. And she had enjoyed every thrilling moment of the climb.

Now it looked as if she must let him go, but she rebelled, for her acquiescence had been strained. She had found her fears about her father were justified, and the last hope that he was alive had vanished; she had seen that she must give up Maud and the career in which she had made some laborious progress. It was obvious that her mother needed her and she had tried to resign herself; but she felt she had borne enough. Her look hardened and her mouth set firm.

"Stayward, not his nephew, injured us," she said.

"All the same, Lisle is his nephew and enjoys the

reward of the other's cunning and dishonesty. Much of the money he inherited was your father's; the invention Stayward stole made him rich. But your father, broken by hardship and poverty, died among strangers, and we do not know where is his grave. Can you picture his wandering about Canada, hopeless, ill, unable to work?"

"Stop!" said Ruth, hoarsely. "I durst not think about it."

"Very well," said Mrs. Creighton. "Teasdale told you I ought to go away, and I knew long since the loneliness and dreariness at Beckfoot were wearing me out. I cannot go; I must give up all hope of getting well, and Stayward is accountable for this. His nephew squanders the money he stole; our money, for which your father labored. Well, we must pay for trusting a rogue, but it is unthinkable his heir and nephew should be my daughter's friend. A small part of his riches might have kept your father alive."

Ruth clenched her hand. She had loved her father, the news of his death, although long expected, had moved her strongly, and her grief turned to passionate anger. She did not see that Mrs. Creighton's arguments were not altogether logical; she saw nothing but her father, wandering, sick and desolate, in a stern country. Afterwards, when she pondered the interview, she thought it strange Mrs. Creighton had talked about Maud and Lisle; one would have expected the news the lawyer brought to absorb her thoughts. Then her appeal against Lisle had been made at a curiously fortunate time; Ruth wondered whether her mother had known this.

"Now I do know who the man is, I shall know the

# RUTH'S PERSUASION

line to take if we meet again," she said, and her eyes sparkled when she got up.

Then, feeling she must be alone, she went to the garden and Mrs. Creighton let her go. She knew Ruth's stanchness. Moreover the girl was not a romantic fool and would do what she ought.

A week afterwards, Geoffrey went one evening to the village and stopped for a few minutes on the wooden bridge outside the thatched post office. The spot was sheltered by the hills and a row of old sycamores checkered with moving shadow the belt of grass between the small white houses and the road. The gardens ran down to a beck and from each a plank bridge led to the green. While Geoffrey lighted his pipe he saw a figure some distance off on the road. It was the girl who wore a big shady hat, and although he could not see her face he knew her pose and step. Dropping the match, he put away his pipe, and went back quickly across the post office garden to a field path.

Five minutes afterwards, he rejoined the road outside the village and sat down under the last of the sycamores. His look was resolute and although his heart beat he meant to be cool. Since he climbed the Stack with Miss Creighton he had seen her in the distance and imagined she had seen him. If she had done so, it was significant that she had gone another way. He had known she would soon find out he was Stayward's nephew, and his uncle had warned him he must reckon on her mother's antagonism. Now it looked as if Mrs. Creighton had worked upon her daughter's feelings.

For all that, Geoffrey did not mean to acquiesce

without an effort. Ruth had gone to the post office, she could not see him in the shadow, and if he waited, he would meet her coming back. He had chosen a quiet spot because the village people were curious and to persuade Ruth their friendship need not be broken might be difficult. The girl was spirited and Geoffrey thought she could be firm. He must try to show her she was illogical.

After a few minutes, he saw her coming up the road. She went slowly, as if in thought, and her languid step and disturbed look indicated that her thoughts were not cheerful. Geoffrey got up resolutely when she advanced, and noted that she hesitated, as if doubtful whether she would stop. There was some color in her face, but he could not tell if it sprang from anger or embarrassment. He admitted that he ought to have let her pass, but did not mean to do so.

"I saw you from the post office," he said.

"Then, you must have crossed the field!"

"I did so. I didn't want to miss you again."

Ruth's eyes sparkled. "You imply that you would not have met me, had I seen you?"

"Something like that," Geoffrey admitted.

"Then, although you imagined I would sooner be alone, you meant to force me to stop?"

"Yes. I expect I ought to have let you go, and perhaps you have some grounds for feeling annoyed, but now and then one can't be fastidious. Besides, you must remember I'm John Stayward's nephew and his bluntness was well known. You see, we're rather an obstinate lot."

Ruth gave him a glance of cold surprise. She was angry, but all the same she liked his pluck. It was obvious he knew his relationship to Stayward was his drawback and refused to pretend he did not. Indeed, she thought he wanted to force her to argue about it, and since she meant to let him go, he was perhaps entitled to know the grounds for her resolve.

"I do remember you are Stayward's nephew," she rejoined. "You must see we cannot be friends."

"I do not see," Geoffrey declared. "I want you to see you're not logical. I've met you three or four times, and until now you were gracious, or might one call it kind? Anyhow, you didn't make me feel I'd done some wrong and must be avoided."

Ruth admitted that he had come to her help when she needed help, and had been her companion in the most exhilarating adventure on the rocks she had known.

"You knew me," she said. "I think you were careful I did not know you. This is important."

"When I overtook you on the moor road I did not know," Geoffrey rejoined. "At the hotel I saw your name in the visitors' book, but until you came into the garden, I did not know you were the girl I had met before and had often thought about. Well, perhaps I ought to have stated that I was Stayward's nephew, but I did not. For one thing, it would have looked as if I felt you ought to be warned——"

He saw Ruth's eyes sparkle, and stopped. "I mean, of course, I wouldn't own my being Stayward's relation was an obstacle," he added.

"All the same, it is an obstacle. Your uncle robbed my father."

"He quarrelled with your father. There was a dispute about the patent. This was some time since. What has it to do with us?"

"Ah," said Ruth, "it has much to do with me! My father was forced to go abroad and died from disappointment and hardship, while his invention made your uncle rich. Poverty has broken my mother's health; but you know our story! It is well known and you have been at Nethercleugh some time."

"I know your mother's story," Geoffrey replied, and when he saw Ruth's color rise went on gravely: "I don't mean to hint she knows it's inaccurate, but the grudge she bore my uncle accounts for something. When you brood over an injury, you exaggerate——"

"She could not exaggerate this injury," Ruth interrupted, and her face got very stern. "My father invented the distilling retorts and died in poverty. Stayward got the reward. Could he have done so, had he not been cunning and unscrupulous?"

Geoffrey pondered. He saw the girl was strongly moved by the wrong she thought Creighton had suffered. To argue that she did not know the truth and enlighten her would not help, but if he said nothing, his silence would imply that he agreed. Geoffrey was stanch and owed Stayward much.

"There was a quarrel and the partnership was broken," he said quietly. "You have heard one side, but not the other. Perhaps it's natural for the loser to think he has been cheated, and Stayward was sometimes hard. For all that, it's well known about the countryside that he was just. People trusted him with goods when he owned he could not pay; men who had been his antagonists came to his funeral——"

He paused and resumed with an apologetic gesture:

# RUTH'S PERSUASION

"We'll let it go! I had nothing to do with the dispute. You cannot hold me accountable."

Ruth's resolve was somewhat shaken. After all, he was not accountable and she approved his stanchness, for she had noted he would not try to placate her shabbily at his uncle's cost. It was plain he did believe Stayward just, and the strange thing was, a number of the dalesfolk had trusted the man. Mrs. Creighton, however, had worked upon her love and pity, and Geoffrey had inherited wealth that was her father's and would have enabled him to live a happy, useful life. One could not forget this.

"All the same, we cannot be friends," she said firmly. "It's impossible; there is too much in the way."

Geoffrey bowed. "If you are satisfied about this, I must agree in the meantime. But I don't agree without some reserve. When you find out you misjudged John Stayward——"

He saw Ruth's mouth get firm, and stopping for a moment, resumed: "There's another thing. We are neighbors and must meet now and then when people are about. What line are we to take?"

Ruth smiled coldly.

"I think you can leave me to indicate the proper line," she said and went off up the hill.

When she turned a corner her step got slow and she felt dejected. She had not shrunk from her duty, but the reflection gave her no comfort and duty was hard. She thought, rather bitterly, her mother ought to be satisfied.

## CHAPTER VI

### THE BROWN CAR

GEOFFREY was occupied with a drill at a bench in the small motor shop at the mining village. Stayward, shortly before he fell ill, had bought a car, which Geoffrey had brought to the garage for some repairs. When he went back the work was not finished, and finding nobody but a boy about, he began to bore a hole for a bolt. While he was engaged the proprietor came in.

"I'm sorry you have had to wait," said the man. "We didn't get all the new parts until a few days since."

"It doesn't matter; I don't need the car," Geoffrey replied. "However, I see you have had her out."

"A trial run. We wanted to put the magneto right before we got at the other job. She wasn't firing well."

"You drove her yourself?"

"For most of the time."

"You ought to be a good driver," Geoffrey remarked. "All the same, I see a dinge on the off-side guard. Looks as if you'd taken a corner too fine!"

The man hesitated, and then noting Geoffrey's twinkle, said with some embarrassment, "Miss Creighton touched the gatepost; as we turned up the Moor Park lonning a dog ran across the road. Reckon I oughtn't

# THE BROWN CAR

to have used your car, but I wanted to try the magneto and when Miss Creighton sent a message mine was out."

"That's all right," said Geoffrey. "Why did Miss Creighton want the car?"

"The doctor told her she must take Mrs. Creighton out and Leadbitter wouldn't let them have his digby. Said his pony was lame, but I reckon it's some time since he was paid."

Geoffrey lighted a cigarette. He had taken off his coat and sat on the bench. His habit was to make friends and he liked men who used engineering tools. Moreover, he knew the dalesfolk talked about everybody's affairs.

"Then, Miss Creighton has some trouble to get a trap or car!" he remarked. "Does she drive well?"

"She will soon. She's steady and has good hands and feet. Then she's keen. Said she'd very much like to hire a little knockabout for a few weeks while the warm weather lasts, but it would cost too much. If I'd had an old thing I hadn't much use for, I'd have let her have it cheap."

"Ah," said Geoffrey thoughtfully, and pondered.

He imagined the other knew all about Stayward's quarrel with Creighton; everybody in the neighborhood knew Mrs. Creighton. To carry out his plan might excite some curiosity, but he thought he could trust the motor dealer.

"I expect you know I've a workshop at Nethercleugh," he said. "Well, I've planned a few useful jobs for the winter evenings; a windmill pump for watering Belle's cattle, a turbine to drive some farming gear, and so forth. However, I've no big tools and thought about getting you to machine the castings when you're slack."

"I'd be glad of the job in winter," the other admitted.

"Very well," said Geoffrey, looking at him hard. "So long as my bicycle runs well, I've no use for the car. Put her right and lend her to Miss Creighton, but she mustn't know the car is mine. Mrs. Creighton mightn't like it—I daresay you understand. Then, although you'll have to state your charge, I don't want them to pay the hire. This will be your business."

The mechanic smiled discreetly. He liked Geoffrey's frankness and imagined he scented a romance, but it was obvious his imaginings must not be talked about.

"I can manage it all right. Mrs. Creighton pays for nothing until you bother her about the bill."

Geoffrey put on his coat and went off, wondering whether he had been rash. Ruth would be very angry if she found out the plot, but he resolved to trust his luck. A week or two afterwards, when he was going up a hill in the dale one afternoon, he heard a horn and his small brown car ran round a bend. Ruth drove and he thought the sweep she took at the curve was nicely judged. The speed had brought some color to her face; she looked confident and happy, as if she enjoyed her occupation.

Then Geoffrey, stepping on the grass by the roadside, saw her look up and imagined she hesitated. The sweep the car made got wider and he wondered whether her grasp had unconsciously tightened on the wheel. Next moment, however, she looked straight in front, and Mrs. Creighton, turning her head with a languid movement, gave him a stony glance. Since he

# THE BROWN CAR 273

did not doubt she knew him, he thought her insolent carelessness was rather well done—Geoffrey felt insolent was the proper word. Her look indicated that he was not important enough for active dislike. Yet he was persuaded she hated him for his uncle's sake.

For all that, he smiled when the car vanished and the dust that streamed about the hedges blew away. He was not going to bother about Mrs. Creighton; he had promised Stayward to leave her alone, and Ruth looked happy. He hoped her meeting him had not spoiled her satisfaction, and, since he was modest, thought it had not. Going on up the hill, he resolved he would try to make some plan that would enable her to use the car as long as she wanted, without her knowing she owed it to him.

So far as he could inform himself in the next three or four weeks, Mrs. Creighton did not get much better; and then a farmer who took milk to Beckfoot stated that she was worse. Geoffrey was sorry for Ruth, but did not see how he could help. In the meantime, the fine weather had gone. In the northern dales, summer is short and when rain begins it rains hard and long. Water flowed down the hillslopes, foamed in the ghylls, and soaked the bogs; the corn sprouted in the fields, and swollen becks brawled across the roads. Here and there in the hollows, the walls were broad and flagged on top, to make a causeway through the floods; at other spots narrow wooden bridges and big stones helped foot-passengers across.

Geoffrey, going to the village one stormy evening, thought he heard somebody behind him, and after a time stopped and looked around. In one place, the sky had cleared and a belt of angry saffron shone above a hill, but leaden clouds with torn edges rolled up from the west and the light was dim. Dark trees shook down big drops on the road, and he heard the noise of falling water. He was rather tired, after a long day with a sheep farmer on the wet moor, and wanted to get back to Nethercleugh. Moreover, he knew the rain would soon begin. Then an indistinct figure came out of the gloom and stopped not far off. It was a servant from Beckfoot.

"What do you want?" he asked, because it looked as if she hesitated to advance.

"I heard somebody on the road," she said. "The beck's rising and I thought it might be over the stones at the water-splash."

A water-splash is a channel across a road, and Geoffrey, imagining she was afraid the flood was deep, told her to come on and he would help her over. After a few minutes, they stopped at the water-splash. The stepping-stones near the hedge were covered by an angry flood. It was getting dark and heavy rain began to fall. The girl looked at the water, and when Geoffrey asked if she must go to the village told him she had been sent with a message. Mrs. Creighton was very ill and Teasdale had said another doctor must be brought from a small town some distance off. Miss Creighton had tried to start her car but it would not go, and the girl hoped to borrow a bicycle at the village and bring a man from the garage. Geoffrey thought for a few moments and then saw a plan.

"You can't get across," he said firmly. "Besides it's nearly dark and blowing hard, and the garage is a long way off. Go back to Mrs. Creighton's and I'll send somebody to start the car."

# THE BROWN CAR

The girl went, and Geoffrey, returning to Nethercleugh, put on his bicycling overalls. Then he looked for a big oilskin cap that would cover much of his face and pulling it down as far as possible, started for Beckfoot. The night was very dark, heavy rain beat upon him, and he heard the streams roar in the gloom.

Ringing the bell at Beckfoot, he stood back out of the light, and said to the servant, "I've come to drive Miss Creighton's car. Tell her I'll put the engine right while she gets ready."

He knew where the car was kept and when he had lighted the lamps it looked as if his luck was good, for after a few experiments with the magneto and sparking plugs he got the engine to go. It was throbbing loudly when Ruth entered the shed, but he let it run, and bent down, pretending to do something with a spanner. Ruth would not know his voice while the noise went on.

"A rough night, Miss," he said. "Better give me t' message and let me go."

"I must go myself," she answered. "You seem to have mended the engine. I suppose you can take me to Mellerby?"

Geoffrey said the engine would run, but the roads were bad and some of the bridges might be under water. Ruth stopped him impatiently.

"Time's important and we must start. Take the shorter road by the Pike."

She got into the car and Geoffrey drove out of the shed. It was very dark and the rain slanted across the beam of the lamps, but he saw the gateposts and turned up the hill, although he would sooner have gone the other way. The road by the Pike was shorter, but it was rough and steep, and he knew the floods were raging down the ghylls. For all that, he must not argue with Ruth; she was obviously determined and if he talked much she might know his voice. He was satisfied to sit beside her and feel her arm touch his when the car jolted.

Now and then a blurred tree leaped out of the gloom and vanished, glistening wet thorns rolled past and presently gave place to rough stone walls. This was all one could distinguish, but when the pace got faster Geoffrey knew they were running down into a hollow where a beck crossed the road. He thought he heard water and began to slacken speed.

"Let her go," said Ruth, and the car rushed on.

Flying water beat upon the screen, obscuring the lamps, and Geoffrey could not see the bridge. He felt the wheels skid among loose gravel, there was a violent splashing, and the car rocked horribly. Somehow he kept her straight and the splashing stopped. He had crossed the first bridge, but the becks were numerous and he did not know about the next. There was an awkward spot at the bottom of a deep ghyll when one got near Mellerby, and he resolved to take a road that turned off some miles ahead and cross by a better bridge. After a time he began to look out for the other road. Speed was perhaps important, but he meant to take care of Ruth. By and by he saw the turning, close in front, and the car had begun to swerve when Ruth touched him.

"No!" she said, sharply. "Go by the Pike!"

Geoffrey's mouth set, for he wanted to rebel but durst not. She thought him a motor driver and it was not a driver's business to argue that she was rash.

# THE BROWN CAR

Then although he liked her pluck her obstinacy annoyed him, and he had hardly time to get the car round. The car tilted as the wheels took the grass, he touched something that broke across the front guard, and then they were speeding on again.

He could not see much. The rain poured down the screen and beat into his face; mud leaped up in showers and some stuck to the lamps. Where the road was straight the walls were faintly distinguishable, but the walls stopped on an open moor and sometimes he took the grass. The car lurched and tilted, and when Ruth was flung against him he thrilled. For all that, he knew he must concentrate on keeping the road, and it was a keen relief to feel the wheels on the stones.

He wondered whether Ruth felt much strain, because she gave no sign. Her dim figure swayed when they went over lumps and into holes; her head was bent as if she tried to follow the road. For the most part, she was silent, and when she spoke he hardly heard her voice. He was highly strung and now they were on bleak, open ground, the wind screamed about the car.

At length, they began to run down hill. The road dipped to a ravine, through which a large stream flowed, and Geoffrey, thinking he heard water, presently slackened speed. Ruth said something, but he was occupied with the controls and fixed his eyes ahead. After a minute or two, the beam of the lamps touched an angry flood and he stopped. He could not see the bridge and it was plain the water ran for some distance across the road. Ruth got up and looked about.

"The bridge wall is very low. It's not important

if it's covered," she said. "Besides, you may see the top when you get near."

"I doubt the water'll get on to engine," Geoffrey replied. "We ought to gan back and take t'other road."

"No," said Ruth firmly. "You must go on."

Geoffrey got down and waded into the water until it reached his knees. The bottom was firm and he knew the flood had not washed the metal away. This was something, but when one crossed the bridge there was a ditch on both sides, and if the magneto went under water the engine might stop. He went back thoughtfully, pulled different ways; he sympathized with Ruth and understood her anxiety to get on, but to try the bridge might be dangerous.

"Well?" she said.

"I doubt if we can get across."

"You must! My mother's very ill and the doctor must be brought."

Geoffrey could hardly see her in the rain, but her voice had an imperious note. He felt he ought to be firm, but Ruth obviously meant to go on, and he started the car.

"Hold fast," he said. "Stick to me if she stops."

They plunged forward, at top speed, and took the water. It leaped about the wheels and splashed from the guard, deluging the glass and lamps. Geoffrey could not see; he must trust his luck and try to feel if the wheels left the road. The bridge was short, and if the metal were washed away on the other side, he would go into the ditch. Yet the rash adventure had a thrill. Ruth was with him and he was carrying out her orders.

## THE BROWN CAR 279

Ahead water tossed in the wavering beam of the lamps, he thought the car was pressed sideways by the flood, and then he felt the rise to the bridge. He was over, but the road dropped a little now, and for a few moments he held his breath. Then the water sank and the throb of the engine got regular. He changed the gear and they began to climb out of the ghyll, but presently the wheel wrenched his hand and the car swerved. Putting on the brakes, he plowed across some yards of heather and Ruth fell against him when they stopped.

"Front tire's burst," he said. "I hope you're not shaken. We must fix the spare rim."

Ruth got down and stood close by when he took a lamp and examined the tire. Its top was badly torn.

"An old fence post with broken nails sticking out, washed across the road by the flood, I expect," he remarked. "I'll get the spare rim and the jack."

He thought she looked at him rather hard, but his head was bent and he had pulled down his oilskin cap.

"Let me help," she said when he returned.

Geoffrey nodded and for a time they were occupied. His hands were wet and slippery, the rain whipped his face, and his soaked coat embarrassed him. He imagined Ruth was wet and chilled, but it was obvious she was not daunted. The light touched her hands and he noted she did not shrink when they got soiled. Then she had something of a workman's firm grasp; Geoffrey knew when one had proper control of one's muscles. Yet although he thrilled to watch her, he said nothing. Now the engine had stopped, he must not talk.

They fixed the spare wheel, he turned the crank, and

gave Ruth his hand when she got into the car. Then as he backed across the road he smiled and wondered whether the small courtesy harmonized with the part he had tried to play. Moreover, a girl who could climb the Stack did not need his help.

"Drive fast," she said and the engine throbbed hard as they rolled up the hill.

## CHAPTER VII

### MRS. CREIGHTON'S WEAK MOMENT

WHEN Geoffrey got back to Beckfoot he put the car in the shed and took off the engine bonnet and part of the floor. Although he had returned by a better road, the run had been hard and he suspected some strain on brakes and steering gear. While he was occupied Ruth came in and stopped, as if dazzled by the light. Geoffrey got up and stood between her and the lamps. He was glad to note she did not look disturbed, and hoped the doctor had given her good news.

"You drive well," she said. "I hardly think I would have reached Mellerby had Jopson sent another man."

"She's a good car, Miss, and you were stiddy," he replied. "It's not as if I'd had a nervous passenger."

"Well," she said, "you drove us through the floods and although you did hesitate, I think it was on my account. But you are wet and it is very late. If you will come in, we will give you some supper."

Geoffrey refused politely. He thought it typical that Ruth had come herself, and not sent a servant, but he was embarrassed. She was looking at him rather hard and he durst not move. He must stay where he was, with his back to the light.

"Then, you cannot refuse a little present you have

very well earned," she said, and moving a pace or two, held out a coin.

He hesitated, but advanced to meet her and used some control when she gave him a half-sovereign. The poverty that ruled at Beckfoot was known and he felt he robbed her of money she needed. For all that, he must play his part.

"Thank you, Miss," he said. "Mayhappen I might ask how Mrs. Creighton's doing?"

"We don't know yet, but I understand she is not as ill as I thought. The Mellerby doctor has helped her to sleep, and we both owe you much for bringing him."

Geoffrey doubted if Mrs. Creighton would own the debt, but Ruth went on:

"I told Jopson we would not need the car now the weather's getting cold. Had you not better take it back?"

"I think not, Miss. If you don't mind, I'll leave her with you. T' garage is small and our cars are not out much."

"But I mustn't run up a longer bill."

"That's aw right, Miss," said Geoffrey, who wanted Ruth to use the car. "We haven't much room and mayhappen it wouldn't bodder you to keep her for us. If you went for a run on a fine day, it would do no harm."

Ruth hesitated and then said, "Very well. But if you leave the car, how will you get home?"

"I've a bicycle," Geoffrey replied. "Car's ready for a run when you want her." He paused and imagining she looked at him curiously, added: "I must get off."

"Of course," said Ruth. "Thank you. It's lucky Mr. Jopson sent so good a driver!"

Geoffrey touched his cap and put out the lamps. It was something of a relief to know Ruth could not see and when he heard her steps on the gravel he shut the door and started down the drive. He was strangely satisfied; Ruth was all he had thought. Although he knew her poverty, she had given him a generous reward. Then she had wanted to give him supper and had thought about his walking back in the storm. She did not send him off like a hired man whose master paid him for his work; he was rather a man who had helped her and to whom she was grateful. Ruth was kind to strangers, and his heart beat as he speculated about her kindness to people she loved.

Then his satisfaction began to cool. He had no grounds for imagining Ruth loved him, and, from her point of view, he had important drawbacks. Moreover, Mrs. Creighton was his enemy and was not likely to be scrupulous. Geoffrey frowned and then braced himself up as he felt for the half-sovereign and put it in a pocket by itself. He was used to meeting and removing obstacles, and did not mean to be daunted. After all, he liked Ruth's stanchness; his business was to persuade her it was illogical and he was not accountable for her father's sufferings. Geoffrey saw he must be satisfied with this. It would not help if Ruth were forced to own that Creighton had robbed his partner and been justly punished.

All the same, he would not hesitate about enlightening Mrs. Creighton, should she compel him. Indeed, he had some time since resolved to do so if he found out that she was circulating fresh stories about his uncle's dishonesty. He had documents, in Creighton's hand, that would silence her. Geoffrey let it go when he came to the water-splash. The beck had risen and the flood looked awkwardly deep. The hedges were covered to half their height and a belt of foam marked the opening left for the stream. When he plunged in, small gravel beat against his legs. It was something of a struggle to get across and he went on to Nethercleugh breathless but exhilarated. Belle had put dry clothes ready and left him some food, and when he had eaten he sat for a time, smoking, by the kitchen fire.

The crumbling peats glowed red and shadows crept across the floor as the candle wavered in the draughts. He heard the wind and rain, but the noise was soothing. Nethercleugh was seldom altogether quiet; the ash leaves pattered and dry boards cracked. The old house was bleak but not forbidding. Its austerity was somehow bracing, and he had not yet altered Stayward's frugal rule. He was rich enough to do so, but he meant to wait.

Geoffrey smoked and weighed his plans. One must let in some light; with wide casement windows, the wainscoted parlor would make a noble dining-room. On the south side one could plant a garden; the east wall kept off the moorland winds. If one cut a round arch and left the old black beams, one could turn the kitchen into a spacious hall; the stairs at one end were broad and the newel posts quaintly carved. Nethercleugh could be beautified, without spoiling its old-fashioned simplicity.

Yet he could not begin until he knew if Ruth approved. She must bring fresh life and joyousness into

## MRS. CREIGHTON'S WEAK MOMENT 285

the brooding calm. Her voice would enliven but not banish the ancient tranquillity; he pictured her graceful figure and soft-colored clothes cutting harmoniously aganst the dark paneling; her light step in the echoing passages. Then he got up and knocked out his pipe. He had some way to go before he brought Ruth to Nethercleugh and there were obstacles in his path.

A week or two afterwards, Mrs. Creighton lay one evening on a couch in the drawing-room at Beckfoot and thought about Geoffrey. She was getting better and Ruth, who had been playing for her, had shut the piano and picked up a book. Mrs. Creighton studied the girl, and got a hint of strain; she thought Ruth's recent calm was rather forced. It looked as if she felt the reaction after an effort. Perhaps it was something of an effort when she agreed that her friendship for Stayward's nephew must be broken off. Mrs. Creighton had demanded this, but now she wondered.

After the Mellerby doctor's visit, Teasdale had been frank. If she were prudent and tranquil, she might live a number of years, but there was a risk. Mental strain and excitement, for example, were dangerous, and Teasdale thought Ruth had better stay at home. Mrs. Creighton weighed this. It meant Ruth must give up her career, and if she did so, she might be unable to start again. For one thing, she must break her partnership with Miss Chisholm, whose help was worth much.

Then George, her lawyer cousin, had called and talked about business. Things were worse than Mrs. Creighton had thought; the dividends on her small investments were getting less, and one could not sell the shares except at a loss; her landed property was mortgaged and, when one allowed for taxes and repairs, hardly paid the interest. Moreover there were debts.

Mrs. Creighton was disturbed. She had hoped to leave Ruth something, even if it were not much, but George had banished the hope; when she died, the girl must support herself. After all, Geoffrey Lisle was rich, and it looked as if Ruth attracted him. In the dale, one could gather news and Mrs. Creighton had informed herself about his haunting the village; indeed, she knew more about him than Ruth and he imagined.

She gave the girl a thoughtful glance. Ruth was reading quietly and her pose was languid. She looked thin and rather worn. Mrs. Creighton knew her work at Rainsfield was hard and it was some comfort to remember she was not going back; but if she gave up her occupation, how was she to live? One could hardly expect her to make a good marriage. For one thing, there were no rich young men in the neighborhood and Mrs. Creighton's friends in town had forgotten her. Besides, Ruth was reserved and proud; she did not use her charm.

Mrs. Creighton frowned and made a rather painful effort to be logical. If she took it for granted that Lisle was attracted, the marriage, in one sense, would be good. The young man's advantages were obvious and she imagined Ruth liked him. Mrs. Creighton tried hard to approve, but found she could not. In fact, there was no use in trying; her morbid bitterness against Stayward extended to his heir. She moved angrily and the shawl round her shoulder slipped down. Ruth looked up and shut her book.

## MRS. CREIGHTON'S WEAK MOMENT

"Does your head ache again? Is there anything I can get you?" she asked.

"No," said Mrs. Creighton sharply. "I want to be quiet. Move the lamp a little and leave me alone."

Ruth put the lamp on another table and Mrs. Creighton resumed her gloomy pondering. For a few weak moments she had vacillated, but her passionate hate was an obsession and could not be conquered. Although Ruth might miss much, she should not marry Lisle. Stayward had brought Ruth and her to poverty and was accountable for her husband's death.

There were, however, other grounds for Mrs. Creighton's relentless grudge. She had not always hated Stayward. She had had some beauty and in the days of the Hassals' supposititious prosperity had been courted and indulged. For all that, she had not met among her father's friends a man who pleased her eye like the rather grim young dalesman with his tall, athletic figure and the face of a soldier-monk; Mrs. Creighton had a romantic imagination then. She was an important landlord's daughter and Stayward was poor, but she tried to hint she might be tempted to forget the difference in their social rank. Yet she had not meant to marry Stayward. The obstacles were too numerous. She wanted to move him and enjoy the thrill of a romantic adventure.

Stayward was not moved. She saw she left him cold. He had something of a monk's temperament. Yet he was not a fool; she knew he had seen her invitation and refused, perhaps with the dry amusement he now and then indulged. The sting that still rankled was there. It was long since, but Mrs. Creighton was a daleswoman and dalesfolk do not forget.

Her health and fortune were broken and, in one respect, her mental balance was disturbed. Her illogical hate dominated a brain that had lost something of its power from long brooding. Her weak moment was gone and she would not vacillate again. Worldly prudence and love for her daughter did not count. Ruth must carry on the quarrel with her enemy's house. For all that, the struggle had shaken her and she got up feebly.

"I'm tired and think I'll go to bed," she said, and frowned when Ruth put down her book.

"Don't bother," she added. "Ring for Jane. She will give me all the help I want."

## CHAPTER VIII

#### THE BROWN CAR STOPS

LONG shadows streaked the hillside and Geoffrey pushed on as fast as possible across the stones and tangled fern. He had been occupied since morning building a derrick at a limestone quarry he had opened, and now wanted to get home. The evening was fine, and the hill commanded a wide view of peaks that cut against a yellow sky, and the shining sea. The green in the valley below him gently melted to blue and he saw far down the road that wound like a white riband along the foot of the hills.

When he got near the bottom, a moving object came round a bend. Its speed indicated that it was a car, but after a minute or two he saw that it was not really going fast. Then the throb that rolled up the slope had an uneven beat and got ominously jerky when the car climbed an incline. Near the top it stopped, and when a girl got down Geoffrey quickened his pace. The light was dim in the valley, but he thought he knew the girl, and if he did so, he knew the car and why it had stopped. All the same, he meant to be cautious and was glad his gray clothes melted into the background of stones and withering fern.

Because of a wet bog he could not reach the road directly opposite the car and he was a short distance off when he climbed a wall and jumped down on the grass. Ruth looked round and then bent over the crank, and her movements indicated that she made a determined effort to start the engine. Her luck was not good, and when she got up as Geoffrey advanced her face was red, but on the whole he was satisfied. He thought he would sooner see her angry than stonily calm, and since she generally was calm, her disturbance implied much.

"I can't make the engine go," she said.

"That's obvious. It looks as if you were trying pretty hard," Geoffrey remarked.

She gave him a quick glance and he smiled.

"Well, perhaps I can help. That is, of course, if you are willing!"

"I'd be ridiculous if I refused! But do you know much about obstinate cars?"

"I imagine I can start this car," he replied confidently.

Ruth looked surprised and he wondered whether he had been rash.

"You see, I know the type of engine," he resumed. "However, we'll begin at the beginning——"

He tapped the tank and Ruth's eyes sparkled.

"I'm not really stupid. There is enough petrol."

"That's something; it clears the ground," Geoffrey remarked and after taking off the engine cover lighted his pipe. "I may have to experiment," he went on. "Suppose you sit on the step while I get to work?"

"If you don't mind, I'd sooner watch. To know what to do might be useful another time."

Geoffrey hesitated. He thought he could start the engine in a few moments, but this was not his plan.

# THE BROWN CAR STOPS

He had been lucky and meant to make the most of his good fortune.

"Very well," he agreed and put down his pipe. "If I'm to explain things, we must, so to speak, proclaim a truce. Of course, it needn't bind you after the engine begins to run."

"Then perhaps you had better smoke. You meant to do so."

"Thank you! When you attack a knotty problem, smoking helps, and one doesn't like to waste tobacco. For a long time I was forced to use economy, and habits stick."

"After the need for economy is over!" Ruth rejoined.

Geoffrey gave her a level glance. "I don't think you ought to be annoyed because I'm no longer poor. The strange thing is, when I was poor you were friendly. I don't know why you take another line now, and hardly think you're logical."

"You really do know," Ruth said coldly.

"Oh, well, we agreed upon a truce," Geoffrey replied. "Suppose we talk about the engine? To begin with, the magneto's often a cause of trouble——"

He got to work and slackened and tightened nuts that did not need adjustment. Indicating covered wires, he told her where they led, and talked about electric currents and circuits. Then he experimented with the valves and after a time leaned against the guard.

"Do you imagine you could start the car if she stops again?" he asked.

"I certainly could not," Ruth rejoined.

"Very well. I must think how I can make the job plainer."

Ruth sat down on the step and he looked about. The sun had set and shadow crept up the dale. All was very calm; one heard the lambs on the hillside and the soft splash of water. Geoffrey wanted to linger. It might be long before he talked to Ruth again and the truce they had not altogether kept had charm. Yet he had found out why the car stopped and fresh experiments might be risky. Beckfoot was some distance off. After a time, Ruth looked up.

"Since you don't seem able to explain what one ought to do, hadn't you better start the engine?"

"I don't know if you're kind," said Geoffrey coolly. "However——"

He turned the crank, the engine rattled, and he opened the door for Ruth.

"Shall I drive you to the village?" she asked.

"I think not," said Geoffrey, smiling. "We must stick to our agreement. The truce was to last until the engine ran."

Ruth turned as she seized the wheel. "Very well! You are fastidiously scrupulous. However, you have started the engine, and perhaps my thanks will not embarrass you!"

Geoffrey bowed and gave her a steady look. "I've been trying to carry out your orders, but it's harder than I thought."

"For all that, you must keep it up," Ruth rejoined and the car rolled off.

When it vanished in the gloom Geoffrey resumed his walk and imagined he had struck the right note. There was no use in urging Ruth yet. Mrs. Creighton's power was strong, but Ruth was independent and by and by a reaction might begin. He must wait and use firmness at the proper time. After all, if he were forced, he could break Mrs. Creighton's antagonism. Ruth's romantic loyalty was the worst obstacle because he must not try to overcome it by proving her father a thief.

In the morning Geoffrey's thoughts were turned into another channel. He had promised Stayward he would live at Nethercleugh, and since it irked him to be idle had soon found an outlet for his energy. There was limestone on the small estate and he was building kilns, and opening quarries to supply the blast furnaces. Then he had examined the lead vein and begun to sink an experimental shaft. Water-power was running to waste and he meant to put up turbines to drive farm machinery.

His plans had kept him usefully employed, and now a letter that promised another occupation had arrived, but he knitted his brows while he weighed the suggestion it contained. To begin with, the industries in the neighborhood, mines, coke ovens, and quarries, were prospering; prices for sheep and wool were high, and large profits were earned. With good trade had come a general desire for improvement, and thoughtful people demanded an extension of public coöperation and control.

The letter invited Geoffrey to contest a seat on the County Council and stated that a deputation would call upon him in the evening. On the whole, he approved the writer's views and agreed that there was much that ought to be done by public effort. All the same, the job would not be easy. The agricultural landlords were old-fashioned country gentlemen and some seemed to imagine the Council's main duty was to make roads that would put up the value of their estates.

Geoffrey put the letter in his desk and went off to his quarry. He resolved to wait until he had seen the deputation and in the meantime he had his new derricks to think about. Soon after he came home, three gentlemen arrived and he took them to the wainscoted room. One was a sheep-farmer from the moors, another owned a brickworks, and the third occupied a post at a colliery. Geoffrey gave them cigars and sat down at the top of the table when they began to talk and smoke.

"I doubt if I'm the proper man to represent you," he said when the brickmaker stopped. "You want somebody well known."

"You're oad John's nivew; everybody kenned him," the flockmaster replied.

"Mr. Bell has given a good reason for our choosing you," the colliery clerk added. "Although we call ourselves Progressives, we like the old standards and don't trust strangers."

"I imagine a number of the old standards are on the other side," Geoffrey said, smiling.

"T' Hassals and such?" Bell remarked scornfully. "Weel, Hassals is gone down and dinnot count. Some of t'others is honest, and some is not, but they're aw for oad ways and willunt try t' new. Then Bells, Staywards, Lisles, and Ritsons was Statesmen lang before gentry came."

Geoffrey knew this was so. The *Statesmen* had owned the land they cultivated, but, for the most part,

# THE BROWN CAR STOPS

were not rich enough to keep up with agricultural development and sold their farms. A few were left and among the dalesfolk to spring from Statesman stock counted for something. The strange thing was, the men who meant to fight for modern methods respected ancient traditions.

Then the colliery clerk began to talk. The opposite party had, he said, a road-making plan they hoped to carry out if they could elect their representative. The thing, however, was a piece of jobbery, and must be stopped.

"Roads and bridges are useful," Geoffrey remarked.

"This road's nea use to anybody but two or three small farmers and landlords," Bell declared. "T' others weel ken that, but they'll put t' through and expect their friends t' do as much for them."

Geoffrey said he imagined reciprocity of the sort was not altogether unusual and the brickmaker smiled.

"Oh, well," he said, "one helps one's friends, but the roads we want will carry motor lorries and develop industrial traffic. It's important that the moor road, which we're against, will unite the opposition in a solid block; not because all like the plan, but because we're getting stronger and they feel their right to rule is threatened. In fact, they won't stop at much to keep out our man. However, we have canvassed the voters quietly and imagine if you'll take office you'll get much support. Although this is, to some extent, for your uncle's sake, I expect folks will soon back you for yours."

After the others had used some fresh arguments, Geoffrey agreed and the colliery clerk remarked: "So far as we can reckon, the miners and furnace-men are all for us, but the village and dalesfolk hold about half the votes and generally follow the landlords' lead; the latter are for the opposition. Although we mean to put you in, we'll have a stiff fight." He hesitated for a moment and then resumed: "Mrs. Creighton will certainly support the other side."

"It's possible," said Geoffrey dryly. "Has she much influence?"

"She's oad Hassal's dowter and that counts," Bell replied. "Some of her friends has dropped her, but t'others hasn't. It's weel kenned Janet Creighton's a manishing woman and tarrible obstinate."

"Bell means she's unscrupulous," the brickmaker interposed. "She'd help our antagonists, anyhow, because she belongs to the old school, but in this particular contest she'll use all her power."

"Mrs. Creighton commands one vote," said Geoffrey.

The brickmaker looked at him rather hard. "I've got to be frank. We all know Creighton and Stayward broke their partnership. Mrs. Creighton tells an awkward story."

"Do you believe her story?" Geoffrey asked, turning from one to the other.

"I'd niver believe it," Bell declared, and the colliery clerk nodded.

"He speaks for the rest of us and all who knew John Stayward well. But what are you going to do about it, if Mrs. Creighton tells the tale again?"

"I don't know yet. You must leave her to me. My uncle's dispute with his partner has nothing to do with my election."

"It may have much to do with it," the brickmaker

rejoined. "You've got to remember you're our man, the party's man."

"All the same, I will not engage in a public quarrel with Mrs. Creighton," said Geoffrey firmly. "If she tries to use a shabby plan, you must not meddle. I will stop her."

The others hesitated, until he smiled and added: "I think I can!"

They went off soon afterwards and Geoffrey lighted his pipe. He sat for some time with his brows knit, but when he got up his look was resolute.

## CHAPTER IX

### RUTH GOES TO NETHERCLEUGH

A FEW days after he received the deputation, Geoffrey got to work and on the whole found his candidature absorbing. He was not much of a politician, but he had something of the constructive talent that had marked John Stayward, and saw that much could be done for the prosperity of the neighborhood by organized effort. New industries had sprung up, roads for heavy traffic were needed, and bridges must be built. These were subjects he knew something about, and he meant to leave educational and political quarrels to others, but soon found that politics must be reckoned on.

There were two parties, the old school and the new; one standing for the preservation of individual rights, and the other for coöperative progress. Geoffrey's stanchest antagonists belonged to the first. In the mining villages, he was promised support, and a number of the farmers received him well for Stayward's sake. Others were obviously on his antagonist's side, and he thought the struggle would be hard. If he won, he would not win by many votes.

Coming home one evening, he saw with some surprise the brown car at his gate. It had begun to rain and the dark clouds that rolled across the hilltops threatened a heavy fall, but he did not think Ruth

# RUTH GOES TO NETHERCLEUGH

would stop for shelter at Nethercleugh. Yet he knew the car, and his heart beat as he went in through the porch.

The big kitchen was shadowy, but he saw two girls sitting by the fire and talking to old Belle. They got up and one advanced and gave him her hand.

"I wonder whether you have forgotten me?" she said.

"Certainly not, Miss Chisholm," Geoffrey replied. "It's not long since we crossed the fells and stopped at the shieling. For all that——"

Maud laughed. "You did not expect to meet me at Nethercleugh? Well, I'm something of an invalid and when Ruth urged me to try your mountain air I came to Beckfoot for a week or two."

Ruth stood quietly in the shadow and Geoffrey bowed. She acknowledged his salute without speaking, and Geoffrey tried to control his curiosity.

"Ruth wanted to see you, and your housekeeper told us you would not be long," Maud resumed. "I hope it will not rain very hard before we get home."

She stopped and they heard the rain on the ash trees. The windows got dark and a deluge beat upon the walls.

"You must wait," said Geoffrey. "I'll put the car in the barn."

He went out and did not return for a few minutes. Miss Chisholm's coming had relieved a rather awkward meeting and he thought she had meant to do so, but he was conscious of keen excitement and wanted to be cool. Something important had brought Ruth to Nethercleugh. When he came back he took the girls to the parlor and indicated chairs.

The dark clouds had passed and although the rain came down in slanted lines the light was stronger. One saw the brown panels, the big dark-green rug, and the old blue china on the wall. Tall brass candlesticks occupied the mantel and a copper lamp hung by heavy chains from a beam. The narrow window commanded a view of a wooded ghyll that seamed the brow of the moor. Miss Chisholm looked about with frank curiosity.

"I like Nethercleugh and this is a noble room," she remarked. "One gets a sense of spaciousness and quiet that's soothing after Rainsfield. Your old fellside houses are dignified but rather stern. Some people imagine one's house reflects one's character!"

Geoffrey smiled. It looked as if Miss Chisholm meant to smooth the way for Ruth and he must play up.

"I'm not accountable for my house; I inherited it," he said. "All I've added to this room is the green rug. An old rag carpet satisfied its last owner and Belle protested when the thing was thrown away. You see, we're a frugal and rather primitive lot."

"It's something to know when you ought to leave things alone," Maud replied. "But Ruth wants to talk to you and I'll go back to your housekeeper. It seems she once spent a thrilling week at Rainsfield with some relations and has a strange admiration for the dreary town."

She went out and Geoffrey waited, looking at Ruth. She was quiet and since she sat between him and the window he could not see her face.

"You did not expect me," she said after a few moments. "In a way, it was an impulse that made me stop the car; Maud and I were driving home and the rain began. However, I really think I meant to come. I felt I ought."

She paused and resumed with something of an effort: "You are standing for the County Council and your antagonist is a friend of ours. Last evening two or three of his supporters met at Beckfoot. I expect you know my mother has promised to help them."

"I imagined she would help," Geoffrey replied.

"At the meeting, they made some plans. You must remember the people who came are not our *friends;* they are men on committees, who know about elections and persuade others how to vote——"

Geoffrey smiled. "I think I understand! You mean one is not fastidious about one's acquaintances when an election's getting near? Well, these men have some influence and they made a plan!"

"Yes, I felt you ought to know——" said Ruth and stopped for a moment. Then she forced herself to go on: "They owned they could not tell who would win. The balance was very even, but if something were done that cost you a few votes——"

"Ah!" said Geoffrey in a sharp voice, "I begin to see! Mrs. Creighton promised to help my antagonist! They're going to circulate the tale about my uncle's robbing your father? After all, however, this has nothing to do with me."

"But it has much to do with you. Suppose it was suggested you were enjoying money that belonged to somebody else? That you knew about, and consented to, its being stolen?"

"The money was not stolen, but we'll let this go.

If I were willing to give up part of my fortune, would Mrs. Creighton accept?"

"You know she would not," Ruth declared. "She would take nothing that was Stayward's and now is yours. Nor would I!"

"Then we have cleared some ground, but I don't understand why you warned me about the committee's plan."

"I want you to withdraw and let your friends choose another candidate. You ought to see you must withdraw!"

"I don't see," Geoffrey rejoined. "In fact, your friends won't get rid of me like that; I have promised to fight this election. Did the people in the plot imagine I'd drop out if you gave me a hint?"

Ruth stopped him. Her face got rather white but she looked very proud.

"Then, you believe my object was to frighten you! Do you think I would let the others use me to force your consent? That I'd let them send me to extort something like a blackmail? I told you it was an impulse. Nobody knows I came."

"I really didn't think so; I know you would do nothing shabby," Geoffrey replied with some embarrassment. "The trouble is, my temper's hot, but Mrs. Creighton's vindictiveness is rather hard to bear, because it isn't justified. However, if you didn't want to force me to give up the contest, I don't understand why you did come."

"But I do want you to give up."

"Then, I'm puzzled," said Geoffrey. "I see no light at all!"

Ruth hesitated and he thought she blushed. "For

# RUTH GOES TO NETHERCLEUGH

one thing, it would be better to withdraw now than wait until your committee asks you to go," she replied after a few moments. "This would be awkward for you and them."

"You mean it would be awkward if Mrs. Creighton got somebody to use the story about my uncle's robbing your father? Well, I doubt if my supporters would ask me to go when they heard the story; but in the meantime it is not important. You, yourself, don't want to injure me?"

"I do not; that is, not *now*," said Ruth with rather strange calm, and then turned and gave him a level glance. "When I heard the plot, I nearly resolved to say nothing and let the others carry it out, though I knew the thing was shabby. When we met at the hotel, you ought to have told me you were Geoffrey Lisle, but you did not; and then again, when we climbed the Stack——"

Geoffrey was quiet for a moment. He remembered Ruth's keen enjoyment of the adventure on the rocks, her frankness and her cheerfulness, but he did not see all that she implied. Since she did not know him then, he thought she had no grounds to blame herself for being gracious.

"Perhaps I ought to have told you," he admitted. "For all that, and although you're angry because I cheated you, you felt you couldn't let your friends put me to shame? You don't hate me like your mother. In fact, if I were not Stayward's nephew, we might be friends?"

"It's possible," Ruth agreed and colored. "But you are Stayward's nephew."

"I don't know if I'd like to be somebody else,"

Geoffrey remarked. "But I want to understand properly. Did you come because you wanted to save me from getting hurt?"

"Not altogether."

"Then, I'm as puzzled as I was at the beginning. You had better tell me. I feel it's important we should be frank."

"Very well," said Ruth in a hard voice. "I warned you because I hoped to save my mother. She has long been ill and feels her poverty. Then she broods about my father. Trouble like this unbalances one. She could not see the thing she meant to do was shabby; but it was shabby, and I wanted——"

Geoffrey made a sign of agreement. "Yes. It's plain now."

He pondered for a few moments, because he was moved and saw he must use some control. He was sorry for Ruth, and sorry he had forced her to confess her object. It was obvious that he had forced her. She had splendid pluck and was all he had thought, but he must be cautious.

"It would help if I retired, but I cannot," he said. "I promised to fight the election and my committee tell me I'm the strongest candidate they could get. It's necessary for me to state this. Very well, I can't disappoint them now when they have not time to get another man. It would be ridiculous to do so and let the opposition win because Mrs. Creighton is illogical."

"Yet if you don't retire, she'll carry out her plan," Ruth declared with a look that indicated she was desperate.

"I think not. I must stop her."

"Can you stop her?" Ruth asked with surprise.

# RUTH GOES TO NETHERCLEUGH

"It's very possible. Anyhow, I'll go to Beckfoot and try."

"But then she will know I told you."

"She will not know," said Geoffrey. "I mean to talk to her about something else than the election; I think it will account for my going and bringing up the old dispute."

Ruth looked at him rather hard and he saw she was puzzled. Indeed, he imagined she was vaguely disturbed.

"You must trust me," he resumed. "Nobody but Miss Chisholm will know you came to Nethercleugh."

"In a way, I ought not to have come," said Ruth, and delicate color touched her skin. "One ought to do things openly. I don't like secrets."

"Do you mean, you don't like to share a secret with me?" Geoffrey asked with some dryness.

Ruth looked embarrassed, but gave him a steady glance. "Perhaps I did mean something like that. Well, I must trust you." She paused and added: "After all, I think I can."

Then she got up and Geoffrey saw the rain was stopping. He brought the car to the gate and Ruth and Miss Chisholm drove off. When they had gone he returned to the parlor and gave himself to careful thought.

To begin with, he knew Ruth's effort had cost her much. She had seen the proper line and had taken it boldly, but he had known her pluck. Then, except where love for her father led her away, she was just, and hated shabbiness. It was impossible for her to approve of Mrs. Creighton's plan. This accounted for much, but Geoffrey wondered whether it accounted for all. Perhaps she had, half-consciously, meant to save him from getting hurt.

He let it go. Mrs. Creighton must be stopped, but she must not know Ruth had warned him. He would have to state some grounds for his going to see her that would not implicate the girl, and he could do so, although it would embarrass him. He meant to marry Ruth if she were willing and had begun to hope he might persuade her if her mother's opposition could be broken. It was plain that Mrs. Creighton had worked upon her feelings. He had, however, seen that he must use patience. Ruth was clever and although she had been carried away by her mother's arguments he thought she would presently find out they had no real weight. All the same, he must see Mrs. Creighton and account for his doing so by stating that he wanted to marry Ruth.

Mrs. Creighton would, of course, refuse, and her refusal would enable him to talk about Creighton's patent. He could soon convince her it would be prudent to leave the old dispute alone and perhaps to own publicly that she had misjudged Stayward. For all that, Geoffrey imagined she really knew Stayward had not injured her and he could not overcome her unjustified bitterness. She might cunningly work against him and use her weak health for an argument to force Ruth to agree.

He must appeal to Ruth and urge his cause as strongly as he could, although he doubted if she were ready yet. He wanted to wait, but could not. In a day or two Mrs. Creighton might begin to circulate her tale, and if he made known the truth, Ruth would be involved in her mother's humiliation. It was obvious that he must do something promptly and trust his luck.

When he got up he was resolved. He must find out how Mrs. Creighton was, and, if she were well enough, demand to see her as soon as she would receive him.

## CHAPTER X

### THE PORTRAIT

IN the morning, Geoffrey, going to the quarry, met Miss Chisholm in a pasture on the hill. She occupied the step of a slate stile, and since she did not get up when he advanced Geoffrey imagined she wanted to talk to him. He noted that she looked thin and rather worn.

"I came out to get some mushrooms, but they don't seem to be plentiful," she remarked, indicating an empty basket. "However, I'm satisfied to sit in the sun and look at the hills."

Geoffrey nodded. The sun was on the fellside and belts of moss shone like emeralds. Withered fern made patches of soft red and the dry bent-grass was touched with silver. In the background, rugged hills rose above a ridge of moor and the broken crags were darkly blue.

"I hope the mountain air will soon brace you up," he said.

"One gets slack at Rainsfield and I rather needed bracing," Maud replied. "Then Ruth urged me to come. I expect you know we are old friends and work together?"

"I understood something like this. Well, the moorland winds are invigorating and Beckfoot's a pretty, quiet spot."

# THE PORTRAIT

Maud smiled. "Remarkably quiet; but I have not known much calm and there is a well-regulated quietness that jars. In fact, it's now and then a relief to go out and hear the becks brawl. You may have remarked that I'm looking for mushrooms where they are not to be found!"

"If you want some mushrooms——"

"I don't," said Maud. "I want the wind and sun. Beckfoot's rather stuffy. I don't mean they keep the windows shut; they're opened by rule."

Geoffrey thought he saw what she did mean and wondered where she was leading.

"Well," he said, "Miss Creighton's your friend and I suppose you fixed on our neighborhood for your holiday because you wanted to see her."

"This really was my object. I wasn't satisfied about Ruth."

"She's well, I think," said Geoffrey. "Anyhow, when we climbed the Stack she was remarkably steady on the rocks and looked fresh when we reached the top." He paused and resumed with a touch of anxiety: "But, of course, it's some time since."

"Ruth is physically strong, but her letters gave a hint of strain. To begin with, I think she felt being forced to let me go and give up her work. She did so for her mother's sake. After all, however, perhaps I oughtn't to be sorry she's not coming back."

"You imply that teaching music is not Miss Creighton's proper line?"

"Yes," said Maud, "I'm bothered about the thing, because I brought her to Rainsfield. Ruth is a good teacher, but you feel the work's an effort and she goes on because she's obstinate. She hasn't the missionary spirit; a real teacher, you know, is something of a missionary. Some of us preach the worship of beauty because we must. It's, so to speak, our vocation, but it isn't Ruth's."

"I think I understand," Geoffrey remarked.

"There are men and women with romantic creeds they're forced to preach. Sometimes we wear ourselves out and don't accomplish much beyond bothering people who would sooner be left alone, but we're satisfied to spend our labor. Ruth is not like that. She tries to hide it, but teaching does not satisfy her. The women whom it does satisfy are not numerous. Then Ruth's talent for music is really not very marked. Nature meant her for domestic life. Her work's to rule a home."

"Yet you hint she is not happy at Beckfoot."

"It's plain she is not," Maud declared. "In fact, this mainly accounts for my coming to the dale. To begin with, I expect you know Mrs. Creighton?"

"I doubt if Mrs. Creighton would confess to knowing me," Geoffrey replied with a twinkle. "For all that, in a sense, I think I know her rather well. However, we were talking about Ruth——" He stopped and gave Maud a steady look when he went on: "I'd hate to feel she was unhappy."

Maud's smile was sympathetic and implied understanding.

"Beckfoot jars me; I think it jars Ruth," she said. "Mrs. Creighton's demands are numerous and the house has a morbid, depressing influence. There are houses like that; you feel they're unwholesome! Then Mrs. Creighton's brooding jealousy is poisonous.

# THE PORTRAIT

Ruth ought not to stay. Yet I wouldn't persuade her to rejoin me at Rainsfield."

"I expect you know I'm the subject of Mrs. Creighton's jealousy," Geoffrey remarked in a thoughtful voice. "It's plain she's trying to work on Ruth."

"Ruth is just," Maud declared. "She has been taught your uncle ruined Creighton, and her mother's influence is strong, but sometimes she rebels. I think she's pulled two ways——"

Geoffrey studied her quietly. Then he said, "Thank you! I must see Mrs. Creighton; I'll go to-day!"

"Then you must be firm," said Maud. "I wish you luck!"

She got up, to allow him to climb the stile, and he resumed his walk. It was obvious that Miss Chisholm knew when to stop, but he admitted that she had said enough. Moreover, although romantic, she was not a fool; he thought she would not have meddled unless she felt her meddling was justified. He was strongly encouraged, but would not let himself be carried away. After all, Mrs. Creighton was a clever antagonist and stubbornly obstinate.

In the afternoon, Geoffrey went to Beckfoot and was shown into the small, lavishly-decorated drawing-room. He noted its rather cheap conventional prettiness and thought he knew what Miss Chisholm meant when she said Beckfoot was stuffy. She had at another time remarked that a house reflected its occupant's character. Geoffrey was persuaded the drawing-room did not reflect Ruth's.

After a few minutes, Ruth came in. She did not sit down and Geoffrey noted that she had a touch of color. He thought her curious and perhaps disturbed, although it was obvious that she meant to be calm.

"My mother cannot see you," she said.

"I rather expected her refusal," Geoffrey replied. "All the same, I must see her in the next few days. It's important."

"You are not easily daunted," Ruth observed with a faint smile.

For a moment or two Geoffrey knitted his brows. Then he said, "Will you carry my message? If Mrs. Creighton does not feel able to see me to-day, I must submit, but the interview can't be put off very long and I must ask her to fix a time. It's necessary, not for my sake so much as hers. In the meantime, I must warn her to say nothing about the Creighton patent."

Ruth looked at him as if she were puzzled. "Then, you mean to talk about the patent? You have found out something fresh?"

"Nothing fresh," said Geoffrey. "I was satisfied about the patent some time since, but I imagine your mother doesn't know how much I know. She may tell you afterwards. Until I have seen her, I cannot."

He waited, but Ruth did not reply. Her look was cold and her mouth was firm. She was very still and her pose had a touch of pride. It was plain that she expected him to go. He began to cross the floor, and then, as he reached a small table that carried a bowl of flowers and some framed photographs, stopped abruptly. Leaning over the flowers, he took a portrait from its silver stand. Ruth turned and gave him a surprised and rather haughty glance.

"Who is this gentleman?" he asked.

"My father," said Ruth.

# THE PORTRAIT

Geoffrey started, but made an effort for control. He looked at Ruth, and then for a moment or two studied the portrait. He saw it had been taken long since, when the man was young and handsome, and much that had puzzled him was plain. Now he understood why he had seen an elusive likeness to somebody he knew when he looked at his camp cook. The fellow was Creighton. Geoffrey saw how this altered things and his heart beat. In the meantime, Ruth waited, trying to control her curiosity.

"Why are you surprised?" she asked. "It's strange you did not know my father. You sometimes went to the coke ovens."

"I ought to have known him, but I did not. The day we met, he was sitting in the shadow by the office door. Then, of course, he wore different clothes in Canada, and the frost had browned his skin——"

"In Canada?" Ruth interrupted.

"In the Ontario bush," said Geoffrey. "I met him in the snow. But you're curious and I have much to tell you." He paused, and looking about the room, went to the long window. "It's ridiculous, but I can't talk about Canada here. Let's go out."

Ruth saw he was excited and his abruptness did not jar. She knew she was going to hear something strange, and tried to be calm. She took him across the narrow lawn to a bench behind some cypresses. Mrs. Creighton would soon know where they had gone and would be angry, but Ruth did not care. Somehow she felt Geoffrey was going to justify the confidence she had once given him. She sat down and he leaned against the rail of the bench, fixing his eyes on her face.

"To begin with, when I met you first on the moor, you were friendly and trusted me," he said. "Afterwards, when we climbed the Stack one glorious day you were frank and kind. We helped each other on the rocks; we were comrades. Is that not so?"

"I think it was so," Ruth admitted with forced quietness, and obeying an impulse, added: "It was a glorious day!"

Geoffrey signed agreement. "Afterwards, things were different," he resumed. "You found out I was Stayward's nephew and Mrs. Creighton talked to you. She urged that Stayward had wronged your father and I had inherited money that ought to have been hers. If you loved your father, you must let me go."

"She did urge something like this," said Ruth, giving him a disturbed glance. "I agreed. But why did you start when you saw the portrait?"

"I'll tell you in a moment; I've been clearing the ground. For your father's sake, you tried to hate me. The thing's ridiculous! He was my friend!"

"Your friend?" said Ruth with a puzzled look. "One feels it's impossible!"

"All the same, it's true. You may remember, when we stopped at the shieling, I told you about our cook, the chemist, who found the valuable metal. Well, this is his portrait."

"Ah!" said Ruth and hesitated, as if she were afraid. Then, with an effort, she resumed: "George Hassal, my mother's cousin, told us he was dead. Was he your cook when you left the mine?"

Geoffrey gave her a sympathetic glance. "No. He died some time before this, when I was at Montreal. On my return, I took him to the settlement for burial."

She turned her head and was quiet for some moments. Then she looked up and Geoffrey saw her eyes were wet.

"It is strange you should do this," she said gently.

"It really is not strange. I told you your father was my friend."

"George Hassal made inquiries and was persuaded he was dead," said Ruth. "We tried to resign ourselves, but after all, I hoped—and now the hope is gone." She paused and began again in a shaking voice: "All the same, I think I really knew I cheated myself. But there is much I want to know."

Geoffrey saw her antagonism had vanished. She no longer thought him her enemy; she was the girl he had met on the moor road and with whom he had climbed the Stack.

He began his story at the camp by the frozen river, where he found Carson in the snow, and told her how the miners approved his giving him the cook's post. Although he doubted if he had much skill for drawing character, he made an effort and his touch got firm and true. He depicted Carson's whimsical good-humor, his habits, and the liking the miners had for him. Then he sketched the background; the rude cook-shack and loghouse, the stiff white pines and the frozen waterfall. Ruth sat very still and her look was grave but gentle. When Geoffrey stopped, she signed agreement.

"He was like that! Even if I had doubted, you would have satisfied me; but I did not doubt. You could not have made so good a sketch unless you were his friend."

"I had time for study," Geoffrey replied. "On bitter winter evenings, when the stove was red hot, we worked together in my shack, weighing and melting down specimens——"

He went on with his tale and related Creighton's laborious experiments, making Ruth realize the man's tenacity and unshakable confidence. He thought she saw something of the pathos of her father's last effort to use his wasted talent, but Geoffrey touched this as lightly as he could. Then he told her about the accident and his journey to the settlement with Creighton's body. He drew the start; the silent men standing with their hats off in the snow, the horses surrounded by a steamy haze, and the dawn breaking behind the pines. He saw she followed the long march, and pictured the sledge and its load drawn close to the campfires in the frozen wilds. When he stopped she was crying frankly.

By and by she looked up. "Thank you! I really knew he was dead, but he was happier than I thought; he found kind friends. Your story has comforted me."

"Then I'm satisfied," Geoffrey answered and waited for a few moments. "There's another thing," he said when Ruth was calmer. "Your father was entitled to a reward for his discovery and you are his heir. I must write to the directors; they're honest people."

Ruth looked up at him with a faint smile. "In the first place, I think my mother will inherit. Will your sense of justice force you to claim the reward for her?"

"I'll own that Mrs. Creighton's getting the reward rather blunts my satisfaction," Geoffrey admitted.

# THE PORTRAIT

"However, I hope I am just. I will write to Montreal."

Ruth got up and gave him her hand. "Thank you again! I must go."

He kept her hand for a moment. "It was on your father's account you felt you ought to dislike me?"

"Yes," said Ruth, but did not look up.

"Very well. Now there is no obstacle to our being friends."

"No," she said and gave him a quick glance. "There is no real obstacle. You were kind to my father. But I think my mother will not be satisfied yet."

Geoffrey smiled. "I'm going to see Mrs. Creighton and expect to persuade her. Will this be some relief to you?"

The color came to Ruth's face and her glance got shy and soft.

"It will be some relief," she said. "I will carry your message. Perhaps she will see you."

## CHAPTER XI

### RUTH REBELS

AFTER Mrs. Creighton heard Ruth's story she went to her room and gave orders that she must not be disturbed. She declared she needed quietness; the news had been a shock, and she must be left alone while she tried to recover. Ruth was sympathetic, although she knew Mrs. Creighton had for some time been convinced her husband was dead. Moreover, although she stated she could not come down for dinner, Ruth found the cook had been instructed to send an appetizing meal to her room.

When it was getting dark Ruth and Maud walked in the garden, and Maud stopped at the bench among the cypresses. The evening was calm and thin mist drifted about the fields and streaked the dark firs behind the house. One heard the beck and the lambs bleating on the hill.

"Let's sit down," said Maud. "I want to talk and can't arrange my thoughts while you move restlessly about. You are restless. Lisle's calling has disturbed you."

"Is that strange?" Ruth asked.

"You knew your father was dead. In fact, you had given up hope before your lawyer relation told you about his inquiries. There's something else."

Ruth said nothing and Maud went on: "Your mother is getting better. By and by she won't need you, and I doubt if you ought to rejoin me at Rainsfield. Your usual calm's deceptive; you're highly strung and teaching would wear you out. It's not your job. Nature gave you another."

"Do you mean you won't take me back?"

"It's possible. Suppose I'm unselfish enough to refuse? What are you going to do?"

"I don't know," Ruth replied drearily.

"What you ought to do is obvious."

Ruth blushed but looked up sharply. "You don't altogether understand and must not meddle!"

"Meddling's my business. I'm something of a missionary and a fanatic. I rage against ugliness, conventional shams, and waste of Nature's gifts. Well, although you have a soberness and balance I haven't got, I've taught you something. I've given you the modern young woman's point of view and made you think for yourself. You're as honest as things allow."

"I don't see where this leads us," Ruth remarked.

"Then you are duller than I thought and I'm going to be frank. To begin with, you cannot stay long at Beckfoot. You and your mother would jar. I can see you rebelling against the strain of forced agreement and conventional pretense. Long since your mother's ambition destroyed your father's happiness; if you stay, her jealousy will destroy yours. Stayward is not accountable for your misfortunes. Bitterness like your mother's is poisonous to everybody about. You can't stay at Beckfoot. It's frankly impossible!"

Ruth was very quiet. Anger would have brought some relief, but she could not be angry; she felt that Maud had not exaggerated much. She had for some time doubted if Mrs. Creighton's jealousy were altogether justified and now she knew it was not. Yet, so long as her mother needed her, her duty was plain.

Maud waited for a few moments, and then resumed: "Your life is yours; a platitude but true. Don't cheat yourself by the illusion that you're necessary to Mrs. Creighton. If you're very resolute and patient, you may bear with her for some time, but the clash must come. When it does come, you may find it comes too late; after you have thrown away a chance of happiness you may not get again——"

"You must stop," Ruth said with quiet firmness, although her face was red.

"I will stop soon. Lisle loves you. He's resolute, modest, honest, and although I doubt if he's clever, he's not a fool. Physically, he's strong, athletic, and rather handsome. What else do you want? Then perhaps it was not for nothing you met him, when you were tired, on the moorland road. One goes far and fronts the hills cheerfully with somebody one can love and trust. It's much if when at length the road runs down into the dark, one does not go alone. Now I'll stop and leave you to weigh my remarks."

Maud got up and went off, but Ruth sat still and mused. It was plain that Geoffrey loved her, and she had not met another whom it would be so easy to love. Moreover, when she had recently glanced ahead, the road she meant to take looked rough and long. Sometimes she felt daunted and sometimes lonely. She might find it lonelier than she had thought and, when the evening came, be forced to own that she had missed the joy of the day. For all that, her mother's claim was strong and there were obstacles in the way of her marrying Lisle. She wondered how he thought to

# RUTH REBELS

satisfy her mother, but saw no light, and when she felt the dew went back to the house.

In the morning, Mrs. Creighton came down to the drawing-room and ordered her invalid's chair to be put near the window. Then she had her cushions and shawls carefully arranged, and when she was satisfied sent for Ruth. When Ruth came she studied her and thought she was pale and looked rather strained. All the same, her mouth was firm and her glance was steady. Mrs. Creighton knew her daughter and wondered whether she was going to be obstinate.

"I have been weighing the story Lisle told you," she said. "In some respects, it is plausible."

"I feel it's true," Ruth rejoined. "There were particulars he could not have invented; the things were characteristic. He knew my father!"

"This is obvious," Mrs. Creighton agreed. "All the same, his knowing your father does not guarantee the accuracy of the rest of the tale. But suppose we admit it is accurate? It looks as if Lisle had copied his uncle. Stayward stole your father's patent; Lisle encourages him to use his skill and then takes his reward! Indeed, he admits he has done so."

Ruth's eyes sparkled. Maud had argued better than she knew and Mrs. Creighton had taken the wrong line. Ruth began to feel her jealousy was poisonous. For all that, she tried to be patient.

"Until Mr. Lisle saw the portrait, he did not know his cook was my father," she rejoined.

"Is this probable? You are not a child and one must use one's knowledge of human nature. So long as Lisle could pretend ignorance, he would not be forced to divide the profit. It counts for much that he is Stayward's sister's son. Margaret Stayward was very like her brother, I knew her long since."

"Oh," said Ruth, "one cannot think everybody is shabby and dishonest! It would be horrible. Besides, the dalesfolk declare Stayward was just. They often talk about him. He was rough but leal, they say. After all, perhaps, your grudge carries you too far."

Mrs. Creighton gave her a look of scornful amusement. "I have lived some time and one soon loses one's romantic generosity. Then I knew John Stayward rather well. However, Lisle admits that my husband, after long and patient experiments, found the metal."

"I think," said Ruth with a touch of passion, "father did not bother about the reward. He was not greedy, and Mr. Lisle declares no bargain was made. He experimented because he was a chemist and felt he must. Can't you see the pathos of it? He was old and had forgotten much; he had no proper apparatus and had lost his skill. Yet it was his vocation; he worked for love——"

"If he did not stipulate about a reward, he was rash and did not take much thought for us," Mrs. Creighton remarked dryly. "All the same, I doubt."

"But you doubt everybody! If Mr. Lisle were dishonest, he would have said nothing. He has promised to write to the directors and see we get a share in the profits of the mine. You cannot refuse this."

"I do not mean to refuse, but before I agree I must know the sum the directors are willing to give and talk to George. He will see I am not cheated."

Ruth knitted her brows and made an effort for control. She felt she had not really known her mother

# RUTH REBELS

until then, and she shrank from the illumination. She saw she must not expect her to be just.

"Mr. Lisle sent a message demanding an interview," Mrs. Creighton resumed. "Do you know what he means to talk about?"

"Not altogether," Ruth replied. "I think he is afraid you might use your influence against his election."

"I shall certainly do so. Lisle is not the man to speak for us at the council. I will give him his interview and make it plain that he must withdraw."

"But you cannot force him to withdraw."

"I have grounds for thinking I have the power."

"Oh," said Ruth, in desperation, "if I could persuade you to give it up! You cannot tell people about father's dispute with Stayward. You must see it's unthinkable!"

"Do you imply I must not carry out my duty to my neighbors, because I need Lisle's help to get money my husband earned? The owners of the mine cannot refuse my claim, and if they tried, George would compel them to pay. Isn't it obvious Lisle offered his help as a bribe?"

Ruth said nothing for a moment, although she was horribly jarred. It looked as if Mrs. Creighton could not realize that her revengeful plan degraded her. In fact, there was no use in arguing. Long brooding had made her mother blind and she could not be helped to see. For all that, Ruth felt she must protest.

"Mr. Lisle's offer was not a bribe. He wanted to help because he's kind."

Mrs. Creighton smiled, a rather cruel smile. "He has a stanch champion. Do you love the man?"

Ruth lifted her head and although her color was high gave her mother a level glance.

"I do not know. He deserves to be loved."

"Then, I expect you know he loves you?"

Ruth did not answer. She was very quiet, but her mouth was ominously firm.

"All the same," Mrs. Creighton went on, "you must let him go. It's impossible for you to marry Geoffrey Lisle. His uncle is accountable for your father's ruin and the hardships that caused his death. Lisle knew, and took the profit Stayward got by theft. You cannot share the fortune stolen from your father. When you meet Lisle, you must make him understand that you and he are strangers."

"I will not," said Ruth and got up, trembling with mixed emotion.

Her mother's hate, founded on an illusion, had grown to something like a mania. While she nursed her supposititious injuries, Mrs. Creighton had lost her mental balance. But Ruth remembered Maud's warning. She was resolved her mother's illusion should not destroy her happiness. She had some right to happiness and she rebelled.

"Mr. Lisle has not asked me to marry him," she resumed. "If he does ask, I do not yet know what I shall say. But so long as he values my friendship, it is his. I will not let him go."

"You may be forced," Mrs. Creighton rejoined.

Ruth looked at her for a moment. Her eyes sparkled and her hand trembled, but with an effort she turned quietly, crossed the floor, and went out. When she had gone, Mrs. Creighton rang for her maid and then sank back in her chair. She was not beaten yet, but her confidence was shaken. Moreover, she had borne some strain. Ruth's selfish obstinacy and ingratitude had hurt; Mrs. Creighton would not own that to be baffled hurt worse. Her disturbance reacted on her physically, and her maid suffered much for Ruth's sake while she helped her mistress to bed. Then she went upstairs and packed her box. She had had enough, she told the cook.

In the morning, Ruth went to the village post office. The post-mistress sold groceries and general goods, the shop was small and dark, and since three or four people were waiting to be served, Ruth stopped at the open door. The others were gossiping and did not see Ruth. After a few moments, one said something that puzzled her and when another replied she started and half-consciously clenched her hand. Her errand was not important, and stealing away, embarrassed, she set off for Beckfoot and met Geoffrey outside the village. When he came round a corner by the water-splash she stopped.

"Whose is the car we have been using?" she asked.

Geoffrey gave her a quick glance. Her eyes sparkled, and she held her head high. He saw he must be frank.

"The car is mine."

"Did Jopson rent it from you?"

"He did not."

"Then you plotted with the man to cheat me?"

"I suppose I did do something like that," Geoffrey owned.

Ruth studied him. She was angry, because she felt humiliated, but he did not look embarrassed. Although his sunburned face was redder than usual, his glance was direct and kind.

"You are honest now," she remarked. "Why did you cheat me?"

"I wanted you to use the car. I heard that Mrs. Creighton must be driven about and you couldn't get a trap. I think that's all. Anyhow, since I thought you wouldn't know, it's plain I wouldn't get much by cheating you. If I'd asked you to use the car, you would have refused, but I don't know if this makes the thing better."

"It does not," said Ruth severely, although she was beginning to relent. He had not thought to gain much; his unselfishness was obvious.

Then she remembered something else that had puzzled her and she thrilled with mixed emotion.

"Oh!" she said, "you drove the car, the night I went to Mellerby for the doctor?"

"I did drive," Geoffrey admitted. "It looked as if you could get nobody else and the need was urgent. Mrs. Creighton was ill."

Ruth's anger vanished and she no longer felt humiliated, although there was much for which she was sorry.

"But I expect you know what my mother thinks about you?"

"It's pretty obvious," Geoffrey replied with a twinkle. For all that, her not liking me wasn't important. She was ill and you were bothered about her."

Ruth turned her head and when she looked up again her eyes were gentle.

"You were generous when we were unjust and harsh," she said. "I wonder why——"

# RUTH REBELS

She stopped and blushed. She had spoken impulsively because she was moved, but she saw she had been rash. Geoffrey gave her a steady glance.

"I think you *know*. If not, I'll tell you when I have seen your mother. She has sent me a note fixing the time."

"She did not tell me this," Ruth replied, turning her head and trying to be calm. "Well, I have kept you and must go."

She went off and Geoffrey started for the village. He meant to be very firm when he saw Mrs. Creighton.

# CHAPTER XII

### MRS. CREIGHTON RETRACTS

THE evening was getting cold, the shadows had crept across the dale, and when a light began to twinkle among the trees ahead Geoffrey looked at his watch. Mrs. Creighton had fixed a time for him to call and he meant to be punctual. So long as he was occupied, he thought he could be cool, but he did not want to wait for the interview.

Geoffrey resolved to take a bold line. He had been patient and tried to avoid a conflict, but Mrs. Creighton's hostility had not got less. She was an unscrupulous antagonist and might work on Ruth's feelings, as she had done before. It was plain her consent to his marrying Ruth must be forced and Geoffrey saw he could not be fastidious. Moreover, she had long slandered his uncle. He tried not to feel revengeful, but Mrs. Creighton could not be allowed to circulate fresh stories about Stayward's dishonesty. She had compelled him to quarrel and he smiled rather grimly as he reflected that she did not know his power.

Lights shone in the windows at Beckfoot when he went up the path. A servant took him to the drawing-room and somewhat to his relief he saw he would not be kept waiting. Mrs. Creighton occupied her invalid's chair and coldly acknowledged his bow. Her face was rather pinched, but she did not look ill. A shaded lamp on a brass pillar stood near the hearth and a man sat in front of a small table. Geoffrey had met Hassal at a public function and knew he was a lawyer.

"I asked Mr. Hassal to meet you because he is my cousin and sometimes advises me," Mrs. Creighton said and indicated a chair.

Geoffrey sat down and thought his chair had been purposely put where it was. The party occupied the corners of a triangle and since the room was small the light was good. He could see the others and imagined they had meant to study him.

"You demanded an interview," Mrs. Creighton resumed. "I can give you a quarter of an hour."

"This is enough for me," Geoffrey replied. "If you should want to lengthen the time, mine is at your command."

He stopped for a moment. It was rather strange to see Hassal. Since the fellow was a lawyer, he would hardly approve Mrs. Creighton's plan, but perhaps she had not told him. On the whole, Geoffrey did not think Hassal knew.

"You know I met Mr. Creighton in Canada," he said. "Since I saw Miss Creighton I have written to the directors of the mining company and urged that his labors deserved some recompense. When their reply arrives I will inform you."

"I suppose you are satisfied the man was Creighton?" Hassal interposed.

"It's impossible to doubt," said Geoffrey, picking up Creighton's photograph, which stood where he had seen it. "However, you can get some copies of the portrait and send them to the mine. I will give you the address."

"When your directors reply we will think about their offer," Mrs. Creighton remarked. "Since my husband's discovery was valuable, his reward must be just."

Geoffrey smiled. "The directors are just, but they will not give you an offer to think about. If they agree to fix a sum, they'll expect you to be satisfied. In a sense, you have no claim. Mr. Creighton did not stipulate he must be paid."

"We have only your statement for this," Hassal interrupted.

"That is so," Geoffrey agreed. "If you doubt me, you must prove a bargain was made. Then, all rests on my statement. The directors knew nothing about Creighton's experiments that I did not tell them. If I'm not trustworthy, Mrs. Creighton's claim falls through."

Hassal made a sign of agreement and Geoffrey went on: "We must wait until I get a reply from Montreal." He turned to Mrs. Creighton. "Now I want to talk about something that does not directly interest Mr. Hassal."

"My cousin will remain."

"Very well," said Geoffrey. "It's my duty to state that I mean to ask Miss Creighton to marry me. I hope you approve."

Mrs. Creighton gave him a steady look. "Does Ruth know this was your object when you demanded an interview?"

"She does not."

"Have you grounds for imagining she will agree?"

## MRS. CREIGHTON RETRACTS 331

"I have none," Geoffrey owned. "I'm taking what I understand is the proper line."

Mrs. Creighton smiled, but her straight, thin lips were firmly set and he got a hint of cruel satisfaction.

"You are honest now; you were not always honest," she said. "At the beginning you cheated my daughter. Afterwards you thought you could persuade her to cheat me!"

Geoffrey colored. In a sense, he had cheated Ruth, but his embarrassment turned to anger. Mrs. Creighton had known more than he thought, and had meant to let him get entangled and then forbid him to see Ruth again. The plot was cruel and risky; so long as he was punished, he did not think she would be much disturbed if she hurt her daughter. Then, from her point of view, he had advantages, and since they did not weigh, her malignant prejudice was stronger than her greed. It was plain that he must be firm.

"You imply that you don't approve my marrying Ruth?" he said.

"I do not approve. Such a marriage is impossible!"

"I must ask why you declare it's impossible," Geoffrey rejoined.

He saw the lawyer glance at Mrs. Creighton and hoped she would not control her bitterness. He had given her a lead, but if she were cautious she might embarrass him. In fact, unless she talked about her husband's supposititious wrongs, he did not see how he could begin the argument he meant to use. Mrs. Creighton was clever, but she did not know how much he knew and revengeful passion carried her away.

"Your uncle cheated my husband, ruined him in fortune and reputation, and drove him abroad," she said in a voice that shook. "He died in consequence of the hardships he was forced to bear, and John Stayward was accountable for his death. You have inherited Stayward's stolen property; you were his heir, and it's possible you knew and consented to the theft. That Ruth should marry the man her father's ruin has enriched is obviously impossible!"

Geoffrey saw she had given herself into his power. There was no reason for his being merciful, but he must be cool.

"You take it for granted my uncle stole Creighton's invention. All turns on this," he said and looked at Hassal. "I'll admit the invention was useful and Creighton sold it for a trifling sum. Would he have done so unless he was forced? Isn't it plain that some rash action, dishonesty to his partner for example, accounted for his not refusing to sell?"

"You imply too much," said Hassal. "Suggestions like this are dangerous. If made publicly, they may cost you something."

"I'll be content if Mrs. Creighton admits they're justified. Since her husband was my friend, I much dislike the line she compels me to take. Well, when Creighton joined Stayward he had nothing but his patent. The specification was bad and did not protect the patent from infringement; in fact it was afterwards infringed by other parties. Then the invention, so to speak, was not complete, and the process Stayward used was a development he worked out after Creighton left him."

"Your unsupported statements would probably be disputed by a patent lawyer," Hassal remarked.

"It's possible," said Geoffrey, who took out some

## MRS. CREIGHTON RETRACTS

documents. "I have plans you can submit to a technical expert, if you like. In the meantime, we'll let it go. Creighton was extravagant and used his partner's money, until Stayward found it was nearly gone. Since he could not trust Creighton, he broke the partnership."

"Creighton was Stayward's partner, and if he did use the house's money, his doing so was not unlawful," Hassal remarked.

"It was ethically dishonest," Geoffrey declared. "I don't know the law, but there were circumstances that made Creighton's later drawings very like fraud. Stayward imagined he could have forced him to refund, but since Mrs. Creighton had spent the money, he used another plan——"

Mrs. Creighton stopped him. Her face was red and she sat upright, with her eyes fixed on Geoffrey. They shone with hate, but he thought she began to be afraid.

"This is slander," she said. "My cousin will advise me how to punish you."

Hassal gave her a warning glance. "I think we will let Mr. Lisle finish his argument."

"Mrs. Creighton's accusation made me my uncle's champion, and the part gives me some advantages," Geoffrey resumed. "Well, I have documents to prove all I state——"

He paused, and putting some papers on the table, began again: "At length Creighton could get no more money from the bank, but money was needed to hide his extravagance. It looks as if Mrs. Creighton had persuaded him to take out a sum that, had it been left, might have helped him to carry on for a time."

Geoffrey turned to Mrs. Creighton. She leaned forward and her look was fixed and strained. He saw she was waiting with keen suspense.

"Well, there was no more money, and Creighton pledged a quantity of coal that was not theirs. Stayward's agreement was needed and Creighton, who durst not ask for it, used his partner's name. Stayward found out and broke the partnership, but paid Creighton a small sum for his patent. I think that's all."

He got up and gave Hassal the documents. "You are used to weighing evidence, and I think you will find my story is well borne out. Anyhow, you'll see Creighton's admission, in his own hand, that he got justice."

He sat down and gave Mrs. Creighton a quick glance. She had sunk back in her chair and he saw she was horribly afraid. He wondered how much she had known, and thought she had known something, if not all.

For some minutes they were very quiet, and nothing broke the strain, except when a paper Hassal picked up rustled. Then the lawyer turned to Mrs. Creighton.

"A closer study of the documents might give some grounds for disputing part of Mr. Lisle's argument," he remarked. "The disputable part, however, is not important. My advice is, agree with Mr. Lisle if he is willing."

Mrs. Creighton looked at Geoffrey. Her face was pinched and white; her hands trembled and her pose

## MRS. CREIGHTON RETRACTS 335

was slack. It was obvious that she knew she was beaten.

"What do you want me to do?" she asked.

"I want you to admit that you misjudged John Stayward and are now satisfied he did not injure your husband."

"I must admit it. I was deceived; circumstances led me to think—— But is this enough? Must I tell people I was misled?"

"Perhaps it's hardly needful," Geoffrey replied with some dryness. "I imagine nobody really believed my uncle stole the patent. Then I won't bother you for a promise not to talk about the invention again. For one thing, you know the truth; for another, I mean to keep the documents."

He took the papers from Hassal and Mrs. Creighton looked keenly relieved.

"I suppose you meant to force my consent to your marrying Ruth?" she said.

"I meant to justify my uncle and have carried out my plan. Then I asked your consent to my marrying Ruth, and you stated the obstacle. The obstacle has been removed and you have no grounds for refusing."

Hassal looked up with a twinkle. "You are taking a very proper line, Mr. Lisle."

"Are you going to tell Ruth all?" Mrs. Creighton asked anxiously.

Geoffrey knitted his brows. "I must tell her something, but I think not all. Anyhow, not yet. Still she is clever; some day she will know——" He paused and added: "I imagine I can leave you to clear the ground."

"Very well," said Mrs. Creighton. "If Ruth agrees

to marry you, I cannot refuse my approval. However, I have borne some strain and I am not very strong."

Geoffrey went off, but Hassal went with him and stopped at the gate.

"In a sense, I'm the head of the family, Mr. Lisle," he said. "If you get Ruth, you will be fortunate; she has virtues that I must own do not mark all her relations. From one point of view, the marriage is good, but it is not altogether because of this I wish you luck. However, it might be prudent to see Ruth soon. To-night Mrs. Creighton is resigned—but I imagine you know my cousin!"

"Thank you. I will come in the morning," Geoffrey replied.

In the morning he returned to Beckfoot and found Ruth in the garden. By and by they went to the bench among the cypresses and Geoffrey leaned against the rail and fixed his eyes on Ruth. He waited, and after a moment or two she looked up with a blush.

"When you had gone my mother talked to me," she said. "She did not really tell me much, but I saw I had been unkind and unjust."

"You were stanch and I liked you for your loyalty," Geoffrey declared. "All the same, it's done with, and since Mrs. Creighton is satisfied, there is nothing to keep you from me now."

"Are you satisfied about this?" Ruth asked, giving him a level glance.

Geoffrey laughed, a joyous laugh. "My dear! Since I first met you on the moor I wanted you. You haunted me in Canada, and thinking about you inspired all my efforts; I meant to come back and look for you

# MRS. CREIGHTON RETRACTS 337

when I had made good. Well, I was lucky and did come back, but there was another battle to be won at home."

"George talked to me," said Ruth. "He said your fight was very fair."

Geoffrey took her hand. "At the beginning I was not very frank, but afterwards I saw I must not use a shabby trick when I fought for you." He lifted his head with a triumphant gesture. "Well, it looks as if I had won!"

"If you really want me——" said Ruth, giving him a shy glance, and he took her in his arms.

# EDGAR RICE BURROUGH'S NOVELS

May be had wherever books are sold.   Ask for Grosset & Dunlap's list.

## TARZAN THE UNTAMED
Tells of Tarzan's return to the life of the ape-man in his search for vengeance on those who took from him his wife and home.

## JUNGLE TALES OF TARZAN
Records the many wonderful exploits by which Tarzan proves his right to ape kingship.

## A PRINCESS OF MARS
Forty-three million miles from the earth—a succession of the weirdest and most astounding adventures in fiction. John Carter, American, finds himself on the planet Mars, battling for a beautiful woman, with the Green Men of Mars, terrible creatures fifteen feet high, mounted on horses like dragons.

## THE GODS OF MARS
Continuing John Carter's adventures on the Planet Mars, in which he does battle against the ferocious "plant men," creatures whose mighty tails swished their victims to instant death, and defies Issus, the terrible Goddess of Death, whom all Mars worships and reveres.

## THE WARLORD OF MARS
Old acquaintances, made in the two other stories, reappear, Tars Tarkas, Tardos Mors and others. There is a happy ending to the story in the union of the Warlord, the title conferred upon John Carter, with Dejah Thoris.

## THUVIA, MAID OF MARS
The fourth volume of the series. The story centers around the adventures of Carthoris, the son of John Carter and Thuvia, daughter of a Martian Emperor.

**GROSSET & DUNLAP, PUBLISHERS, NEW YORK**

# FLORENCE L. BARCLAY'S NOVELS

May be had wherever books are sold.   Ask for Grosset & Dunlap's list.

## THE WHITE LADIES OF WORCESTER

A novel of the 12th Century. The heroine, believing she had lost her lover, enters a convent. He returns, and interesting developments follow.

## THE UPAS TREE

A love story of rare charm. It deals with a successful author and his wife.

## THROUGH THE POSTERN GATE

The story of a seven day courtship, in which the discrepancy in ages vanished into insignificance before the convincing demonstration of abiding love.

## THE ROSARY

The story of a young artist who is reputed to love beauty above all else in the world, but who, when blinded through an accident, gains life's greatest happiness. A rare story of the great passion of two real people superbly capable of love, its sacrifices and its exceeding reward.

## THE MISTRESS OF SHENSTONE

The lovely young Lady Ingleby, recently widowed by the death of a husband who never understood her, meets a fine, clean young chap who is ignorant of her title and they fall deeply in love with each other. When he learns her real identity a situation of singular power is developed.

## THE BROKEN HALO

The story of a young man whose religious belief was shattered in childhood and restored to him by the little white lady, many years older than himself, to whom he is passionately devoted.

## THE FOLLOWING OF THE STAR

The story of a young missionary, who, about to start for Africa, marries wealthy Diana Rivers, in order to help her fulfill the conditions of her uncle's will, and how they finally come to love each other and are reunited after experiences that soften and purify.

GROSSET & DUNLAP,   PUBLISHERS,   NEW YORK

# ETHEL M. DELL'S NOVELS

May be had wherever books are sold. Ask for Grosset & Dunlap's list.

## THE LAMP IN THE DESERT

The scene of this splendid story is laid in India and tells of the lamp of love that continues to shine through all sorts of tribulations to final happiness.

## GREATHEART

The story of a cripple whose deformed body conceals a noble soul.

## THE HUNDREDTH CHANCE

A hero who worked to win even when there was only "a hundredth chance."

## THE SWINDLER

The story of a "bad man's" soul revealed by a woman's faith.

## THE TIDAL WAVE

Tales of love and of women who learned to know the true from the false.

## THE SAFETY CURTAIN

A very vivid love story of India. The volume also contains four other long stories of equal interest.

GROSSET & DUNLAP,     PUBLISHERS,     NEW YORK

# ELEANOR H. PORTER'S NOVELS

May be had wherever books are sold.    Ask for Grosset & Dunlap's list.

## JUST DAVID

The tale of a loveable boy and the place he comes to fill in the hearts of the gruff farmer folk to whose care he is left.

## THE ROAD TO UNDERSTANDING

A compelling romance of love and marriage.

## OH, MONEY! MONEY!

Stanley Fulton, a wealthy bachelor, to test the dispositions of his relatives, sends them each a check for $100,000, and then as plain John Smith comes among them to watch the result of his experiment.

## SIX STAR RANCH

A wholesome story of a club of six girls and their summer on Six Star Ranch.

## DAWN

The story of a blind boy whose courage leads him through the gulf of despair into a final victory gained by dedicating his life to the service of blind soldiers.

## ACROSS THE YEARS

Short stories of our own kind and of our own people. Contains some of the best writing Mrs. Porter has done.

## THE TANGLED THREADS

In these stories we find the concentrated charm and tenderness of all her other books.

## THE TIE THAT BINDS

Intensely human stories told with Mrs. Porter's wonderful talent for warm and vivid character drawing.

GROSSET & DUNLAP,    PUBLISHERS,    NEW YORK

## "STORM COUNTRY" BOOKS BY
# GRACE MILLER WHITE

May be had wherever books are sold. Ask for Grosset & Dunlap's list.

### JUDY OF ROGUES' HARBOR

Judy's untutored ideas of God, her love of wild things, her faith in life are quite as inspiring as those of Tess Her faith and sincerity catch at your heart strings. This book has all of the mystery and tense action of the other Storm Country books.

### TESS OF THE STORM COUNTRY

It was as Tess, beautiful, wild, impetuous, that Mary Pickford made her reputation as a motion picture actress. How love acts upon a temperament such as hers—a temperament that makes a woman an angel or an outcast, according to the character of the man she loves—is the theme of the story.

### THE SECRET OF THE STORM COUNTRY

The sequel to "Tess of the Storm Country," with the same wild background, with its half-gypsy life of the squatters—tempestuous, passionate, brooding. Tess learns the "secret" of her birth and finds happiness and love through her boundless faith in life.

### FROM THE VALLEY OF THE MISSING

A haunting story with its scene laid near the country familiar to readers of "Tess of the Storm Country."

### ROSE O' PARADISE

"Jinny" Singleton, wild, lovely, lonely, but with a passionate yearning for music, grows up in the house of Lafe Grandoken, a crippled cobbler of the Storm Country. Her romance is full of power and glory and tenderness.

*Ask for Complete free list of G. & D. Popular Copyrighted Fiction*

GROSSET & DUNLAP, PUBLISHERS, NEW YORK

# KATHLEEN NORRIS' STORIES

May be had wherever books are sold.  Ask for Grosset & Dunlap's list

SISTERS. Frontispiece by Frank Street.

The California Redwoods furnish the background for this beautiful story of sisterly devotion and sacrifice.

POOR, DEAR, MARGARET KIRBY.

Frontispiece by George Gibbs.

A collection of delightful stories, including "Bridging the Years" and "The Tide-Marsh." This story is now shown in moving pictures.

JOSSELYN'S WIFE. Frontispiece by C. Allan Gilbert.

The story of a beautiful woman who fought a bitter fight for happiness and love.

MARTIE, THE UNCONQUERED.

Illustrated by Charles E. Chambers.

The triumph of a dauntless spirit over adverse conditions.

THE HEART OF RACHAEL.

Frontispiece by Charles E. Chambers.

An interesting story of divorce and the problems that come with a second marriage.

THE STORY OF JULIA PAGE.

Frontispiece by C. Allan Gilbert.

A sympathetic portrayal of the quest of a normal girl, obscure and lonely, for the happiness of life.

SATURDAY'S CHILD. Frontispiece by F. Graham Cootes

Can a girl, born in rather sordid conditions, lift herself through sheer determination to the better things for which her soul hungered?

MOTHER. Illustrated by F. C. Yohn.

A story of the big mother heart that beats in the background of every girl's life, and some dreams which came true.

*Ask for Complete free list of G. & D. Popular Copyrighted Fiction.*

GROSSET & DUNLAP,   PUBLISHERS,   NEW YORK